PRAISE FOR

SAY YOU'LL BE MINE

"I couldn't put down this page-turner. A warm, smart, sexy, and absolutely charming debut with the most important lesson at its center: real love is built on courage. Meghna and Karthik's happily ever after is the new *When Harry Met Sally*. Naina Kumar's *Say You'll Be Mine* has it all."

—COLLEEN HOOVER

"With poignancy, humor, and heart, [*Say You'll Be Mine*] unpacks the ways in which personal and external expectations can derail our best intentions and champions the courage and growth true love really requires."

—*Entertainment Weekly* (Grade A-)

"Fake engagement—one of the romance genre's most stalwart, dependable tropes—reigns supreme in Naina Kumar's *Say You'll Be Mine* . . . an insightful look at how cultural and familial expectations can shift even the best-known love stories."

—*ELLE* "One of 2024's Best Romances"

"Charming . . . brilliant."

—*New York Post* (A Best Book of February)

"The strength of this sweet debut lies in the relationships with family members and friends and how they are tempered by cruel realities and the thorny path to true love. Kumar is a writer to watch."

—*Booklist*

"Perfect for fans of grumpy-sunshine pairings and mostly closed-door romances."

—*Library Journal*

"Kumar debuts with a swoon-worthy contemporary that marries a grumpy-sunshine romance with a deep exploration of familial relationships."

—*Publishers Weekly*

BY NAINA KUMAR

Say You'll Be Mine

Flirting with Disaster

FLIRTING
with
DISASTER

FLIRTING
with
DISASTER

A Novel

NAINA KUMAR

DELL

New York

Published in the United States by Dell, an imprint of Random House,
a division of Penguin Random House LLC, New York.

DELL and the D colophon are registered trademarks
of Penguin Random House LLC.

ISBN 978-0-593-72390-6
Ebook ISBN 978-0-593-72391-3

Printed in the United States of America on acid-free paper

randomhousebooks.com

1st Printing

Book design by Debbie Glasserman

To Houston, and the brave, kind, resilient people who live here.
There's nowhere else I'd rather call home.

FLIRTING
with
DISASTER

SEVEN YEARS AGO

I open my eyes to a face entirely too close to mine. I can't take in the full picture, but I catalog the features I see. A large nose. Morning stubble. A firm mouth that's partly open, releasing small, warm breaths that puff against my skin.

The room is dark, but there must be light filtering in from somewhere because it's reflecting off of something. Glitter. Specks of gold. Something that sparkles in a streak down the curve of his throat.

A very attractive throat.

I register the too-warm blanket on top of us, or maybe it's the heat radiating off of him. His leg's thrown over both of mine, and my body's tucked against his, his hand resting on my hip.

I don't want to move. I want to stay here, all wrapped up in him. But my eyes are so dry it hurts to blink. And my mouth tastes like cotton.

Water. I need water.

I squint in the direction of the nightstand, spotting the half-empty, very crinkled plastic bottle sitting there.

As I reach for it, light bounces off of something else, but it's not glitter this time. It's . . . a ring.

A diamond ring. I pick it up off the table, running my thumb across the solitaire. I suspect it's not real, and when my nail accidentally scrapes the metal, pieces of gold varnish flake off, confirming my suspicion.

Who knows where we got this from? Last night is a blur. Maybe it came out of a slot machine. Maybe it was a prize. Some cheap, plasticky bauble. I set it back down, but at this angle I notice there's a bit of engraving on the inside.

I peer closer, raising it higher to get a better look.

I read it once. Then read it again.

And my stomach turns to lead.

Viva Las Vegas. On their own, those words would be fine. My memory's coming back to me in pieces. I know we're in Vegas. And I know the man beside me is the man I'm falling in love with, but that doesn't mean I'm prepared for the two words that follow.

Wedding Chapel.

Viva Las Vegas Wedding Chapel.

"Nikhil," I whisper, shaking his shoulder gently. "Nikhil."

His eyes are hesitant to open. They flutter a couple of times, his body fighting for more sleep, before finally giving in. He blinks in confusion, and then a moment later, recognition sparks.

As he meets my gaze, his mouth curves in a warm, lazy smile, and I feel it low in my stomach. Desire pierces through my panic, curling within me like smoke.

"Good morning," he says, his voice all gruff and hoarse. He always sounds like this when he first wakes up, and it's quickly become my favorite alarm. I love the way he whispers in my ear. The way he follows it by brushing his lips along my cheekbone.

I've never known anyone like Nikhil. I've never *been known* by anyone like Nikhil. I've never had anyone see all the broken, scared, awful parts of me and choose me anyway. This summer should have been the worst of my life with all my anxiety surrounding preparation for the bar exam. And there has been plenty of that. Nikhil saw me at my lowest when I was studying. Crying and stressed and unsure. But somehow, he made it better. Just by being with me. Listening to me. Making me take breaks. Forcing me out of my room and into the sunshine. Cheering me up with his smiles. His jokes. And just . . . his presence.

Being around him makes everything better.

"Morning," I tell him. The panic that disappeared a little while ago has fully returned. I have to know what happened. I have to know if it's true. "Do you . . . do you remember anything about last night?"

His brows crinkle. "Not much. We had dinner with your friends and then . . . I remember saying goodbye to them, and after . . ." He frowns. "Did we come back here? I think that's what we were going to do, but . . . I'm not sure."

"Okay," I say. "Okay. Umm, don't freak out." Really, that message is for me as much as it is for him. "But do you remember anything about this?" I grab the ring, showing it to him.

His eyes grow wide. "Oh my god." His gaze bounces between me and the ring. "We actually got married? That . . . that was real?"

We stare at each other for a moment, both of us processing the shock as the news settles in. A vague memory of me wearing a scratchy white veil floats through my brain. It was attached to some kind of firm plastic headband, and I remember it really hurt my ears. I rub one of them absently, though there's only a bit of dull pain now. Nikhil was standing in front of me, I think. I don't remember what he was wearing. This foggy image appearing in my mind could easily have been just part of a dream, if not for the ring I'm still grasping tight in my hand.

And then . . . Nikhil does the strangest thing imaginable.

He laughs, all bright and sunny and deep. It sparks something within me, and suddenly, I can't help but laugh in return.

"We're married," he says.

"Yeah."

"You're my wife." Wonder rings loud and clear in his voice and it washes over me like sunlight. It warms me, scattering the dark and anxious feelings I had moments before.

I'm somebody's wife. I'm *Nikhil's* wife.

I don't fully know how I feel about that yet. But the idea doesn't sound as scary as it did when I first woke up.

He watches me, hesitation creeping through his expression. "Are you . . . are you okay?"

"Yeah," I say, surprised to hear myself say it. Surprised that I mean it. "Yeah. I think I am."

He draws me closer, his arms coming around me, his forehead resting against mine. We stay like that for a while until my entire body relaxes, leaning into his.

"I love you, Meena," he says, and my heart jumps at the words. It's not the first time he's said them, but it still feels unreal. I don't think I've fully wrapped my mind around it. That this kind and patient and wonderful man actually loves *me*.

"I know this is fast," he continues. "And it's not something we planned. And I know how you like your plans."

I laugh, and he leans back to watch, grinning in return.

"But I'm in this. I'm in this with you. Whether there's a signed piece of paper or not. We can get rid of it. We can rip it up and file the proper stuff and go back to the way we were. Or we can keep it.

I don't care. None of that changes anything for me. You're it. You're it for me. I'm here. And I'm yours. For as long as you want me."

Something clicks in this moment. Something right and sure slides into place. I want Nikhil. I won't ever stop wanting Nikhil. I won't ever stop wanting to be around him. Whether there's a piece of paper or not.

"You're it for me too," I whisper back.

A bit of hair slips in front of my face, and Nikhil reaches out, tucking it behind my ear.

"I'm guessing we made vows," he says. "But I don't remember any of them. And I don't remember most of the traditional ones either, but I want to make some now." He takes a deep breath, his face growing solemn and tender.

"Meenakshi Nader, I promise to be there for you."

"And I promise to be there for you."

He pauses. "You don't have to—"

"I want to." I want to promise this man everything he's promising me. I want to show him that I mean it. That we may have entered this whole thing accidentally, but I'm choosing to stay in it. I'm choosing him.

"Okay." His hand finds mine, his thumb rubbing over my palm. "What's mine is yours," he continues.

"What's mine is yours."

"In sickness and health, and rain and shine, and bad times and good. I promise to share all of it with you. All of it. For better or worse."

"For better or worse," I repeat.

He smiles, wide and beaming, and I feel it all the way in my chest. "Now, I think this is the part where I get to kiss the bride."

Laughter bursts out of my mouth and he catches the sound, his lips sliding against mine. His hands come up to cradle my face, and I reach for him in return, running my hands along his arms, his neck, threading my fingers through his hair.

What Nikhil said earlier was true. I've never really deviated from my plans before. Never really done anything reckless. But this doesn't feel reckless. This just feels right.

I love him and I don't care what it takes. The two of us are going to be okay. We're going to go back home. To Houston. And we're going to make this marriage work.

PRESENT DAY

I step out of Houston's Hobby Airport and walk straight into hell.

Literally. Figuratively. Emotionally. I'm in hell in all ways.

Part of me is tempted to turn right back around. Southwest has a steady handful of flights between here and D.C. I'll just march to the counter, buy a new flight, and be on my way. No one will know about this out-of-character burst of irrationality. No one will know I was ever here, in my hometown, the one place I promised I would never return to. I'll leave the past where it belongs and just . . . move forward.

Except, I can't. That's why I'm here.

I pull out my phone and check the Uber app. The ride I called the second the wheels made contact with the runway is still a good twelve minutes away. *Of course.* The universe knows how much I don't want to be here, how quickly I want to get this all over with. So, it's doing the exact opposite. Slowing things down. With my luck, we'll end up hitting traffic on the way there, dragging things out even more.

I check my work email, firing off a few quick responses as I walk to the designated pickup spot.

Call the Speaker's office and ask for Sonia. If she can convince him to adjust the language on paragraph 3A back, he may just find that he has a majority for that highway bill he's been dying to pass.

Yes to the meeting with the Section 8 housing nonprofit, and a hard no to the natural gas group. (Putting aside the fact that our climate advocacy clients might actually kill us, we're just not that kind of firm.)

Just got confirmation that they're pulling walking human nightmare Judge Bates off the short list for that opening on the 5th Circuit (thank god). Good work, everyone.

I'm moving to slip my phone back into my purse when something sharp collides with the middle of my back. I stumble, my phone falling out of my hand. I wince at the *thwack* it makes as it hits the concrete.

"Sorry," a man's voice calls. "Sorry about that." I turn to face the perpetrator, but I only catch a glimpse of a dark-haired man, his hand holding tight to a young girl's. They're navigating through the crowd, walking quickly toward the entrance of the airport, and it's only then that I notice the number of people that are moving alongside them.

Houston's crowded. It's a big city. It's not unusual for the airport to be busy, but still, something in the air feels off. It kind of reminds me of my usual morning commute. People move at a quick clip, a slightly frenzied, caffeine-induced adrenaline spurring their steps. But it's not the kind of crowd I expected to find here, on a Saturday morning. The energy is strange. Almost . . . frenetic.

I squat to pick up my phone, dusting it off and grimacing when I flip it over and see the large crack now running across the screen. *Great.* The universe strikes again. Or maybe I really am in hell. The blistering heat from the sun and the slight scent of sulfur invading my nose certainly make it seem that way.

I swipe toward the rideshare app, trying to see how much longer I'll have to wait for my car. The image is all blurry, the screen distorted because of the fall. The phone buzzes in my palm, some kind of notification banner flashing across the top. I squint, but the text is unreadable. I think it's an emoji or icon. Something gray and round. Maybe a cloud? I pull it closer to my face, trying to make it out, but before I can the phone vibrates again, a little green symbol popping up. An incoming call. I answer, even though I can't quite read who it's from.

"Hello?"

"Meena, why the hell is your location set to Houston?"

"Shake, what—" I break off, completely shocked. I haven't heard from my ex since he dumped me about three weeks ago. I'd concocted this whole plan right after our breakup, intending to call him once I finished all of this and got back to D.C. I hadn't expected him to find out about it already.

"What are you doing tracking my location?" I ask.

"You never took me off Find My Friends," he says. "I called your office, and they said you were out of town, and—"

A white Toyota Camry pulls up, and though I can't confirm it in the app, I'm almost certain it's for me.

"Hey, hang on," I say. "I think my car's here."

"Wait, Meena, I'm saying I don't know if you should—"

The driver steps out of the car, and I pull the phone away from my ear, though Shake's voice continues faintly.

"Meena?" the driver asks, and I nod, meeting him near the trunk and handing him my carry-on bag.

I climb into the backseat and place my purse near my feet before I return to the call. Shake's still talking, and though I've missed the last few seconds, I can guess what he's said.

"Look, maybe I should have told you about this before I came down here," I interrupt, clicking my seat belt over my chest. "But with everything you said last time . . . I thought I'd just fly here and finish things and then we could figure out if there's anything, well, if there's anything *left* for us to figure out."

Shake's silent for a moment. "So . . . you're actually doing it? I mean, you've made up your mind?"

I pause. Abhishek "Shake" Das and I have been friends for years, ever since we were introduced and I gave him a hard time over his chosen nickname. We both worked on the Hill and ran in the same circles, and fell into an easy, banter-filled friendship, but there was never anything romantic back then. When we first met, Shake had a girlfriend he was beyond devoted to, but even if he had been single, I hadn't really been in the right headspace to date at that time.

But after Shake's relationship went up in flames—in the most public, embarrassing way imaginable—I was there for him. I'd sympathized, having known exactly how that kind of heartbreak feels, and the more I'd gotten to know him, the more I'd realized how similar the two of us are. We share the same goals, the same dreams, the same drive. We just get each other on a fundamental level. And over the years that friendship naturally transitioned into something else.

I'd dated other men, but Shake was the only one who understood both my ambition and my slow, cautious nature. He understood that when your heart's been broken, it doesn't heal back quite the same. He had always been satisfied by the feelings we had for each other, by the way our relationship was. Calm and quiet. Soft and comfortable. He understood that we didn't have to feel capital *L* Love for each other. He agreed that *loving* each other was enough.

When he broke up with me, my first thought was how hard it would be to find someone else who would understand me that same way, who would be satisfied with only that much. On top of that, my family loves him. In fact, my parents think he's perfect. They couldn't stop talking about him after they met him, saying he was exactly the kind of man they'd always pictured for their daughters. They'd be devastated if they found out we broke up.

"Yeah," I tell Shake. "I'm sure. Look, I'm flying back tonight, so maybe we can talk about all of it then."

I had booked the latest flight available for tonight out of Houston. Maybe it was optimistic of me, thinking this would take less than a day to sort out, but I'm a good negotiator. It's a key part of my job. And there's no reason we can't both be professional about this. At the end of the day, this is a deal like any other. There's something I want. And though I don't know what it is, there must be something he wants too. And once I figure that out, I'll make him an offer he can't refuse.

I almost smile at the thought. He's never seen this side of me before. Never seen me go all *Godfather* on somebody. He doesn't know what I'm capable of. But after today, he will.

"You're . . . you're flying back tonight?"

I frown. "Yeah," I say. "That was the plan at least, and so far nothing has changed."

"Really?" Shake's voice sounds more normal now. There's a hint of relief in it that wasn't there before. "That's great. So, everything's okay, then? That's why I was calling, because it sounded like things were going to be bad. Like, really bad. I wasn't sure . . . But if you're still going to fly back tonight, maybe it's not . . . maybe it's not what I was thinking."

My frown deepens. Has my lawyer been talking to Shake? Sharing information with him? I mean, they are friends. Shake is the one who referred me to him. But if there is news, neither of them has shared it with me. My lawyer only told me that there'd been no response. He hadn't given any indication that things would be particularly bad once I got here. Unless . . . Is Shake jealous?

It seems absurd. After all, he's the one who broke up with me. I'd always been honest with him about my situation. He'd been fine with it, until we started talking about plans for the future. I'd told him I was going to make things official, that I was sending the papers, and that had appeased him for a while. He started organizing some meetings with political advisory groups for us. Our first was scheduled to take place in just a few days, to talk about the viability of the two of us running for office. We'd planned on framing it as a joint run, hoping to capitalize on the novelty of a couple running together for two open seats.

And then he'd found out that the papers weren't signed.

"How long have you been sitting on this? It's been months, hasn't it?" he'd said, his eyes wild. "Have you . . . I mean, we're supposed to meet with the team in three weeks. We're supposed to talk with them about running— God, Meena we've talked about getting *engaged*."

I'd tried to tell him I'd been working on it, but in truth, I hadn't followed up as much as I should have. I'd cared about it. I'd wanted it over just as much as he did. I'd just kind of let it fall by the wayside.

"I'll do it," I'd told him. "Before the meeting, I'll get it done."

He'd just shaken his head, his hand trembling as he ran it over his mouth. "I can't do this. You need to . . . you need to fix this. You need to do whatever it takes to sort your shit out, because otherwise . . ." He'd let out a rough breath. "I can't be with you like this, waiting for you to make up your mind. I can't jeopardize everything I've been working toward. I mean, this run, this meeting, we've talked about doing all of it together, and if we can't do that, I need to figure out something else. I can't just—" He'd stopped, looking at me as if I was a stranger. "We're done. Until you get this figured out, we're done."

And I'd just watched, my mouth parted in shock, as he'd walked out the door.

This trip was supposed to be my way of showing I'd taken everything he'd said seriously. But it's also for me. This is a chapter I have to close before I can start a new one. And I'm ready for that now. I'm ready to move on.

"So, we'll talk later tonight?" I ask him again.

He clears his throat. "Yeah. Okay. And just . . . be safe. If things look like they might get worse, just get out of there. Maybe look at booking an earlier flight?"

"Sure," I reply, even though I'm not quite sure what he's talking about. Does he actually think I'm going to be in danger here? With *him*? I almost scoff at the idea, but then the car turns down a familiar street, and the sound dies in my throat.

The trees are taller. I don't know why that's the first thing I notice, but it is. When we first moved into this neighborhood, everything was new. The sidewalk was freshly paved. Little saplings lined the block, each one at a perfect distance from its neighbors. And they all had a nylon band circling the trunk, connecting each one to a stake in the ground. The stakes must have been there to give the trees support or something. To help them grow.

Whatever it was, it clearly worked, because none of the trees have them anymore. They all stand alone. Strong. With nothing tying them down.

"Shake, I have to go." He responds with a goodbye, but I barely hear him. My mind's too busy playing a weird game of past versus present.

Mrs. Patterson used to live in that house. That small, one-story home with the wraparound porch. I used to see her gardening, her gloved hands pulling up weeds, her large hat blocking out the sun. She waved at me every time I walked down this way, which was rare. I was in a strange sort of self-imposed exile in those days. I locked myself in my room with my bar prep materials, studying at all hours of the day, fueled by dread and panic that I might fail the bar exam. Again.

Goosebumps prickle up my arms, and I rub them away. She probably doesn't live there anymore. The bushes in the yard are overgrown. Scraggly. She wouldn't have ever let them get that way.

The car turns left, drawing us farther into the maze of this suburban subdivision. Drawing us closer to the cul-de-sac where I once lived.

I was surprised when I found out *he* still lives there. Not just in the same neighborhood, but in the same house we'd rented. From the property records I found he bought it a few years ago, but I can't understand why. Back then he'd always called it a "starter home." I'd hated that. The way he made it sound temporary from the very beginning. As if it was just a stepping-stone to something bigger and better. I'd liked our home as it was. At one point, I thought it was perfect.

Warm red brick. A fireplace with a mantel. A backyard with a tall old tree, Spanish moss dripping from its branches.

A tiny kitchen with barely any counter space. A living room

with a secondhand couch, and two bedrooms on the second floor. In the guest bedroom, where I spent a great deal of time, there was a large window facing out onto the street. I angled my desk to face it so I could glimpse the outside even if I couldn't be a part of it.

The house was small, but back then it was my whole world. Back then, it was ours.

I blink as that house comes into view now. It takes me a second to recognize it. It's the same shape and size, with the same driveway to the right leading to the garage.

But it's just . . . wrong. It's so wrong.

The car pulls to a stop, and I leap out, barely remembering that I need to grab my bag from the trunk before I storm to the front door.

I rap my knuckles against the hard surface, but no one comes to greet me. Instead, I'm met with the loud creak and screech of the garage door opening around the corner. I rush in that direction, every cell within me thrumming with energy, with the need to confront him.

But that fire slowly dies as I draw closer. He's facing away from me. His form is slightly shadowed in the dim light of the garage, but I can tell he's bending over. He lets out a grunt as he grabs hold of something. A large pallet or crate of some kind.

I'm about to announce myself, but then the back of his shirt rises, exposing a strip of warm, tan skin. My mouth goes dry. Did he always have a lower back like that? With . . . with . . . ridges? Can human beings even form muscles like that there? How can that be possible?

"You painted the house?" I ask. The words rush out, as if my mind's desperate for anything that will change the direction it was heading in just a second ago. "You painted all that red brick white? Why would you do that?"

He turns around immediately, whirling so fast that the pallet of bottled water wobbles in his arms. It tips to the side, almost falling, before he adjusts and catches it.

"Meena?" His voice is hoarse. His eyes are wide with shock. But I don't bask in his surprise the way I thought I would. I don't get to savor it, relish the moment. Because whatever shock he's experiencing, my body seems to be echoing it. My heart is thumping, beating wildly. The sound of blood whooshes fast in my ears.

I didn't properly prepare for this. Sure, I did my research and fine-tuned my negotiation strategy. But I didn't prepare for the full force of him. I didn't let myself imagine what it would be like to see him face-to-face.

It's been years. And logically, I knew that, but I didn't think about the toll those years would have had on him. In my mind he was preserved in amber. A relic. Static. Unchanging. But he's aged.

He's broader now. Still just as tall, but his shoulders seem to have expanded, his chest widened somehow. And his arms are slightly thicker too. They strain under the weight of the water he's carrying, making his veins stand out in sharp relief. He looks good. The same eyes, the same nose, but his hair's different. He'd always done that longer on the top, shorter on the sides thing when he was younger, but now it's long all around. Dark, tousled waves that end at the tops of his ears.

I want to run my hands through it. I want to see if it's just as soft as I remember. I want to feel it against my skin.

He blinks, his eyes slightly glazed, and I realize he's been watching me back this whole time, his gaze traveling over me from head to toe.

I flush, thinking about how much I've changed over the years too.

I lift a hand to my hair before I realize it, and try to play it off by tucking a piece behind my ear. Does he notice the occasional strand of silver sparkling here and there? The sharp cheekbones that were once hidden beneath the fuller, rounder cheeks of my youth? Time has changed me, though it shouldn't matter. I shouldn't care what he thinks. But it's been six years. I'm not the girl he remembers. And for some reason, I care.

"Meena?" he asks again. His brows crease, new lines I've never seen before forming on his forehead. "What . . . what are you doing here?"

When I thought of this moment, I imagined doing something dramatic. Like pulling out the papers and waving them in the air. Telling him he needed to sign on the bottom line or he'd be sorry.

But all of that sounds silly now.

His gaze flickers, flitting down toward my left hand. I'm tempted to curl my fingers into a fist, but I leave them loose, relaxed at my side. As if I don't know what he's doing. What he's checking for.

Shake and I are nothing if not practical. We may not have been ready for that step, but we'd already talked about rings. We'd set up email alerts for sales at a few jewelry stores, but then we'd broken up, so there's no engagement ring for Nikhil to stare at. Nothing for him to ask questions about. Nothing for me to explain.

"Nikhil," I say, and his eyes shoot back to mine. "It's been weeks and you haven't responded to anything. None of my emails. None of my calls."

He scoffs. "Right. *Your* emails. *Your* calls." His words are harsh. Mocking.

"My lawyer's emails," I amend. He rolls his eyes, and I immediately regret my attempt at a conciliatory tone. "You know what I mean."

"I don't," he shoots back. "I never do."

Oh. So, it's going to be like this. I square my shoulders. "You need to sign them, Nikhil. We need to just get this over with."

He shifts his weight to one side, leaning his body against the garage wall.

"What's the rush?" he asks.

I resist the urge to cringe. I'm usually smoother than this. Subtler. I know how to play it cool. To pretend like I don't need anything. All my negotiating tactics, all my skills seem to have vanished. I've let him glimpse the one card I was supposed to hold on to.

It's like being back around Nikhil has reduced me to the age of the person I was back then. Emotional and volatile and so . . . young.

I change the topic. "Why did you paint over the brick?"

He watches me, studying my face for longer than feels comfortable, then shakes his head. "Why do you care?"

"I don't," I reply, but we both know I'm lying.

"Look, this will only take a few minutes," I say. "You sign it and I promise you'll never have to see me again. I'll head right out of here, go straight back to the airport, and—"

A flash of surprise crosses his face, but it quickly disappears as his mouth sets into a stern, thin line. "You won't," he says. He pushes off the wall, and heads toward the door. "Grab a crate, will you?" he calls over his shoulder.

I stare at his retreating form for a second, then scramble after him. "What do you mean I won't?"

He balances the bottled water on his hip, freeing his hand to turn the door handle. When he steps inside, he glances back at me and groans. "You seriously didn't grab anything? We're going to need to bring all of it in."

If this is a delay tactic, it's the strangest one I've experienced yet.

"What are you talking about?" I ask as I follow, jumping when the heavy door swings shut behind me. He still hasn't changed that, then. He always said he would, but it's the same old door that we used to have. Always slamming shut when I least expect it.

He finally puts the water down, dropping the pallet onto a stack of similar crates assembled on the floor. "Don't you read the news?"

My jaw almost drops. Is he kidding me? The man who rarely picked up a newspaper, who barely paid attention when I watched the news or put on NPR is asking *me* if I ever read the news.

"You know I do."

He lifts a shoulder. "Well, things change. People change. It's not like you and I know each other anymore."

Ouch. That hurts. It shouldn't because he's only stating the truth, but it stings. Like a manicurist rubbing acetone over a paper cut. "Well, I haven't changed," I say, before I quickly correct myself. "Changed in that way, I mean. Of course I read the news."

A muscle twitches in his jaw. "So, you came here. To my house. Fully knowing what was about to happen."

"Knowing *what* was about to happen?"

His brows snap together. "There's a hurricane in the Gulf, Meena."

"It's hurricane season," I reply. "There's always a storm in the Gulf." But even as I say the words, I know they're coming from a place of denial. *No. No, no, no, no, no.*

I pull out my phone, and the cracked, distorted screen is filled from top to bottom with blurry images. Messages I can't read. Notifications I can't make sense of. But I don't have to be able to read them to know what they all say.

I rack my brain, trying to recall whether I read or saw anything about this. Nothing popped up when I booked my flight here. No warning indicating that a storm was on its way. I vaguely recall a headline about a hurricane forming off the coast, but after some time, the headlines about these things start to run together. For good reason. Most of these storms don't materialize into anything. They tend to dissipate before reaching the shore.

Still, if something was close to Houston, surely I would have noticed it. Surely someone would have told me.

"Was your flight canceled?"

My eyes dart up. I expect him to look smug or cocky. But his expression is almost gentle. More relaxed. Open.

I lift a hand to my forehead, trying to rub the tension out of it. "I don't know. My phone's not working. I can't tell."

"When was it supposed to leave?"

"At ten."

He nods, but from that stiff, stilted movement I can tell he thinks there's no way that plane is leaving tonight.

"But everything was fine," I say. "Earlier. Everything was okay. I . . . No one mentioned anything about a storm when I left—"

"It was veering east," he says. "No one was predicting it would come this way until midmorning." He ducks down, removing a water bottle from the plastic wrapping and handing it to me.

I twist the cap off and gulp it gratefully.

"I had stocked up," Nikhil continues. "At the beginning of the season. Just in case. So, I've got plenty of water and food. And we have hours until it makes landfall. It's supposed to get here tonight, so we'll have more than enough time to board up the windows and move some things up to the second floor . . ."

Oh, no. I'm not staying here. I'm not staying here with *him*. There's no way. We won't survive it. I'd rather take my chances with the hurricane.

I turn back to my phone. I can find a hotel. There must be something available. Somewhere. I press the icon that looks like my travel app, but I know I've tapped the wrong thing when Olivia Rodrigo's last album starts playing instead.

"Shit." I press the same icon, but instead of stopping, the music seems to only grow louder.

"Here, let me," Nikhil says, reaching for it. I yank my arm away, but not before his fingers lightly brush against mine.

It's fleeting. Over in less than a second. But electricity tingles at my fingertips, sending tiny shocks toward my elbow. I shake my hand, trying to get rid of the sensation, which somehow, miraculously, silences my phone. I look down in surprise, then groan when I see that the screen is now pitch-black. This thing is officially broken.

"Maybe I can switch to an earlier flight," I say. "If I could use your phone. Or your computer. I could . . ."

"People are evacuating, Meena. Those flights are going to be booked."

The small hope that had been building within me dies a quick death. He's right. I hate that he's right. Now I understand the mad rush at the airport.

"It'll be okay," he says gently. "We'll get through this. The house is in good condition, and like I said, we have everything we'll need. Flashlights and radios and I even installed a backup generator last year. It doesn't always work, but it should kick in if we lose power."

I nod along as if I'm listening. As if it's the *storm* I'm worried about and not the fact that I'm about to be stuck sharing a house with the man I'm trying to sever ties with once and for all.

Turns out I was right before. I am in hell. But it's worse than I thought. Because now I'm trapped here. With the one person I hoped I'd never have to see again.

My *husband*.

Nope. I take that back.

I refuse to be trapped here. I refuse to accept it.

"Can I borrow your phone?" I ask. Desperation swims through me, but I do my best to hide it. To keep it buried deep, deep down.

Nikhil's forehead creases, but he doesn't say a word as he pulls his phone out of his back pocket and hands it to me.

I clutch it like a lifeline and my hand shakes a bit as I check every airline I can think of. Unfortunately, it takes only a few minutes to confirm that Nikhil was right. Almost everything is booked. And prices are sky-high for the few seats that remain—there's a flight to D.C. going for north of $1,000 right now and really, we need stronger legislation to prevent corporate greed during a time of crisis like this—but even with those prices, almost everything is gone.

"How many hours until it gets here?" I ask, switching tracks and trying to search for rental cars. Only it seems like everyone must have had the same idea, because when I select "Houston" as the pickup location, the page freezes. I refresh the page, but the traffic must be overwhelming, because a 404 error alert pops up. I groan.

"Meena, what are you—"

"Your car," I say, walking toward the garage, pausing in the hall-way and swiping the keys off the hanging shelf instinctively. I don't even think twice about it. It's only when I reach the garage door that I register what I've just done. And what I just saw out of the corner of my eye.

I look back over my shoulder, a bit stunned. It's the same hang-ing shelf Nikhil had installed when we first moved in. And it's still hanging in the exact same spot. He'd made it back then, out of some leftover wood he'd brought home from a construction site. And then we'd painted it together.

Pale green. With a border made out of little vines and flowers. The colors have faded a bit with time, but the scrawled script in white is still legible.

Welcome to M&N's

We'd debated what to put there. We hadn't wanted to be too cringey. Like something you'd find in the discount aisle at a T.J.Maxx.

"'Home is where the heart is,'" I'd joked after we'd struggled to come up with a better option.

"No, that's too long," Nikhil had said. "There's not enough room on the shelf. We have to pick one of those one-word ones, like 'Gratitude,' 'Peace,' or 'Love.'"

I'd gasped. "It's so simple, Nikhil. It's been staring us right in the face. I can't believe we didn't see it until now. 'Live, Laugh, Love.' It's timeless. A classic for a reason."

He'd laughed, and I'd grinned.

"What about, 'Welcome to Our Home'?"

"Or 'Welcome to Meena and Nikhil's'?" I'd suggested. "It's a little more personal?"

He'd beamed and I'd basked in it, in the warmth that had radiated from him. It hadn't mattered that the words were too long, that we'd had to shorten our names to just our initials. We'd both thought it was still perfect.

Things had been so easy in those early days. When we'd come back from our honeymoon. When we'd first moved into the house. When everything had felt so bright and possible and new.

"We can't take my car," Nikhil says, snapping me back to the present.

"Why not?" I ask, before I can correct him. *We* aren't taking his car anywhere. *I'll* be taking the car somewhere.

I mean, if he really wants to evacuate, he could come with me. I wouldn't leave him stranded, but he's clearly prepared to ride out the hurricane here so I'm sure he'll be fine. Actually, I'm sure he'd *prefer* staying here, and he'd definitely prefer me being far, far away from him. After all, it's how we've been for the majority of our marriage. He's clearly preferred it all these years so I'm sure he'd prefer it now.

"It's bumper-to-bumper traffic out there," he says. "It's all over the news. They're saying it's almost as bad as it was during Hurricane Rita."

I deflate.

I'd been in middle school during Rita, but I remember the way the entire city had rushed to evacuate. Hurricane Katrina had devastated New Orleans just weeks before, and people here had naturally been terrified. My family had somehow managed to secure a flight out, but those who had planned to evacuate to nearby Austin or San Antonio had been stuck. The resulting gridlock had been a nightmare, turning a drive that would normally take three to four hours into something that took more than twenty. Cars stalled and ran out of gas, fights broke out on the highway, and many people gave up and went back home after being on the road for nine hours and still not making it out of the city.

"When is landfall?" I ask, grasping at straws, trying to think of any other solution.

"Tonight. By the time it reaches us it'll probably be late, but we'll start feeling the beginnings of it around six or seven. Could be earlier or later than that though. It's just an estimate."

My mind buzzes, trying to think through other options. I ask to borrow his phone again, and he passes it to me.

A quick search shows that there are a few hotels close by that have remained open. I almost book one, typing all my information in, overjoyed to see a way out, but at the last moment I hesitate. I don't have food. Or water. Or anything that would help me get through a storm like this. I don't even have a working phone or a flashlight.

I could try to do a last-minute run for supplies, but the thought of fighting my way through a pre-storm grocery store with ravaged, empty shelves and long lines makes me recoil in horror.

I wish I knew someone who still lived here, but I didn't do the best job of keeping in touch with childhood friends. I have no idea who stayed in Houston. And even if I could miraculously remember someone's number from back then, I don't think I could call them now, out of the blue, and ask to crash with them. We'd once had a robust community here. My parents used to have so many family friends, uncles and aunties whom I'd known my whole life. Who would've hosted me in a heartbeat. But that was before they'd had a falling-out. Well, really, that was before my parents had been *pushed* out, basically ostracized after everything that had happened with my sister.

At least I don't have to worry about them right now. My parents left Houston a couple years ago and retired to New Jersey so they could be closer to my aunts and uncles, who are mostly scattered throughout the tristate area. My family doesn't know I'm here or that I flew to Houston at all. And I'm planning on keeping it that way.

I swallow, my throat dry and scratchy. "Could I . . . Would you be willing to . . . You said you stocked up, right?"

Nikhil lifts an eyebrow, but doesn't respond.

"On supplies," I say. "You stocked up on supplies, right?"

He nods.

"Do you have any extra? Would you be willing to give me some of it?" The words fly out of my mouth, jumbled and rushed.

A bewildered expression crosses his face. "Umm, yeah. Of course. You can use whatever you want."

The tightness in my chest eases. "Thank you. I'll pay you back. For whatever I take."

His confusion only grows. "You don't have to pay me."

"Oh. Thanks, but I will. I'll Venmo you. And maybe I can borrow your car? If not, I can take an Uber and—"

"You're leaving?" There's shock in his voice, but there's something else too. It's barely there, just the slightest hint of it, but it almost sounds like . . . he's hurt? No. That can't be right.

"It'll be better this way," I say quickly. "If I go to a hotel. But I'll come back. After the storm. And we can sit and figure everything out then, but it's probably best if we don't—"

"You're going to a hotel," he says, his voice rife with disbelief.

"Yeah, there are a couple that are staying open and—"

He scoffs, the sound harsh and quick. "You can't stay in a hotel during a storm like this. What are you going to do if the power goes out? You think the Holiday Inn Express is going to have a generator?

What if there's flooding? What if you get stuck there for days on end?"

"I'll be fine," I snap back, even though the idea of being by myself in a hotel room in the dark for an indefinite amount of time is a little terrifying.

He shakes his head, his eyes dark. Thunderous. "You don't even have a working phone, Meena. You can't . . . Do you know how bad this one is supposed to be? You think the hotel staff is going to be able to take care of all its guests if something happens?" He pauses, and some of the anger leaves his face, replaced by a flash of something raw and vulnerable. "You'd really rather be there? You'd really rather go through all of this alone?"

I'm tempted to say "yes." To fling that word out there and stand my ground, but the idea of being by myself in a shabby hotel while violent rain and winds pound at my window has lost a good amount of its appeal.

I need to be honest with myself. As much as I hate it, escape is not an option.

"No," I say quietly, acceptance and dread traveling through me. "That makes sense. I'll . . . I'll stay here."

Nikhil watches me blankly for a moment. He opens his mouth, as if he's about to say something more, but he must change his mind because he shuts it, nodding instead.

He turns away, heading farther into the house, and I have no choice but to follow after him.

A jittery sensation buzzes beneath my skin, but I clamp down on the panic by engaging in the one activity that always calms me down: making a list. In order of priority, I need to make sure that I

1. inform my boss that I'm going to be in Houston longer than I had planned;

2. assist in whatever hurricane prep Nikhil thinks we need to do; and

3. survive the storm while keeping as far away from my ex-husband as possible.

Well, soon-to-be ex-husband. Once I can get him to sign off on these divorce papers. We still haven't discussed the divorce in detail, which I suppose is understandable under the circumstances.

It's strange. I've been trying to figure it out, but I don't understand why Nikhil wouldn't just respond to the papers in the first place. We haven't been in touch in six years. Haven't seen or talked to each other in all that time.

In the early days of our separation, I'd been so sure he'd come after me. That we'd reconcile. That it had all just been a misunderstanding. I'd imagined him flying up to D.C. and making some big grand gesture, apologizing, and trying to win me back.

But he never did.

He's never once reached out. He obviously hasn't wanted to and is obviously not interested in having a relationship with me at all. So, why won't he sign off on this divorce? It wouldn't change a thing between us. It would just make our separation official.

It's the next item on my to-do list:

4. Figure out why Nikhil's been holding out, get him to sign the papers, then leave and never come back here again.

Nikhil is rattling off instructions about the prep we need to do before the storm and I'm nodding along until he comes to a sudden stop and tilts his head. "Are you listening to me?"

"Yeah, yeah. I am."

He crosses his arms. "Really," he drawls, long and slow. "You weren't just tuning me out and making some kind of pro/con list in your head?"

"No," I say sharply, a bit unnerved by how close he got to the truth.

"Ah, a to-do list, then. Or maybe you're mentally rearranging your work calendar. I'm sure all of this," he says, waving a hand in the air, "really threw a wrench in your plans."

He's watching me with an all too knowing look on his face. As if after all these years, he still understands the way my mind works. As if he can still figure out exactly what I'm thinking. As if he still somehow has a right to.

The back of my neck grows hot, and I feel prickly. Irritated.

"It did," I snap. "Trust me, I wasn't planning on being here a second longer than I had to. I'm leaving as soon as this storm is done. As soon as you sign the papers."

His expression darkens. "Well, if you're hoping to make it out of here in one piece, you're going to need to pay attention. I was saying that we'll have to stay away from the windows.

"We're going to board up the big ones, but I don't know if we can get to all of them. And the boarding may not even help that much. The glass might shatter regardless."

"Fine," I say.

"And because we need to stay away from windows, we're going to have to figure out what parts of the house we'll stay in during the storm."

"Makes sense."

"The bedrooms are off-limits, obviously. The windows are supertall there. And most of the first floor won't work either. The only room that has no external exposure is the closet upstairs. The pantry and the bathrooms don't have any windows either, but it's not like we could sleep there comfortably—"

I freeze.

"I'm not sleeping with you."

His eyebrows jump, and my cheeks warm. I guess I could have phrased that differently.

"We'll put sleeping bags in the closet," Nikhil says, exaggerating the *s* in "bags," hissing like a snake.

My stomach twists. He seems to be just as adamant as I am about not sleeping together, which is good. Great, even. Perfect. Nice to know we're on the same page.

"I think it's really the only option we have," he continues.

A picture of the closet pops into my head. The floor space is limited. Even with separate sleeping bags, the bags will be touching. And how thick can sleeping bag material be? I don't remember. I can't remember the last time I slept in one. But I don't think it'll be thick enough to hide the outline of his body against mine.

The curve of his leg. His thighs, thick and firm. Those back muscles I accidentally glimpsed earlier.

No. Nope. This isn't going to work. "I'm sleeping in the guest bedroom."

"The guest bedroom," he repeats flatly. "The one with that huge window facing the street."

"Yes," I snap. "Good to know you haven't changed that part of the house at least."

He lets out a sound of frustration, and I grit my teeth. I know that sound. It means he's conceded the argument for now but will revisit it later.

It's time to up my game. Time to be strategic.

Okay. So, a hurricane is bad. Bad news all around. But there's a bit of a silver lining here. It's not just that I'm trapped with Nikhil; Nikhil is now trapped with *me*. I can use this. Twist it to my advantage.

This hurricane is giving us time alone together. Time that I can use to get him to sign the divorce papers. No distractions. No outside world. I'll wear him down. Pester him until he has no choice but to—

I jump. The phone I was so sure was dead has come back to life, vibrating loudly in my hand. The screen is still black, but I can hear some noise coming out of it. I lift it to my ear tentatively. "Hello?"

"Meena, thank god. I've been trying to reach you, but none of the calls were going through. I know what you said before, but everyone's reporting that the storm's going to hit Houston tonight. You need to get out of there. I was looking at flights and everything's booked, but I'm going to call the firm's travel agent next. They can usually swing something."

Soon after we'd met, Shake had stopped working on the Hill. His ex-girlfriend had cheated on him, which would have been devastating enough on its own, but her infidelity hadn't been a small, private indiscretion. She'd been sleeping with Shake's boss. A high-level congressman. A high-level *married* congressman.

Shake had needed a fresh start, so he'd gotten out of politics and joined a classic white-shoe law firm that could not be more different from mine, as evidenced by the fact that his firm keeps a travel agent on retainer. The midsize, boutique public interest firm I work for could never afford to do that. "Okay," I say, risking a glance at Nikhil.

He's watching me, his eyes steely. Sharp. Like flint. As if the smallest movement might spark something. Set everything aflame.

I half turn away. I don't know if he can hear everything on the other end of the conversation, but I'm hoping Shake's voice doesn't carry.

"My phone's not really working though," I tell Shake. "Not reliably. So, if you do book something I may not find out about it."

I guess I could give him Nikhil's number. I could tell him to call me there if he's able to book a flight, except . . . I'm not ready to tell Nikhil about Shake yet. I'm not sure why, but the idea of it makes me a little nauseous. Though, do I really need to tell him about Shake at all? I'm hoping Shake will want to get back together once all of this is done, but I don't know that it'll happen for sure. Besides, I don't *have* to give Nikhil my reasons for the divorce. Actually, it's probably better if I don't. It's better if he doesn't find out why I need this divorce so badly.

No, telling Nikhil about Shake is not an option. I'll stay. I'll use this time to get the divorce, and then I'll be done. A clean break. With Nikhil being none the wiser.

"Okay," Shake responds. "But . . . are you going to be okay? I mean, besides the storm. Because he's there, right? You're going to be staying with him?"

My cheeks flare with heat, growing even hotter when I feel Nikhil's gaze burning against the side of my face.

"I'll be fine," I say quickly. "Don't worry about me."

He pauses. "I'm sorry. About a lot of the things I said and how I . . . I've been wanting to talk to you, but I know now's not the best—"

"We'll talk when I get back," I say firmly. "Hopefully I'll be back by Monday, but if not, could you call my office and tell them the situation?"

He says he will, telling me to be safe and that he's still going to try to get me out, but we both know the odds are slim.

I hang up, letting out a sigh.

"Who was that?" Nikhil asks. He says it nonchalantly, but his tone is careful. Too even and measured to be casual.

"No one," I say, and his eyes narrow. "Just my sister."

Nikhil never met my sister. He once met my parents in passing, but I never formally introduced him to any of my family. Even though we were married—*are* married—they never knew about it. Or him.

His face hardens, as if he remembers that fact.

"Huh," he says. "Her voice is deeper than I thought it would be."

Damn it. So, he did overhear.

"Yeah, well . . ." I trail off, hoping he'll just let it go. "So, the windows. Is that what we need to do next?"

He holds my gaze for a second, before scrubbing a hand across his face. "Yeah. Sure."

He stalks back toward the garage door, grabbing a toolbox along the way. Then he leads us to a pile of plywood.

"I already measured everything and cut these to size," he says.

"I'm just going to need some help positioning them over the windows so I can drill them into place. And if we have time to do the second-story ones, I'll need your help with the ladder."

I nod. He grabs a few pieces of plywood, slinging them under his arm in one smooth movement. He's strong. He's always been strong. And this is his area of expertise. He used to work in construction. Still does, I think.

I get my hands around a piece of plywood, and half carry it, half drag it to the front. In the time it takes me to do that, he's finished lugging the rest of them.

We start on window number one, and fortunately it's not too difficult. I just have to hold the board in place while he does all the work. It's not a bad arrangement. Though there's tension between us. Something staticky. Prickly.

We settle into a rhythm. An uneasy temporary truce. The only words we exchange are related to our task.

When I lose my grip and the plywood slips slightly, he grunts out a "You got it?"

I get the board back into position and mutter back a "yeah."

When he asks me to pass him the drill, I do it carefully. Delicately. Making sure our hands don't accidentally touch again.

I follow his instructions, shifting the board whenever he asks me to, and when it comes to his part, he's quick. Efficient. I try not to watch him as he works. Try not to notice the intense expression of concentration as he drills. The sweat that beads near his temples. The way he wipes it away with the back of his arm.

I used to love watching Nikhil at his job. He was always so serious. So focused. Sometimes it felt like a role reversal. Here, he was the rule follower and I got to be the fun one. Here, I got to feel free. I still remember how he'd looked the first time I'd shown up at one of his construction sites, back when we'd started dating. He'd had a bright yellow hard hat on top of his head, and a wary expression on his face as he'd handed me a hat of my own.

"If you're going to visit me," he'd said, "you're going to have to follow the rules."

"Rules, schmules," I'd joked, teasing him just for the fun of it. Everything had been so new back then. Every smile I'd wrangled out of him had felt like a gift. He was generous with them, but I'd counted them up anyway, saved them like treasures, guarded them deep in my heart.

He'd slipped the hat over my head, fastening it under my chin.

"There," he'd said. "Now you're OSHA compliant."

"I'm not an employee here so I'm pretty sure those regulations wouldn't apply . . ."

"Law nerd," he'd said affectionately.

"Safety nerd," I'd shot back with a grin.

He'd laughed, leaning to give me a kiss, and laughed even harder when the hard plastic of our hats had collided instead.

I didn't realize until later how much of a role reversal those moments had really been. That his job had made him as stressed and miserable as studying for the bar had made me. That it had twisted his natural light and joyful state of being into something else. Something sadder. Something he never quite let me see.

I shake my head, returning my focus to what we're doing. And before I know it, we've finished the last first-story window.

We're about to head back into the garage when a voice sounds behind us. "Boarding up the windows, huh?"

I turn around. A white man of medium height and build is watching us. A grin on his face.

"It's a good idea," the man says. "A very good idea. But I don't think I'm going to do it. Not this time." He swings that smile in my direction. "Nikhil knows, but the last storm we got I went all out.

Moved all my furniture to the second floor. Boarded every window. Took every precaution. And how did that turn out?"

The mystery man booms out a laugh. "All we got was a light sprinkle. Could barely call it rain, really."

"This one looks like it's going to be worse," Nikhil says.

The man shrugs. "That's what they said about the last one too." He extends a hand toward me. "I'm Alan. I live in that house over there." He points to the house at the very center of the cul-de-sac, about four houses down from ours.

Ours? I mean Nikhil's. Four houses down from Nikhil's.

"Nice to meet you," I say, shaking his hand. "I'm Meena and . . ." I look back at Nikhil. "I'm just visiting."

Alan chortles. "Bad timing for a visit."

Yeah. Thanks, Alan. I know.

The house Alan pointed out is a nice one, but I'm pretty sure it was empty the whole time I was here. I remember a perpetual For Sale sign hanging in the front yard.

"You'll be in good hands with Nikhil," Alan continues, slapping Nikhil on the back. "He's a pro at this kind of thing. Though I think he's a little too paranoid. He even installed a generator if you can believe that."

Nikhil's lips stretch. I guess it's technically a smile, but the expression is grim. "I like to be prepared," he says. "And a couple other people in the neighborhood have them too."

"Right, right," Alan says. "Fair enough. You know, I understand how important it is to be prepared. I am an astronaut after all."

He . . . he is? I've never met an astronaut before. I don't know what I was expecting, but Alan isn't it.

Alan must register the surprise on my face. "Oh, did Nikhil not mention that?" he says. "I work for NASA. It's not far from here. Just a couple minutes away. A nice, easy commute. I've worked there awhile. Been to the International Space Station a couple times." He shifts his weight, his expression growing solemn, the pitch of his voice lowering. "You know, when you've been to space, when you've seen what I've seen . . . you learn a lot. So, if you two need anything, you just let me know. Issues with plumbing, electricity, feel free to call me. I've done it all."

"Umm, thanks," I say. I'm not sure how much plumbing and electricity work astronauts do in space, but what do I know?

Nikhil rubs his hand over his mouth. His classic move when he's trying not to laugh.

Alan doesn't seem to notice. He plants his hands on his hips, looking at the windows thoughtfully. "What kind of plywood did you use? A quarter-inch thick?"

"Five-eighths of an inch," Nikhil responds. "Anything thinner and it won't hold up."

"Ahh, right. Smart. That's smart. Good thinking. And the drill? You used a . . . a . . ." Alan blinks.

"A power drill," Nikhil says. "Yes, that's right."

"Good, good," Alan replies. "Exactly what I was going to say. Just couldn't remember the word."

"No worries," Nikhil says. "We all *space out* from time to time." This time Nikhil's lips twitch and I'm the one fighting to hold back a laugh. Despite my best efforts, one escapes and I attempt to disguise it as a cough.

Nikhil's eyes catch mine. And even though he's not winking at me, it feels like he is. Like he's saying, *It's fun sharing this moment with you.* Or *I'm happy you're here.* Or *Isn't this guy ridiculous?*

But then his expression turns cold. All trace of amusement vanishing. Though it's possible I just imagined the whole thing.

"I appreciate your offer to help, Alan," Nikhil says. "And the same goes for you. If you need anything, just let me know. You still have the same radio as last time?"

"Yup. Set to the neighborhood frequency."

"Great." Nikhil wraps things up, explaining that we need to get going so we can board up the rest of the windows, and Alan saunters off on his way.

"Nice guy," I offer, as Nikhil and I lug the ladder out of the garage.

Nikhil makes a low, noncommittal sound in response.

"Has he lived here long?"

"Can't remember."

"Kind of cool he's an astronaut."

Nikhil's hands are full with the weight of the ladder, but he still somehow manages to lift his shoulders in something that resembles a shrug.

I take the hint. Whether it's because we're back in hurricane prep mode or because I'm the one attempting to jump-start the conversation, he doesn't want to talk.

We set the ladder against the house, and I hold it steady, looking straight ahead. I'm definitely not stealing glances at the sight above me. Definitely not sneaking peeks at the way Nikhil climbs, at the way his muscled thighs and butt and *everything* move in those jeans.

We finish with the front of the house, and then the windows at the back. We bring in the remaining crates of water, and the potted plants and other small objects scattered in the yard.

After dragging the last one in, we trudge back inside. I collapse at the kitchen table, resting my head in my hands. I'm bone-tired. And it's not just from all the lifting.

It's like my body has forgotten how to cope with these temperatures. And though I know there's a storm coming, the weather right now would fool anyone. It's late August. The tail end of summer, but it feels like the peak. There's hardly any cloud cover to block the sun. And the humidity. I'd forgotten about that too. It makes it so no matter how absurdly hot it gets, you can't sweat any of it off. It sticks with you. Combining with the moisture in the air. As evidenced by the way my T-shirt clings to my skin, all damp and disgusting.

"I need to take a shower," I announce.

"That's not a bad idea," Nikhil mutters.

I bristle. I know I'm not exactly smelling like roses, but he doesn't have to jab at me like that. I open my mouth, fully intending to lob something sharp and harsh and barbed right back at him, but then he continues.

"We may lose running water once the storm hits. Doesn't always happen, but we should probably use it while we still can."

The anger that had been building within me deflates, and a prick of guilt takes its place.

I really have been assuming the worst from Nikhil. It never used to be like that between us. There was a time when we only brought out the best in each other. Nikhil knew exactly how to shake me out of my dark spells and make me laugh. He made things light when they felt heavy, and I added weight when it was needed.

"You ground me," he'd told me once, his eyes bright and earnest. "Sometimes I feel . . . I feel untethered. You know how, with my mom, her job made it so that we had to move around a lot? And it's just every time I started at a new school, every time I felt like I was just starting to fit in, we'd have to leave. I'd have to figure out a new city, a new school, and new friends, and then at the end of the year, I'd have to do it all over again.

"But you . . . you make me feel like I can . . . like it would be *safe* to put down some roots. You're so determined. So sure about what you want out of your career and your life. You never hesitate. You never waver. And if you're sure that . . . if what you want is me—"

"Of course it is," I'd said, my hand on top of his, the pad of a finger traveling over his skin.

He'd swallowed. "But it's okay if it's not. I don't want to assume. I know we got married under strange circumstances and it's not something we've talked about since. It wouldn't be wrong if you've changed your mind. It's only been a few weeks and we can still—"

"I want you, Nikhil," I'd told him. "I want you."

Relief had flooded his face, but it had given me pause. Had he somehow doubted me? Had I done something to make him think I wasn't in this with him? Did he not know how I felt? Did he not know that every day with him made me feel like I'd won the lottery? Something I'd never expected. Something I'd never believed could actually be mine.

I'd opened my mouth to tell him, to try to explain just how much I'd wanted him, but then his lips had met mine, and we'd just showed each other instead, with our mouths, our hands, our bodies.

He'd traced every part of me like it mattered, running his finger over my sternum, placing his palm flat against the center of my chest. Sometimes he'd press his ear to that spot, listening to my heartbeat as he brushed his lips against my breast.

The weight of his body, the pressure of it, had soothed my every nerve. In those moments, he quieted my mind. Made me feel blissfully at peace, with no worries about the future, no worries about anything. Even now, at night, when I'm too tired to hold the memories at bay, I can feel him. A phantomlike sensation. The way he pressed against me. The way he moved against me. The way he brought me to heights I'd never experienced before, and the way he held me as I came back down. Liquid heat spreads through my body and I scoot back from the table, my chair emitting a loud screech as it scrapes against the floor. Nikhil flinches and I offer an apologetic grimace before fleeing up the stairs toward the guest bedroom.

I need a shower. Really what I need is to get out of here. To get away from this house. From him.

I shut the door behind me, my skin burning as I flip the shower handle all the way to the left, making the water as cold as I can get it.

We're not the same people anymore. I'm not that person anymore. The Nikhil who lives in my suppressed memories is not the man sitting at the table downstairs. That man is a stranger to me, and he needs to stay that way.

Because I have a life waiting for me back in D.C. I have to go back and show Shake I'm serious. The two of us are going to build something together. Something stable and good. Together, we're going to achieve everything we've always wanted.

I need to remember the plan. I need to stay focused. I need to get what I need and get out.

I can't let Nikhil derail my future.

Not again.

4

I switch off the water and wrap a towel around me, feeling incredibly grateful that I just happen to be the kind of paranoid person who travels with an extra pair of underwear no matter what.

I didn't pack much more than that since I never planned on being here for more than a few hours. But still, I'm grateful. In this moment, clean underwear is enough.

I towel-dry my hair and attempt to finger-comb the tangles but give up after accidentally yanking a few too many snarls. I should put my old clothes back on, but I'm not ready for that gross, sweaty T-shirt to touch my skin again, so I delay. Huddling in my towel, I stalk around the guest bedroom.

Nikhil really hasn't changed much about it. He's replaced the beat-up futon with a real bed, which is a nice upgrade, but otherwise this room's remained the same. Almost exactly the way it looked seven years ago. Back when I spent hours and hours in here. Back when I was using it as my study space.

I was sitting at that exact desk in the corner when I discovered

I'd failed the bar exam. I'd pulled up the results, control-F'd to find my name, and had almost thrown up when I'd realized that my name was not on that list. My job in D.C. was contingent on my passing. Everything was contingent on my passing. I'd never felt like such a failure.

Nikhil was so sweet in those weeks. So supportive. He was there when I had to pick myself up off the ground. When I had to start bar prep all over again. Every time I felt like I couldn't do it, he encouraged me. Held my hand. Believed in me.

We had been married only a few months at that time. He'd come home from work and find me here in this room, at that desk. He'd lean in the doorframe and ask me how studying was going, his voice bright and cheery, and I'd try to match his tone even though my brain always felt scrambled, my skin tight with electricity.

But slowly, around him, I'd start to feel better. He'd run his hands over the tense muscles in my shoulders and make me laugh, telling me something funny about his day. Sometimes, he'd insist on going on a walk around the neighborhood, which was good. It was often the only time I got some fresh air. He'd wave at some of the people we passed, exchange chitchat with others, and one day I'd been so curious.

"Do you know them?" I'd asked, our hands swinging, my fingers interlaced with his. We'd moved here only recently, and we hadn't socialized much in our first few weeks. We'd been so wrapped up in each other, floating through a haze of early wedded bliss. We'd rarely left our bedroom, let alone the house. And then, once I'd gotten the results back, our free time had vanished. Mine consumed with bar prep, his consumed with work.

He'd shrugged, the gesture pulling at our joined hands. "Some of them. I've done work on a couple of these houses." He'd gestured toward a place a few spots down from ours. "I did their roof a while back. Laura and Jody. They're supernice. I've been meaning to go over there and say hi. Maybe invite them for dinner, but—" He'd glanced over at me, his expression a little unsure. "But maybe later would be better?"

I'd attempted a smile and nodded, because I'd understood exactly what he meant by *later*. He meant post bar exam. Post me being this version of myself. And I couldn't blame him. I didn't enjoy my own company these days. Why subject others to it as well?

"Yeah," I'd said, a bit halfheartedly. "Later. Though we'll be moving to D.C. around then, won't we?"

"Right. Yeah," he'd replied, the word an exact echo of the way I'd said it, and we'd both let the topic drop.

A soft *thud* sounds at the door, shaking me back to the present. Not quite a knock, but not an accidental noise either. I creep in that direction, open the door a crack, and see something lying on the ground. A white bundle. I snatch it and shake it out.

It's a T-shirt. A clean white cotton T-shirt.

I could almost kiss it. In fact, I bring it to my face to do just that, when I catch a whiff of something woodsy and earthy.

Vetiver. Nikhil's cologne.

I'd bought him a bottle of it for our six-month anniversary, but there's no way that same bottle has lasted him till now. And I can't imagine that he'd keep rebuying the scent. I know I wouldn't want any reminders of that awful day.

I wave the T-shirt in the air, hoping some of the fragrance might drift out into the ether. But when I slip it around my neck, the scent envelops me. I can't get away. And despite how much I want to hate it, it's almost . . . comforting.

The shirt's long enough on me that I technically could wear it without pants. But as nice as it sounds to skip putting on my tight, restricting jeans, there's no way in hell I'm walking around like that.

So I force my legs back into them, push my hair away from my face, and head downstairs.

The familiar, homey smell of garlic and onion immediately floods my nostrils. It could be the beginning of any dish, but because it's Nikhil cooking, I'm almost positive he's making pasta.

"Thanks for the shirt," I call. During my shower, I decided on a new strategy: plan "kill 'em with kindness." Snapping at him hasn't been getting me anywhere, and I can at least try to be cordial. Try to find some common ground.

"No problem," he replies. He's facing away from me, stirring something together in a saucepan.

"What are you making?" I ask. My stomach chooses that exact second to grumble. Loudly.

He snorts. "Why? Are you hungry?" He turns around with a grin, and for a second I'm dumbstruck. Frozen in place. It's not the wide smile he used to always wear, but it's close.

I take it in. Savoring it. The crinkles near his eyes. The tiny, barely there dimple that you wouldn't notice unless you already knew to look for it. This is the first unguarded look I've seen on Nikhil since I got here. Warmth creeps through my chest.

Then he swallows. Hard. Breaking the magic of the moment.

His eyes bounce around. To the hem of my shirt—*his* shirt— where I've bunched the excess length with a hair tie. To the sleeves that I've folded over a couple times. To the collar that's a little too wide, dipping a bit low, exposing my collarbone.

I shift my weight, my skin heating under his gaze. Now I'm warm for an entirely different reason.

The saucepan bubbles noisily, and Nikhil spins in a hurry, lowering the flame. "I'll just, uh, finish this up. Want to grab some glasses of water for the table?" He pauses. "Unless you want something else to drink. I don't have much, but you can check the fridge . . ."

"Water's fine." I open the cabinet door to my right, only a little surprised to find the glassware right where I expect it. Right where we always kept it. I don't comment on it though. I just grab the glasses, fill them up, and duck out of the kitchen to set them on the table.

It takes no time at all and then I'm back. Feeling awkward and uneasy. It's strange to be in this house and feel as if I'm a guest. In this space I helped curate. Helped create.

"What else can I do?" I ask Nikhil as he finishes straining the pasta over the sink.

"Nothing." He doesn't look at me. "Unless you want something else to go with this. I have bread. If you want to heat that up. Or put it in the toaster."

Finally. A task. I peek in the fridge and pull out some garlic and butter, along with the bread.

We work in silence. Like we have all afternoon. But this time I'm determined to find a way through the tension.

"So, what have you been up to?" I ask, my voice light and breezy.

Nikhil's hand freezes, his wooden spoon halting midstir. "What do you mean?"

God, he sounds so suspicious. So untrusting. I slather the bread with my softened garlic butter and pop it in the toaster oven. "Nothing," I say. "I'm just asking how you've been."

He's quiet for a beat. Then he clicks off the flame. "Fine." He sounds so curt. So harsh. But his next words are softer. "I've been fine."

"Good," I say. "Glad to hear it. The house looks great, by the way. You've done a really nice job with it." Minus the painting over the brick, which I'll never understand, I mean it. At first glance not much has changed, but the furniture's been updated. And rearranged. A midcentury modern layout right off the pages of a magazine.

It's exactly Nikhil's taste. His style. It's how he would have decorated it then, if we'd had the money to afford it.

He shoots a look my way, as if to make sure I'm not joking. Or being sarcastic. But he must realize I'm being sincere because he mutters a quiet "thanks" before scooping the pasta into a large bowl.

We make our way to the dining room table and it's only then that I get a good look at what kind of pasta he made.

"This is all I had in the fridge," he says quickly. "I just threw it together."

I nod. Maybe he eats this all the time. Chicken and broccoli and pesto. Those are common enough. But the cavatappi? That weird corkscrew pasta shape? It was always my favorite. Still is. I don't remember him liking it. Maybe he stocks up on all kinds of pasta, just in case he has guests with a particular craving.

My stomach churns at the idea of Nikhil making pasta for other people. For other *guests*.

I spear a piece of broccoli, stuffing it in my mouth. "It's really good," I say, a moment later.

Nikhil only grunts in acknowledgment.

My hopes start to plummet, but I have to remind myself that this is still heading in the right direction. We're sharing a meal together. Peacefully. We're not chatty. Or friendly exactly. But this is better than before. I need to keep it up.

Only I've run out of all possible topics of conversation. Asking how his work is going seems like too much of a loaded question. Though he'd always ask me about bar prep, he rarely told me what was going on with him, sharing only select things about work. Goofy antics, light moments, client reactions when they finished projects early or on time.

It was only when he came home with a slight limp that I'd recognized the pattern.

"What happened?" I'd asked immediately, reaching toward him.

He'd waved me off, his mouth stretching into a smile that looked a lot more like a grimace. "It's nothing."

"It's clearly not *nothing*, Nikhil. You're hurt."

"Just a sprain," he'd said, forced cheer in his voice. "It'll be fine tomorrow."

"But how did this happen? Did you get it checked out? Do you need to take some time off or—"

"It's fine," he'd said again. "How was your day?" He'd smiled wider, even as his forehead glistened with sweat, the pain he was feeling so obvious. "That rule against perpetuities still giving you a hard time?"

It had hurt. We were supposed to share everything. We had *promised* each other that we would share everything. But I'd learned that day that there was a whole world inside his mind I couldn't access. The way I shared things with him, the way I leaned on him, was something he wouldn't reciprocate. No matter how much I pushed or prodded for more, there were walls I couldn't climb over, until finally, I just stopped trying. I reach for the garlic bread, biting off a large chunk of it. What's a safe subject to talk about? What's something I could ask that would—

A loud, deep laugh breaks my train of thought.

Nikhil is shaking his head, a hand over his mouth. I stare at him incredulously and he lets out another chuckle.

"What's so funny?"

"Nothing," he says, though his lips twitch, proving him a liar. "It's just . . . you still eat your toast like that?"

I pause, looking down at my hand. The garlic bread is upside down, the garlicky-buttery side facing the floor. As it should be.

"Like what? The *right* way?" I respond.

He laughs again. "You are literally the only person who thinks that."

I grin, shaking my head. "Then I'm the only person with common sense." We'd talked about this once before. The first time I spent the night at his place, I think. He'd made breakfast in the morning and he'd laughed then too when he saw the way I'd eaten my toast, but my rationale makes perfect sense.

"The side with butter or jam or whatever has to face down so that more of it hits your tongue. That way you get the most flavor out of it. Otherwise, it's just a waste."

The right corner of his mouth tilts up. "A waste?"

"Yes. A waste. Why would you want to taste the dry, bland side first?"

He leans forward, his arms resting on the table. "But what if you have a lot on there? What if you put too much jelly? All of it would fall off."

I huff. "Well, obviously I wouldn't eat that kind of toast that way. Be serious."

The slight tilt of his lips transforms into a full-blown grin. "I wouldn't dare to be anything but serious about this."

He takes a bite of his pasta, his smile muted, but still there, and for a moment, I'm pretty happy with how my new plan is working. We're being pleasant. Amiable.

But then he strikes unexpectedly, throwing my earlier question back in my face. "So," he says. "What have you been up to?"

Something icy and cold travels up my spine. The question feels so loaded. I hadn't meant it to be that way when I'd asked it, but on the receiving end . . . I want to run. Retreat. Raise a white flag.

All of that would be better than giving him an honest answer.

I'm trying to win back my ex. My wildest dreams for my career might finally be within reach. And you and this marriage are threatening all of it.

I sip my water, drawing out the moment for as long as possible. "Oh, you know," I say lightly. "Same as usual."

He stares. He's waiting. Expecting me to say more. When I don't, his eyes flicker. "And what is usual?" he asks.

I shrug, doing my best to hide my inner panic. I don't know why this is getting to me. Why this simple question is burrowing under my skin. Making me sweat.

"Work," I reply. I force a light laugh. "That probably sounds boring, but that's what takes up most of my time."

"Good," he says. "That's good." He looks away, but a few seconds later his gaze returns to me. "And it's going well?" he asks. "Work, I mean. Is it everything you wanted it to be?"

I can tell he tried really hard to make that question sound neutral, but a bitter undertone still snuck its way through. It raises my hackles. "Yes," I snap. "It is."

He nods, looking down at his food. His fork aggressively scrapes across the plate and I wince.

"Is yours?" I ask, before I can help myself.

His brows furrow. "Is my . . . ?" he repeats.

"Your work. Is it everything you wanted it to be?" It's a bad move. My doubling down on this. On a topic that has always been a minefield for the two of us.

But to my surprise, his expression softens. The lines of his mouth relax. "Not yet," he says. "But I think it will be."

Surprise sparks through me, the tension within me fizzling away, leaving my chest buoyant. Light.

"Good," I tell him. I open my mouth, then pause.

I want to know more. Is he still in construction? Is he doing something else? Starting his own business like he'd once wanted to? What exactly is he looking forward to?

And strangely, I want to tell him that I'm kind of . . . proud?

That I'm happy for him. Happy he's found some kind of joy in his work.

But those words belong to a different Meena. A younger Meena. I don't have a right to say those things now. "That's good," I say instead.

We return to eating, the only sounds in the room the clinking of our silverware and the light rain that's begun outside.

I squint, trying to look out the window, but it's gotten too dark to see clearly. Still, I know what this rain means. The outer bands of the storm are here.

"Looks like it's starting," I say, gesturing toward the back door.

He casts a worried glance outside, then fishes his phone out of his pocket. He studies it for a few minutes before turning it around, showing me a storm map.

"It'll take some time for the worst to get here," he says. "Probably early morning. They're projecting sometime around two or three."

"Oh," I reply. Sounds like neither of us will be getting any sleep tonight.

Silence descends again. Though it's broken a few minutes later when Nikhil coughs.

My head snaps in his direction, and I'm shocked to find him staring at me. His eyes fixed on my left hand. On my fingers drumming against the table.

I go still. I hadn't realized I'd been doing that. "Sorry," I mutter.

"It's fine," he says hoarsely.

That sound, the sandpapery quality of his voice, sends shivers down my spine.

I clear my throat. I need to regain control of myself. I need to regain control of this conversation. I need to remind myself why I'm here. "Well," I say. "Since we have some time, I was wondering if you maybe had a chance to look everything over. The papers, I mean. Though I understand if you haven't had time yet. I'm sure you've been busy, but really the whole thing is pretty short, and the terms are superstandard. I promise. Though I'm not saying you just have to trust me. You can consult with whoever you want, assuming you haven't already. Or you can ask me questions. I'm happy to discuss any of it and—"

"Meena," he interrupts. His voice is still rough. Slightly ragged, but then his lips stretch into a smile I'm all too familiar with. I wonder if he knows how pained he looks. How that smile conveys just how miserable he actually is. "I don't want to . . . Let's not do this right now."

I wait a beat, trying to be calm. Trying to be patient. Trying to show him how reasonable I can be, but then he rubs the side of his neck and averts his gaze, staring down at the table. And my temper flares.

He's checking out. Retreating.

I hate it. Even after all these years, it still feels so familiar. An echo of so many conversations we had. Me trying to broach a sensitive topic, and him brushing it away instead of engaging. Trying to defuse the situation with a joke, a change in topic, or that sad attempt at a smile. Sitting right in front of me, but still making me feel so alone.

I snap. "Well, we have to talk about it sometime. And I don't get it. I really don't. Is there something else you want? Something not spelled out in this draft? Because these terms are open to negotiation. All of this is just a starting point. We can discuss it."

"It's not that," he says, still looking away. Still not looking at me.

"Then what?" I ask, thoroughly exasperated. "Don't you want this to be done? Don't you want this to be over?"

His head moves back. Just the smallest movement. It's not quite a wince, but as I struggle to figure out how to classify it and what it means, his eyes return to mine. He raises his glass to his mouth and god, I wish I could look away but I'm transfixed. By the way his lips part, the way his throat flexes as he swallows.

The shape of his mouth is still so familiar to me. If I closed my eyes, I'd still remember exactly how it looks. Exactly how it feels.

"I need to ask," he finally says, but then he stops. He takes a deep breath and licks his lips. My pulse jumps in my throat.

"I need to ask you . . ."

Suddenly, his face disappears. I can't see his mouth anymore. I can't see anything. The room is pitch-black.

Nikhil whispers a curse under his breath, and only then do I realize what's happened.

The power's gone out.

5

A bright light shines directly in my eyes. I blink, raising my hand to block it.

"Sorry," Nikhil says, sweeping his phone away. My vision takes a few seconds to adjust, then slowly things come into focus.

The room is still dark, but the light from Nikhil's phone helps. I can make out the table. The couch in the corner. And Nikhil. He's standing. Facing away from me, inching toward the backyard.

"Where are you going?" I ask, pushing my chair back, following the source of the light.

"The generator," Nikhil replies. "It's in the back, but obviously it's not working." He breathes out a sigh. "Last time we had a power outage it turned on for five minutes, then crashed. It's under warranty, and I had the guys come out, but they swore nothing was wrong with it. That it was just a fluke." He slides the back door open.

I watch him a second, still confused. "If they couldn't fix it, why do you think you can?" I call.

"And what would you suggest?" he says. "That we just sit here in the dark? With no AC. Or power. Or light. That we just let all the food in the fridge and freezer go bad? That we just give up? Without even trying to fix things?"

"No, I'm just saying . . ."

He forges ahead, his phone's flashlight cutting a path through the drizzly dark.

I watch from the doorway, tempted to follow after him. To continue this conversation. To push back against his not-so-subtle statement about our marriage.

I wasn't the one who first gave up on us. I wasn't the one unwilling to fix things.

His shadowed form stops beside a large metal rectangle and he pops some door or latch open. He starts fiddling with something, and the more time I spend out here, standing in the doorframe, exposed to the elements, the more I understand his point. The lack of light is one thing, but this heat. It's sweltering. Even though the sun is gone, the night is so thick. And heavy. It's almost hard to breathe.

I'd forgotten how essential AC is down here. We absolutely need to get this thing up and running.

"Anything I can do to help?" I call out.

The tinkering, the scraping of metal against metal, comes to a stop. "No," he says. "Not with this. But there's an emergency preparedness box in the pantry. Should have a couple flashlights and maybe some candles. You want to grab those?"

"Sure," I respond. I start to move in that direction, a little worried about how I'm going to navigate to the pantry in the dark, when the lights miraculously flick back on.

"Success," Nikhil calls from outside, closing the metal latch with a satisfying click.

I fetch the box, bringing the whole thing to the table. I don't know what all we'll end up needing, but it seems like a good idea to keep the emergency preparedness stuff within arm's reach.

I'm arranging the items, pulling out a couple flashlights, walkie-talkies, and candles, when Nikhil comes back in, slamming the sliding door shut.

He pushes a hand through his rain-slicked hair, and I immediately wish to be plunged back into darkness. Because there is no earth on which it's fair for Nikhil to emerge from the humid outdoors looking like *that*.

While the dampness in the air has made my hair frizz and poof to twice its normal size, it's only managed to make Nikhil's better, bringing out his slight curls. The waves that swoop perfectly. Almost like those of a cartoon prince.

But he's not boyish enough to be mistaken for one of those cartoons. At least not anymore. His skin's gotten a bit more texture over the years, no longer baby smooth. And he wears his stubble longer now. It's not quite a beard, but it's almost there. A perfect shadow. My palm itches with the urge to rub my hand across it.

I'd always wanted him to grow a beard, but he never did. He'd said it would be too prickly and uncomfortable. For me. I'd never pushed him, but now I'm desperate to know if he was right. My cheeks burn imagining his mouth moving against mine, his stubble sliding against my skin. Would it be soft? Or scratchy? Would I hate it? Or like it too much?

Nikhil moves subtly, and the light catches his hair, showing the tiniest hints of gray shining through. At his temples. And along his jaw. I imagine he'll only get more salt and pepper over the next decade, which is entirely unfair. It shouldn't be possible for this man to continue to get better looking with time.

I push the candles and everything I gathered back into the box, unable to take my frustration out on anything but these poor inanimate objects. "Guess we don't need these anymore," I say.

His hand drops on my arm, stopping my movements. The touch burns. I feel it. Everywhere.

His eyes grow wide, as if he's feeling it too, the electric current coursing between us.

I yank my arm away quickly, and he throws his hands up in front of him.

"Sorry," he says. "I only wanted to keep the candles out. And the flashlights. Just in case."

I sink back into my chair, but don't say anything. Not as he arranges the candles in the center of the table. As he sets the lighter by his place mat. As he returns to his meal, then gets up to microwave his plate. I don't even respond when he politely asks if he can microwave mine as well. I just nod, using all my energy to hold back a loud exhale of relief when he leaves the room.

I wish I could call my mom and get her advice, but even if my phone somehow started working again, I can't tell her that I'm here. In Houston. And I can't tell her about Nikhil. She doesn't know anything about him. No one in my family does. I couldn't tell them about our impulsive, whirlwind relationship. Not when so much was riding on me. Not when I'd seen how they'd responded to my sister. Not when I'd silently promised I'd never turn out the same way.

Nikhil comes back from the kitchen, a plate in each hand. He sets mine down in front of me, and I force myself to take a bite even though I'd lost my appetite a while ago.

Nikhil doesn't seem to suffer from the same issue. He tears into his meal with a vengeance, coming to a stop only when the lights above us flicker.

I glance up, hesitating for a moment. "Do you think—" I start, but I don't need to finish my question. The lights go out again, clearly providing an answer.

"Is everyone okay?" a deep voice says, coming out of the box on the table.

I jump as Nikhil turns the flashlight on his phone back on. He reaches into the box, pulling out a lantern-looking thing, then presses a button on the side. "We're all good here," he says. "Did everyone else lose power too?"

"We did," a woman replies, "but we're good. Generator isn't kicking on though."

"Mine isn't either, Elizabeth," Nikhil says. He picks up the lighter and lights the two candles between us.

A laugh travels over the radio. "Well, if Nikhil can't get his to work, I don't think there's any hope for the rest of us."

"We still have power," a man says. "If anyone needs anything, let us know. We could take in four or five people if we had to."

"Let's hope it doesn't come to that," Elizabeth replies. "Everyone on the low end of the street evacuated, right? So, I think we should all be fine."

"I didn't," a different man says.

The line goes quiet for a beat, and I watch as Nikhil scrubs a hand across his face.

"Alan?" Elizabeth asks. "What are you . . . You didn't leave?"

"Nope," Alan replies cheerfully. "But I think it'll be fine. But if anyone else needs help, let me know. In fact, Nikhil, I could stop by and try to fix that generator for you?"

"Oh, no," Nikhil says quickly. "Thanks, but that's okay. We can manage."

"Let's all keep checking in, all right?" Elizabeth says. "We'll stay on this frequency."

People sign off, agreeing and saying their goodbyes, and Nikhil flips a switch, placing the lantern back in the box. "So," I say, "that was . . ."

Nikhil looks up, the candlelight playing across his face. Light and shadow. In one moment, I can't see him. And in the next, his skin is warm and golden, almost aglow.

"The neighbors," he replies. "We've been through a couple storms now, so Elizabeth—she has a background in disaster prep— she set up this line for us to keep in touch. Just in case anyone needs anything."

The skin over my ribs stretches tight. *Who is Elizabeth?*

I swallow, my throat suddenly itchy. "And the generator? It's not going to . . . It's definitely not working then?"

He takes a sip of his water and shakes his head. "I did a full reset last time. And if that didn't fix it . . . I don't know what will. I could try it again, but I'm not sure how many resets this thing can take without breaking once and for all." He sounds resigned, but underneath it all I can hear the barely restrained frustration. He's trying hard to hold it back, but I can tell he's upset. That he's mad his fix didn't work.

"It'll be fine," I say, adopting a cheery tone, but it sounds all wrong. Like grape-flavored cough syrup. Artificial and sickly sweet.

"Right," he says, and his voice rings just as untrue and false as mine.

"How are your parents?" I ask, trying to regain a sense of normalcy. Though Nikhil never really knew my family, I'd gotten to know his. His mother, like my parents, had immigrated to the United States from India. She'd initially moved here for college, and she'd met Nikhil's father, a white, outdoorsy midwesterner. They were nice, or nice enough. I didn't get to know them that well.

His parents had finally settled down in one place once Nikhil was in his junior year of high school. His mother had gotten a tenure-track position after years of hopping around to different colleges across the country, but even though they lived in the same city, Nikhil and I hadn't seen them that often, except for the occasional birthday or holiday.

We'd driven by campus once, back in the early days of dating, and Nikhil hadn't said anything until later that night, when his head had rested on the pillow beside mine, my fingers running through his hair.

"I dropped out of college, you know?"

I'd turned on my side, watching him. His face had been uncharacteristically tense, his jaw clenched in a way I'd never seen.

"Yeah?" I'd said carefully.

"Yeah," he'd replied. "It just wasn't for me, you know? But my parents . . . my mother . . . she wasn't too happy about it."

"Why?" I'd asked, but he'd fidgeted, barely meeting my gaze.

"Does it bother you?" he'd asked, changing the topic. "That I dropped out?"

"No," I'd said, a bit puzzled. "Why would it?" I'd known what Nikhil did for work. I'd met him *while* he was at work. I'd kind of assumed some of this already. But his question . . . It almost felt like he was asking something else. Something I couldn't quite figure out.

His brow had furrowed, and I'd pulled my fingers from his hair, running them over that spot instead, trying to undo the tension. And when that hadn't worked, I'd pressed my lips there, kissing his forehead.

He never answered my question. Never talked much more about school or his family after that, but as I'd lain next to him, holding him to me, his body had begun to relax. Like he'd realized that I'd meant what I'd said.

"My parents? They're good," he says, short and to the point. "And yours?"

"Mine are fine. They're happier since they moved up north. I think they miss certain things about living here—the weather and H-E-B, of course—but they're closer to family and it's easier for me to visit them now too."

"And your sister? And Ritu? How are they?"

"They're close by too, both in Jersey. But Ritu's actually planning on being even closer after graduation. She's looking for jobs near D.C., so I'll get to see her more often. If it all works out."

He stares at me a moment. "Ritu's graduating?" he finally says. "From college?"

I laugh at the surprise etched across his face. "I know! I can hardly believe it myself." In my mind, my niece is still the little baby I'd met all those years ago.

He shakes his head, and the candlelight flickers, showcasing his cheekbones, the shadows along his jaw. "That's wild. I think the last time I saw her . . . saw a picture of her, she would have been fourteen? Maybe fifteen?"

"Yeah, she was just starting high school." Ritu had been so nervous back then. She'd called all the time, asking questions about how many AP classes she needed to take, what extracurriculars she should be involved with, and always wondering when I'd make my next visit. The two of us had always been close, the twelve-year age gap erasing some of the distance, making her feel more like a younger sister than a niece, but we weren't so close that I could tell her the truth back then. That the real reason I was staying in Texas longer than planned was that I'd failed the bar. That I was married. That I had no clue what I was doing with my life anymore.

"She's changed a lot since then," I say, thinking of the artsy, creative twenty-one-year-old she is now. "I don't know if she'll like living in D.C., and I don't think she knows what she wants to do yet, but she's got time. I keep telling her there's no rush, that she doesn't have to have it all figured out yet."

Nikhil snorts, though he attempts to school his features when I glance up at him.

"What?" I ask, unsure what he's finding so funny.

"Nothing." He picks his fork back up, rooting around the pasta on his plate, but he's barely hiding a smile. His teeth glint in the candlelight, completely giving him away.

"What?" I ask again.

He shakes his head. "Are you telling me *you* didn't have it all figured out at twenty-one?"

"Well, that was different," I say, my voice sharp and defensive.

"Why?"

"Because it was. I *had* to." I'd formulated my life plan much younger than twenty-one. I'd actually already started law school at twenty-one, but it wasn't because I'd *wanted* to. I'd needed a path. A sure thing. Something that would tell my parents that I'd be fine. That they didn't need to worry about me. That I wouldn't turn out like . . . well, like my sister.

I'd shared all of this with him once, confided in him about the root of all my anxiety around the bar. He'd seemed understanding then, but from the way he's looking at me now, it's clear he thinks something about this whole thing is funny. He's smiling. Mocking me. Except the smile on his face is a little too gentle for that. Almost . . . indulgent.

"I know you did," he says softly, and I realize he's wearing that same look again. The one that says he knows me, that he gets me. That even though it's been years, he knows some true, core version of me that very few people do.

Goosebumps travel up my arms.

"But you were very much the exception," he continues. "Most of us were floundering around at twenty-one. Some of us were floundering around for a lot longer after that." He lifts his glass, peering at me over the rim as he takes a sip. "Well, you were there, so I guess you know."

"Know what?"

"How lost I was. How I was so . . . directionless."

I frown. "I never thought of you that way."

He watches me for a long moment, something flickering in his eyes. "You don't have to say that."

"I mean it though. Of the two of us, you were the only one with a real job back then. If anything, *I* was the lost one." I look down at my plate and take a bite. "I mean, I'm sure you remember how I was after I found out about the bar."

He's quiet for a second. "I remember it was hard. I remember there were some bad days, but mostly I remember the way you got right back up. The way you started prep again the very next week. The way you committed and the hours you put in studying. You never wavered, and I always admired that. The way you didn't give up. I was . . . in awe of it, really."

Our eyes meet over the candlelight.

"Really?" My voice is low, disbelieving, the word escaping on a breath.

He nods, leaning toward me. "Really."

There's something so tender in his expression, something tentative. An olive branch. A cracked door.

I'm tempted to push at it, to see what might be behind there, but . . . this whole idea he has of me? It's based on a misconception. He'd seen only what I'd wanted him to see back then. He hadn't seen the truth.

I shake my head. "It's only because I was scared," I say. "The way I worked so hard. The way I was studying for my next attempt. It's only because I felt like I had no other choice."

His expression shutters, and it's like the sun has set. The room grows darker. I feel as though I've made an error. A multiple-choice question, and I picked the wrong one.

"You all done?" he asks a few moments later. He barely waits for my reply before taking the plates into the kitchen. We put all the leftovers away, and to my relief the fridge is still cold. I know it won't be that way for long with the power out, but it'll preserve what we have for at least a couple hours. Maybe even through the night.

We finish tidying up, and I try to keep myself busy, try to keep myself distracted, but I can't stop the dread settling in the pit of my stomach, growing with each task we complete. I wipe down the counter, take a deep breath, then turn around to face Nikhil. There's nothing more I can do to put off the inevitable.

I have to figure out where to sleep tonight.

6

"Y ou are not sleeping in the guest bedroom." Nikhil's brows are sharp, drawn together. He's not angry exactly. More like bewildered. Confused.

But we've already had this conversation. The romantic energy between us may be dead, but there's all kinds of *other* energy between us. At least on my part. Though maybe he doesn't sense it. Maybe he doesn't feel it the way I do. Maybe that's why he thinks his plan is so perfect.

"Well, I'm not sleeping in the closet," I shoot back. "The guest bedroom is perfectly fine. And we boarded the windows, so I don't think that's a . . ."

"It's not foolproof, Meena. The thing can still break. It's not safe for you to be . . ."

"It's fine." I march up the stairs, cutting him off before he can say anything more. I head straight toward the guest bedroom, because no matter what he says, I know Nikhil. He won't force things. He'll state his point, but he won't actually *do* anything about it. He won't follow after me once I'm in the bedroom. He won't pick me up out of bed and carry me with him. He won't cradle me in his arms and . . .

My mental walls slam shut, firmly stopping the direction of those thoughts.

His voice carries after me, explaining all the ways the window can still break. Something about wind and force and pressure and how plywood can only do so much, but when I cross the threshold of my room, mutter a quick "good night," and close the door, his voice grows softer. Muffled as it travels through the wall between us.

I turn, leaning my back against the hard surface of the door, and close my eyes. I'm not sure what I'm waiting for. Not sure why I'm standing here instead of climbing under the covers and getting the sleep my body so desperately needs.

But then I hear it. The loud sigh Nikhil exhales from out in the hallway. Just a few inches away. And then he retreats, his footsteps growing softer and softer until I can't hear them anymore.

This is what I wanted. I didn't want to share the closet with him. Didn't want to sleep next to him. Didn't want him to fight me too hard. I didn't want any of that.

But as I pull back the covers, as I lie down and close my eyes, there's the tiniest voice in my head. I try not to listen to it, even as it calls me what I know I am: *Liar*.

When I first met Nikhil Chopra-Wright, I was fresh out of law school and stressed out of my mind. I had moved back into my parents' house in Houston, fully intending to do nothing for the next two and a half months but study for the bar exam. Thanks to hard work, determination, and sheer fear of failure, I'd made stellar grades in law school, and at the beginning of my third year, I'd gotten the permanent job offer I'd been hoping for. A first-year associate position at the public interest law firm that had launched dozens of political careers. The place so many of my idols had started as baby lawyers.

The position was contingent on my passing the bar exam, which of course I would do. There was no reason to think that I wouldn't. I'd never failed anything before.

And then, I met Nikhil. Really, it was more like I *saw* Nikhil. Because the distraction he caused started weeks before I technically met him.

My parents had been expanding the first floor of their house, adding on a new bedroom for my grandparents since they were finally moving in with us from India after years of my parents begging them to. Construction had started a couple weeks before I'd moved back home, and I'd been frustrated, concerned that the noise would prevent me from concentrating on bar prep. I hadn't anticipated that the real distraction would come from another source altogether: one of the men working on the project.

I heard him before I ever saw him. I'd been knee-deep in contract law and parole evidence when a deep, warm laugh from outside had floated up toward my bedroom. I'd been irritated at first, upset that my concentration had been broken, and then I'd seen him and nearly fallen right out my window. It's not an exaggeration. I truly was seconds away from self-defenestration. My fault, really, for leaning so far forward, trying to catch a glimpse of the tall, handsome man walking up our driveway.

He'd been joking with a co-worker, and fortunately hadn't noticed me or the way I was staring, but I hadn't been able to look away. His smile had captured me, wide and beaming and . . . secure. Like he was sure of himself. Comfortable in his own skin. That smile, his clear and apparent joy, had sparked something within me. It'd made me greedy. I'd wanted to be on the receiving end of that smile. I'd wanted to bask in it. I'd wanted to understand that joy and be a part of it. I'd wanted *more*.

These memories must have somehow infiltrated my dreams because I'm sitting in that childhood bedroom right now. I'm in that strange space where I know what's happening, where I know this is all a dream, but as much as I try, I still can't control any of it. There are bar prep books stacked on my desk, but when I pick one up, the words begin to blur. Letters jumble together, forming words that don't mean anything.

Panic floods through me. I have to make sense of this. It's important. I have to figure it out. If I can't . . . if I can't . . . I can't remember what will happen. I can't remember anything. My anxiety increases, my breaths grow shallow.

The gravel outside crunches, and I glance out the window to see Nikhil walking right toward the house, just as he did back then, but he's not the young, smooth-faced version I remember. He looks older. Gruffer. The way he looks now. And this time he notices me.

He raises a hand, the corners of his mouth lifting into a smile. The same smile I'd seen that day. One I haven't seen in years.

Something within me eases at the sight and I'm leaning. Leaning toward him. Waving back at him from the window. But then his smile transforms into something else. Worry. Concern. He cries out, and suddenly, I understand why. I'm falling. I've leaned too far, and I'm falling and falling and can't stop. I'm Alice down the rabbit hole. The distance between the window and the ground seems endless, and—

Thunder booms and my eyes fly open. My heart thuds, the soles of my feet tingling as if I'm still flying through the air. I place a hand over my chest, trying to force my heartbeat to slow down, and take deep breaths, holding each inhale for a few seconds before letting it out.

I haven't had a nightmare in years. I'm not even sure this qualifies as one. Not in the traditional sense, but I'd felt so out of control. Stuck in a free fall I couldn't escape.

The rain's gotten louder now. Heavy. Pelting. And the wind has blown past a whistle into a full-on howl, making the hair on the back of my neck stand up straight. The sound isn't haunting; it's harsh. Angry. Like something outside is trying to rattle us. A giant that wants to pick up the entire house, turn us upside down, and shake all the contents out.

Lightning flashes, illuminating the room for a half second, but before I can peer out the window, before I can fully process, before my mind can catch up and realize that if light from the outside is permeating the room, something's gone wrong, a loud crash sounds.

Pebbles of glass stream toward me and I scream.

I'm unable to move. Unable to understand what's happening. It's so loud. Wind roaring in my ears. Water spraying through the air. And my skin stings. Along my arms. And the side of my face.

Instinctively, my hands rise in front of me, my body forming some kind of protective crouch, trying to safeguard my face from the onslaught of glass and rain. Whatever spell had been on me before is broken, and I'm ready to leap from the bed, ready to make a run for it, when a pair of arms comes around me. One beneath my knees, the other behind my back.

I tense, pulling away in surprise, until a familiar voice screams over the sound of the storm, directly in my ear, "Meena, it's me."

He moves before I can respond, carrying me to the hallway in three large strides, then slamming the door behind us. He sets me down on my feet and his face is thunderous. Furious. I'm bracing for an *I told you so* when his gaze shifts. Scanning over my features, stopping at my right cheek. He stares, and it's almost like I can feel something there.

I lift a hand, brushing that spot, the backs of my fingers sliding against my rain-soaked skin. I'd forgotten about the stinging from before, but now it's worse. The pressure of my fingers adds to the pain. I flinch.

I wouldn't have thought it possible, but Nikhil's expression grows even darker. He takes a half step toward me but stops when I instinctively take a step back.

"I thought the window was—" I start, attempting to explain that I'd thought the boarding would have been sufficient. That I hadn't really thought it would break. That I hadn't really *thought* period, other than hoping to escape sharing tight quarters with Nikhil. But he doesn't let me finish.

"You're hurt," he says. He's looking elsewhere now. The light of his flashlight following the tilt of his head. I glance down, tracking the movement, slightly surprised to see little lines of red running across the back of my hand.

When I look up at him again, my head rears back. I blink, not quite sure what I'm seeing. I'd thought he was holding a flashlight before, but now . . .

"Are you . . . You're wearing a . . . What is that?"

He flushes. At least, I think he does. The light and shadows are hitting his face at odd angles.

A laugh climbs up my throat, because really, it's ridiculous. Whatever he's wearing. And the exhaustion, the nightmare, the window, the fear, all of it has taken a toll on me. Everything has been so heavy, and I'm desperate for something light.

"It's a headlamp," Nikhil says, and I have to hold back another inappropriate giggle at the absolute misery, the embarrassment, in his voice.

"You look like you just came back from a hard day at the mines."

"It's practical," he says. "It's hands-free."

"When did you even—" I stop, as the laugh I'd been trying to suppress a few moments ago finally escapes. "When did you even buy that?"

"I told you I'd prepped for this season. I bought everything months ago."

"Right," I say. "Standard hurricane season prep. Canned goods. Bottled water. Flashlights. All makes sense. But a headlamp?"

He stares a moment, then his shoulders droop in resignation. "It came free with the radio," he mutters. "I'd thrown it on my dresser. I hadn't planned on actually using it."

I grin. "Well, I'm glad you did."

He shoots me a skeptical glance. "Really?"

"Yeah. I mean, look at how useful it ended up being. Besides, it suits you. You should wear it more often. Out on walks or while running errands. Soon everyone will be copying you. You'll be a trendsetter."

"Oh yeah?" A corner of his mouth creeps up, and I have this strange, brief sensation of victory. "Then I'll have to get you one as well," he continues. "We can't have you missing out on the latest fashion statement."

"Oh, no." I laugh. "I don't think so. I'd never be able to pull it off."

"Huh." He watches me for a long second, and when his eyes light up with mischief, I'm struck by how familiar that expression is. How familiar this all feels. The lightness and teasing and pure fun of being around him. With a click, he unbuckles the headlamp, and it's only then that I realize I might be in trouble.

"Nikhil—" I say in warning, but he only smiles wider, slowly advancing in my direction.

"Don't you think you need to try it on? Just to be sure?"

"No, that's okay. We don't have to—"

"C'mon. Since you love it so much, let's just see how good this thing looks on you." He reaches for me, and I dodge, letting out something between a squeak and a laugh as he catches me. He slides the lamp around my hair, his hands coming to the back of my skull. But right when I think he's going to fasten it, he stops moving, his whole body growing still.

He takes the lamp back, slipping it onto his head, then he raises his thumb to my chin. Slowly, he turns my head to the side, and I watch all of that mischief, all of that levity, drain from his face.

"We need to get you cleaned up," he says, his voice flat and gray.

"Okay." My arms prickle with goosebumps, the hallway suddenly feeling cold.

He closes his eyes, squeezing them tight for a second before meeting my gaze. "Why would you— Do you know what could have— Seriously, what were you thinking?" He speaks quietly, but that doesn't make his words sound any less hot and acidic.

A spray just as stinging and harsh as the wind and pebbles of glass.

I know I'm in the wrong here. He'd warned me plenty, but I didn't take his warnings seriously. I probably should have listened to him, but hell if I'm going to admit that.

"Meenakshi," he says, and I go still. He doesn't add anything else. He doesn't have to. Because Nikhil doesn't use my full name. Ever. It's happened only twice in my life, and neither of those moments is one I want to relive.

So I don't respond. I don't say anything. The silence lingers for a few seconds, and then he tries again.

"Meena," he says, as if the last slip hadn't happened. "You can't just—" But he doesn't finish the rest of his sentence. He only shakes his head, and turns and walks away.

"Come on," he calls over his shoulder. The beam of light bounces slightly with each step he takes, and I follow him, the path to the primary bedroom somehow feeling both familiar and foreign.

In the bathroom, he's pulling open cabinets and drawers, searching for something, and I perch on the edge of the bathtub. Waiting. I idly track the scrapes and cuts on my arms, alarmed at the glinting I see when the light catches just right. There are specks of glass there. That makes sense. That's what's caused the stinging and the light trails of red. Though now they look almost pink, diluted by the water coating my skin.

Nikhil returns with a large brown bottle, cotton balls, and tweezers. He squats in front of me, pulling my arm across his knee. With the light shining from his head and the tweezers in his right hand, he looks a bit like a surgeon preparing to cut.

He turns my arm, studying it for a bit. And then he squints.

He needs his glasses, I think. I scan the counter, looking for them. He always left them lying around. By the sink or on the kitchen table or right by the bed. Wherever he happened to be reading. I almost crushed them once. He'd left them lying on a cushion on the couch, and I'd nearly plopped right down without looking. He'd bought some extra reading glasses that day.

"I didn't break them," I'd said, absolutely incredulous as he'd pulled four pairs, all in different colors, out of a plastic Walgreens bag.

"But you could have," he'd said. "So I got backups. Just in case."

After that, instead of one pair of glasses scattered around the house, there were four. At least he said there were only four. I could have sworn there were a lot more. It felt like the number just kept growing. Like they were multiplying. Spreading through the house like a plague.

But I haven't seen any today. I twist, trying to scan the rest of the bathroom, but his grip on my hand tenses, holding me in place.

"Where are your glasses?" I ask.

The lines on his forehead crease. He lifts the tweezers. "You need to hold still," he says. He places the slanted edges around a small piece of glass, and I force myself not to move, not to wince, as he lifts it away. But after it's over, I realize it wasn't too bad. I've had splinters that hurt worse.

"Where are your glasses?" I ask again. Because though I'm thankful he's helping me get rid of these shards of glass, I'd prefer that he see clearly while he does it.

His mouth goes flat and thin. "I don't need them."

"You don't need them?" I don't understand. The man couldn't read anything without them. He'd kept a pair in the kitchen because he couldn't even read the labels on the spices. He'd once accidentally swapped cumin with cinnamon, and to date that black bean chili is the worst thing I've ever eaten.

"I got a procedure," he says, using my distraction to weasel out another piece. And then another.

"What kind of procedure?"

He fishes out another bit of glass. He's moving at lightning speed and I can't help but appreciate the efficiency. "It's similar to LASIK but has better results for people who need correction for their near vision."

"Was it safe?"

He slants me a look, as if he wonders why I care. Or why I'm asking. And honestly, I'm not sure why I am either. It's just . . . I never knew he wanted his vision corrected. The reading glasses had been cute. And each color had been a surprise. Dark green frames. And blue. And tortoiseshell. Though his red ones had been my favorite. I'd loved the way he'd looked in them. So intellectual. All wise and sophisticated.

He'd been wearing frames like that the first day we met. Even though it had been blazing hot that summer, I'd started taking daily mental health walks around lunchtime. Not because it was when the crew took their break or because I always spotted Nikhil from my window around that time, going to his car to grab his lunch and a book, then retreating to a shaded spot under the tree in our side yard.

I'd just needed some fresh air. Some time to stretch my legs and get out of my room. If I happened to leave out the back door so I could cut through the side yard and pass by Nikhil, well, that was just a coincidence. Not that I actually ever planned on talking to him. I was in full, awkward do-not-approach-me mode, with my clunky headphones clamped over my ears and my phone tucked into the embarrassing cousin of the now-trendy belt bag: a fanny pack.

For the first few days, he'd just dip his head when he saw me. A friendly nod. But then he started waving. The first time it happened I'd had a mini panic attack and nearly sprinted away, but I soon began to respond like a normal person and not a child with a schoolyard crush. About a week later, he'd spoken to me for the first time.

"What are you listening to?" he'd asked, sitting at the base of the tree, book open on his lap. I'd stopped right in my tracks. Then cringed.

I hadn't wanted to confess that I was listening to an audio recording of a BARBRI course on property law at 1.6x speed, so I'd lied and just said, "Music."

The right corner of his mouth had kicked up, and my stomach had swooped like I was on a roller coaster.

"What kind?"

I'd tried to come up with a generic singer, but finally gave in and told him the truth, explaining that it wasn't music exactly. That I was listening to lectures because I had a big exam at the end of the summer.

He'd stood up, dusted some dirt off his pants, then leaned against the side of the tree. It was criminal really. That lean. No one had a right to be that tall and handsome and devastating and somehow become even more attractive with just a *lean*.

He'd asked me about my exam, and I'd told him about law school and the bar, and even though I'd worried that I was boring him several minutes in, he'd seemed genuinely interested, asking more questions whenever I paused. Slowly, my anxiety around him had faded.

I'd asked about his book and he'd shown me the cover: *Turning Your House into a Home*. It wasn't what I'd been expecting.

"Why interior design?" I'd asked, and his face had lit up.

"I'm renting, but there's still something nice about designing a space. Even if it's only somewhere I'll be for a little while, there are things you can do to make it feel more permanent. To make it feel more like home."

"Like what?" I'd asked, genuinely interested, and he'd explained. Telling me about color theory, space planning, even the shape and size of furniture. He'd described pieces he'd made for his space—chairs and bookcases and floating shelves—and his passion had captivated me. He told me it was all just a hobby. That it had nothing to do with work. That it was just something he did for himself, and I found it fascinating. To see someone so moved by something they were doing just for fun. I didn't quite understand it, but I wanted to.

After a couple more run-ins and discussions about design and law and everything under the sun, he'd asked me out. We'd gotten ice cream one day after he'd finished working, and I'd fallen hard.

I'd joked about all of this with him once. Told him that it was his glasses that had first caught my eye. That I'd really been digging his whole professorial vibe. But instead of laughing in response, he'd just looked at me strangely. He hadn't worn that pair as often after that.

"Yeah," he finally says, responding to my earlier question. "It was fine. The procedure worked."

He switches to my other arm, but there aren't as many scratches here.

"I got LASIK," I offer, and his eyes shoot up to mine. "Got it a few years ago. I was kind of nervous about it, but it ended up being a breeze." He nods, but he's quiet, still watching me. As if he's examining my eyes, looking for some kind of change. Any difference between then and now.

I look away, staring at the white tile lining the floor.

"So, no more contacts," he says.

"Right," I respond. "No more contacts."

He releases my arm and picks up a cotton ball, holding it to the opening of the brown bottle, then flipping the bottle upside down.

"This is going to sting," he says, and before I can even take a full inhale, he wipes the hydrogen-peroxide-soaked cotton ball up my arm in one swift movement. I curse, the burning quick and unexpected, but try not to do more than that.

He's only trying to help. Not torture me. Though maybe he is getting a bit of pleasure out of my pain. It's not like I would know. His face doesn't reveal anything, but he always was a pro at keeping things hidden. Keeping his true feelings buried deep down.

He sets aside the used cotton ball, and now that my arm has been cleaned, I can see the cuts were tiny. And not that many had been bleeding. The few that were have stopped now. Aside from the slight burning and a bit of tenderness, it doesn't hurt that bad at all.

I expect Nikhil to move on to my other arm, and I mentally prepare for that area to hurt as well. So I'm shocked when he lowers his head instead. His mouth moves toward the back of my hand, like he's a courtly knight trying to earn the favor of a princess.

But instead of a kiss, his mouth forms a perfect "O." And then . . . he's blowing. A steady stream of cool air. My arm goes tense, my hand clenching into a fist, but if he notices, he doesn't say anything. Or stop. He just goes higher, that breath traveling up and down my arm. It's over in a matter of seconds, and only once he's moved on to the other arm do I fully understand what he was doing: he was trying to ease the sting.

That realization hits at the same time he streaks a new cotton ball across my other arm and a shocked sound escapes me. He gave me no warning this time, and I'm not sure if that was better or worse.

"Sorry," he mutters, before blowing against the few tiny wounds on this arm. He's faster now, but even though it's fleeting, the sensation of his breath against my skin short-circuits my brain.

I try to stand up as soon as he's done. I need to get some distance. Need to look at something else besides him. I need a break from . . . all of this, but then his hand taps my knee.

"Wait." His fingers lightly come beneath my chin. "There's a little left." He tilts my head, studying it in the light. "Looks like the glass just grazed you here, so it's only a scratch."

He dabs another cotton ball in the solution, and then his left hand comes back to my face, his palm cradling my uninjured cheek, holding me secure. It burns, just like all the others, but this time I don't have the luxury of watching his expression. My face is turned to the side, away from his. Though after the last few minutes, I can picture him clearly. See it all in my head. The way his mouth purses as he concentrates. The way his brows crease in sympathy when I tense and do my best not to jerk away. I can picture the shape of his lips as he blows cool air, just as he's doing right now, only a few millimeters away from my skin.

Finally, he's done, the cotton ball discarded, joining the pile of used ones beside me. But he hasn't dropped his hand. It's still there, spanning the side of my face. His thumb tucked beneath my chin. His fingertips threading into my hair. He holds still for a beat, and then his thumb inches up, rising from my chin, coming to a stop right below the curve of my bottom lip.

His pupils are large, and they grow larger as I suck in a breath. The movement makes my mouth part, bringing my lip into direct contact with the pad of his thumb.

And slowly, he tilts my face down.

He's going to kiss me, I think as he rises toward me, bridging the space between us.

My eyes instinctively slide shut, and the scent of him fills my lungs. Sawdust and warmth and earth. I lean farther into it, wanting more.

Now. His fingers tighten in my hair. I feel him exhale against my lips. *It's going to happen now.*

But then, his arm retracts. My eyes pop open to see his hand fall loosely to his side, his fingers flexing once, then forming into a fist, while I'm left with slightly stinging wounds and the residual warmth from his palm against my cheek.

He stands back up, and I spring up as well.

"Thanks," I say. "I . . . I appreciate it."

"Yeah," he responds. And then his eyes flit down to my shirt. Really, *his* shirt. The fabric is pretty damp, not completely drenched, but it definitely shows the aftereffects of the ministorm that happened in my room, making the shirt mold to my body, clinging to my curves. His headlamp follows his gaze, and it's as if a spotlight is shining right there, highlighting my chest. A second later, he seems to realize his error. Seems to realize that the headlamp has given him away, because he snaps to attention, his head swinging up fast.

"I'll get you another shirt," he says. He retreats to the bedroom, coming back a moment later with a twin of the shirt I'm wearing: another plain white cotton tee. I take it from his outstretched hand, and for a split second I'm tempted to sniff it, to see if it carries the same vetiver scent, but Nikhil's watching me.

"Thank you," I say. I raise the new shirt, waving it slightly. "I'm just going to . . . uhh, change, so if you could . . ."

"Yeah, yeah," Nikhil says. He backs away quickly. "Sure."

He exits the bathroom and closes the door behind him, but with the absence of his headlamp, the room is sent into sudden darkness.

"Nikhil," I call. The door opens up a crack. "Could you leave the light? Or actually, do you have another flashlight?"

He lets out a puff of breath, something between an exhale and a laugh. "Why? Don't you want to wear the headlamp?"

"Umm, not particularly."

He huffs again, though a second later he's handing a slim flashlight to me.

"Thanks." I flick it on and change quickly. Obviously, I misread the moment. Maybe it was just muscle memory or the remnants of the attraction that used to be there, but I doubt Nikhil actually wanted to kiss me. He's probably still furious with me about the guest bedroom. To his credit, he hasn't done that much I-told-you-so-ing, but he absolutely could have.

Shame prickles the back of my neck. I owe him an apology. Maybe I can offer to make it up to him. There has to be a way I can repay him for getting me out of there. Maybe I could cover the cost of repairing the guest room?

I go out to present my offer to Nikhil but stop when I see him wrestling with some kind of blanket in his arms. The material's shiny. Reflective. Which I can see clearly because he's still got on that headlamp.

"What are you doing?" I ask.

Nikhil fumbles a second, then lets out a sound of relief. He yanks on something and a zipper comes undone.

"The thing was stuck," he says. "For a second I thought we might only have one sleeping bag."

Right. The closet. The sleeping bag*s*. The plan Nikhil had all along. "But we don't, right? You have another one?"

"Yeah, mine's already set up in there." He nods in the direction of the closet. "I knew I had an extra, but it took me a minute to find it. And then I couldn't get it open. But it's fine now."

He opens the closet, bending down and placing the sleeping bag on the floor.

The closet space is just as tight as I remember it. Though it's larger than the coat closet downstairs. That thing wouldn't fit one sleeping bag, let alone two. But these sleeping bags take up all the floor space. There's not going to be a whole lot of wiggle room.

And with the two bags next to each other and the lantern-radio on the floor in between, this setup is . . . cozy. Like some intimate couple's camping trip. The back of my arm itches. The stress must be breaking me out into hives.

I scratch absently, then hiss.

Nikhil turns around, his eyes wide. "What happened?"

"Nothing. Ignore me. I forgot about the . . ." I gesture toward my arm, waving at the tiny scrapes there.

He frowns. "Are you okay?"

"Yeah, yeah. It's nothing." I clear my throat. "Actually, I wanted to tell you that I'm—"

A loud *crack* sounds, and I almost jump out of my skin. I cast a wary glance toward the bedroom window, which I'm thankful to see is still boarded up.

"Probably just a branch," Nikhil says calmly, but his forehead is creased. He's worried. "Still, we should both get inside."

I step into the closet and don't say anything when Nikhil closes the door behind us. I don't point out that the noise outside sounded a lot more like an entire tree toppling than a branch snapping. I don't continue my apology from before. I don't even breathe.

Unlike the sharp beam of light protruding from Nikhil's forehead, the lantern on the floor is soft, emitting a warm, almost golden glow. But that's not what gives me pause. It's the fact that my back is pressed against something hard and firm. Nikhil's chest. I can feel it rise and fall as he lets out a breath. Somehow both hot and cool as it settles on my skin, moving through my hair. I hold back a shiver.

His hands come to the tops of my shoulders. "Meena," he says, and the shiver I've been suppressing climbs up my spine.

He presses lightly, using the pressure to maneuver me a step forward. "You're blocking the way," he says curtly. He takes a tiny step around me before dropping to the floor and sliding into his sleeping bag.

I mirror his movements, mechanically, getting into my bag and zipping it around me. I'm frazzled and out of sorts, but that doesn't necessarily have anything to do with Nikhil. I haven't gotten much sleep. I'm stuck in this house I'd never thought I would visit again. And there's a literal hurricane going on outside right now. I'm allowed to be frazzled. It's understandable under the circumstances. Any rational person going through this would be.

I turn onto my side, facing away from him, and blow out a breath.

"You good?" he asks, the pitch of his voice sounding lower than usual. Or maybe it's the acoustics in this tiny room.

"Yeah. Fine."

He waits a beat. "You were going to tell me something," he says. "Before."

"Oh. Right." I shift. The sleeping bag provides more cushion than I thought, but I can't remember the last time I slept on the ground. It's not exactly comfortable. "I was going to say that I'm . . . well, I'm sorry."

Heat floods my cheeks, but fortunately I'm still turned away. Really, it should be socially acceptable to do all apologies this way. With our backs toward the wronged party. Though I'm still embarrassed, though I still *hate* having to do this, not having to see him or gauge his reaction is making it all easier.

"I should have listened to you," I continue. "About the guest bedroom. About not sleeping there."

He's quiet for a few seconds. Probably because he's so unfamiliar with the concept of an apology. He'd never reached out after the fight, never told me he was sorry for any of it.

"It's fine," he finally says.

"No. No, it's not. Actually, I wanted to, uh, offer to pay you back. You know, just let me know how much damage there is to the room, and if there are any repairs, you can send me the bill. I'll take care of it and—"

"I don't need your money, Meena."

"Oh. Yeah. I know that, but I want to—"

"I don't *want* your money, Meena. Keep it." The words are strained, as if they're barely escaping through clenched teeth.

"I'm just trying to say sorry." Though to be honest, it's more than that. He helped me, and I'm not going to leave here with a debt unpaid. With my owing anything to him.

"You got hurt," he grumbles. "And the window would have blown in even if you weren't there. There's nothing you need to pay for."

"You don't know that," I say, attempting to lighten the mood. "Maybe the plywood would have stayed in place if I wasn't here. You'd probably have had a better assistant helping you than me."

"I wouldn't have had an assistant. I would have done it myself."

His serious reply sinks my attempt at levity. "Right," I say. "That makes sense."

The closet reverts to silence, broken only by the rustle of the synthetic sleeping bag material next to me. He's probably rolling over. I wonder which way he's facing, but I don't give in to the temptation to sneak a peek over my shoulder.

"Actually," he says, "I should have boarded the windows up earlier in the day. I ended up having to do them faster than normal. It's possible I missed something."

"I'm sure you didn't," I say. I don't know why I'm trying to console him, but I don't want him thinking I blame him. At least not for this. "And it's not like you had a ton of notice."

He pauses. "I had enough time. It's just . . . as soon as I heard the news I . . . I had another property I had to board up first."

"Oh." For a second I think Nikhil is saying he owns another house, but then I realize he's talking about work. "Well, that's important," I say. "I understand why you'd prioritize that."

"You . . . you do?"

"Yeah. It's not like you can just tell the boss you're not going to show up."

He's quiet for a long moment, and I feel the need to clarify.

"I just mean that if you had a site you had to prep first, then that makes sense. It's what you had to do."

"A site," he repeats slowly, like he's unable to understand what I'm saying.

"A construction site?" I try, the words unintentionally coming out like a question. Is that not a commonly used term? I swear I've heard him say it before.

A few seconds pass. "Right," he says. "Sorry. Yes, that property is under construction." He moves again, the material crinkling. "We should get some sleep."

As soon as he says it, I register how heavy my eyelids are. How exhausted my body is. Whatever adrenaline has been fueling me, it's completely gone now. "Good night," I tell him, closing my eyes.

I'm asleep before I hear any kind of response.

A loud alarm blares. My arm shoots out on instinct, slapping about in the direction of my night table, searching for the snooze button. But instead of my phone, I make contact with something else.

"Ow," a deep voice says, less than an inch away from my ear. "What the hell was that for?"

My eyes swing open. I'm not back home in my apartment. I'm here. In Houston. With Nikhil. And he's sitting up, clutching his nose with one hand and silencing his phone alarm with the other.

Trapped in this closet, I can't tell what time it is or how long we've been asleep, but it doesn't feel like it was anywhere near long enough.

"Sorry," I say. "Reflex."

He snorts, then winces, lightly rubbing the bridge of his nose.

I watch the rhythmic movement of his fingers for a moment, the way they lightly stroke up and down.

Before Nikhil, I'd never found a nose attractive. I'd never really thought a whole lot about them. Noses are functional. They serve a purpose. But Nikhil's nose . . . For some reason, it was different. Large, and strong, and prominent. Right in the center of his face, perched above the wide, ever-present smile he used to wear.

During our fourth or fifth date, he'd told me he wasn't seeing anyone else. His foot had been tapping underneath the table, the nervous energy thrumming through his body clear, but so incredibly endearing. He'd swallowed and said he wanted us to be exclusive, and I'd never felt so giddy. So light.

"I'm not seeing anyone else either," I'd said, placing my hand on his knee, squeezing it tight, telling him he wasn't alone in the way he was feeling. "And I want that too."

"Yeah?" he'd breathed, and I'd nodded, mutual relief and joy settling into the space between us. After dinner, he'd walked me back to my car, and I'd practically floated that night, the air hot, the sky hazy, with the occasional star peeking through.

This moment . . . It's crystallized in my mind. I can still feel the humidity, the way the thick, warm wind had felt against my skin. I remember the press of his palm against mine, the way our fingers intertwined as I thought, *This is a beginning. This is something new.*

And when we'd reached my car, when he'd pressed my back against the driver's side door, when he'd leaned down to kiss me good night, I'd felt wild and hopeful and ridiculous.

So, I'd stretched toward him, impulsively kissing the very tip of his nose.

A startled laugh had exploded from his chest, flipping my heart inside out, and I'd reached up and kissed him again.

"What was that about?" he'd asked.

I'd smiled, dizzy with a feeling I couldn't quite name. "I like your nose." *And you. I like you.*

He'd laughed again, then nuzzled his nose into the curve of my neck, tickling me until we were both laughing so hard we lost our breath.

"I like yours too," he'd said, against my skin. "I like yours too."

Nikhil's phone beeps, shaking the memory away, and I realize I've spent the last however many seconds staring at him. I can tell Nikhil's noticed because he's watching me quizzically, his mouth open as if he's about to ask me a question.

But I beat him to it. "Why did you set an alarm?"

"I didn't," he says grimly. He flips the screen in my direction. "Tornado watch." A National Weather Service alert is displayed prominently across the top. We don't have tornado sirens in Houston—at least, I can't remember ever hearing any growing up— so I guess this is how they share the news.

"What does that mean? What are we supposed to do?" I'd forgotten that tornados could happen in the middle of a hurricane. I hadn't considered the possibility that we might end up experiencing more than one natural disaster at a time.

"We're supposed to get on the ground floor when these alerts go out," he says. "In a room without windows."

I wait for Nikhil to get up, for him to usher us out of the closet, but he just stretches his arms out in front of him. And gingerly scrunches his nose. "You pack quite a punch, you know?"

"It was just a slap," I say. "And it wasn't on purpose." I look over at him, and hesitate. "It doesn't really hurt, does it?"

He shakes his head. "No." He slants a look at me. "But maybe I should have expected something like this. You always were a little weird about my nose."

A surprised laugh escapes me. "I wasn't *weird* about your nose."

"Please," he says, the corners of his mouth rising. "You absolutely were. In fact, this all probably happened because you were just looking for an excuse to touch it."

My face warms. "That is not—"

"It's okay," he says. "I get it." That subtle lift of his mouth grows into a full-out smirk. "I've been told I have a very attractive nose."

I blush even harder, but god, it's true. He does. He has an attractive *everything*. Especially when he's smiling like this, the dimple in his cheek winking in and out. I want to press my thumb to it. I want to say things that keep him smiling, just so I can feel it appear and disappear.

"But don't worry," he says, lying back down. "I always liked yours too."

Without thinking, I lift my hand to touch my nose, and that smirk on his face softens into something smaller. Something tender.

I pull my hand away, only now noticing he's fully encased in his sleeping bag. I stare at him for a moment, confused. "Are we . . . We're not going downstairs?"

"We can," he says, "but we'll be better served by getting some sleep. These are going to keep going off all night. And this kind of alert means there's potential for a tornado. Not that one's necessarily been spotted."

"Shouldn't we just stay downstairs then? I mean, is it even safe to be here?" I hadn't taken any of this seriously enough before. I'm not making that mistake again.

He rolls onto his side, facing me. His brown eyes appear almost golden in the dim light of the lantern. "We don't have a lot of options downstairs. The pantry, maybe. Or the guest bathroom. But both are standing room only. And I wasn't exaggerating, these tornado alarms are going to keep happening. We could run up and down each time they go off, but that's not exactly safe either."

"Then what do we do?"

The corners of his mouth tilt up again. Gentle and sweet. And my heart thuds dangerously. I can't remember the last time we were like this. Face-to-face, lying together in the middle of the night. It's so familiar. A position we've been in hundreds of times before. But it feels new.

Now that he's close, I can catalog even more changes. Like the tiny nick under his bottom lip where he must have cut himself shaving. And the grizzled grays growing in his stubble.

I'm struck again by the desire to feel it. To see how different the sensation would be now. His skin was always so smooth against mine. The curve of his jaw always so soft—gentle—when it traveled over my neck, my chest, my stomach, my thighs. My cheeks flush as I remember the first time. The way we'd fumbled with our clothes, with buttons and zippers, and then with each other. Somehow, what should have been a little awkward and unsure felt different with him. Learning each other, figuring out what drove the other wild, all of that felt like a joy and not a burden. *He* made it feel like a joy.

I can still picture his face, the way he'd looked up at me, his hand wrapped around my thigh. His eyes intense, and focused. Like he was studying me.

"Here?" he'd asked after some time, his mouth, his tongue tracing patterns that made it hard for me to think. I'd babbled something incoherent in response, and the way he'd laughed, all bright and sunny and sure. It had warmed me through and through.

"Now what?" I'd said afterward, completely wrung out and content in a way I'd never experienced before.

"We go back to sleep," Nikhil says, and I blink, trying to make sense of his words from the past echoing in the present. He's answering my earlier question, I realize. About what we should do in response to the alerts.

My cheeks burn hot, my heart gallops in my chest, and I hope he can't tell what I was just thinking about. I hope he can't see right through me, that he can't figure me out the way he once could so easily.

I nod, and a piece of hair falls over my face. The hair situation has been hopeless since I arrived, and it has only gotten worse with each exposure to the humidity and rain and wind. I usually wrangle my hair into submission with a combination of products and styling tools, but I've got none of them here, so my normally pristine lob is a giant mass, completely out of control.

I lift a hand to push it away, but Nikhil's hand is outstretched too. He's reaching for the piece, as if he intends to tuck it behind my ear.

My heart thuds again, so loud I swear he can hear it. But the touch I'm anticipating never comes. Nikhil freezes, his hand suspended in the air. Then he snaps it back and turns away.

I take a deep breath, trying to make it as quiet as possible. Trying not to let him know how affected I am by all of this. By him.

I turn as well, my back toward his, and close my eyes. Soon, all of this will be over. Soon, I won't have to think about any of it ever again.

Nikhil hadn't been lying about the repeated tornado alerts. Over the next few hours our sleep is interrupted multiple times by that irritating blaring sound. I ask Nikhil to put his phone on do not disturb mode, but he's hesitant. Worried that we'll miss a real, true warning, and it's hard to argue with that.

But the next time we're wakened, it's not by the robotic siren-like noise I've gotten used to. It's a voice. Loud, but staticky and tinny. Like it's traveling from a great distance away.

"Hello? Hello?" the voice says. "Is anyone there?"

Nikhil shoots up, grabbing the lantern. "This is Nikhil. I hear you. Everything okay?"

"Nikhil, thank god," the voice replies. "I've been trying and trying, but no one's been answering. I thought I had the frequency wrong."

"No, this is the right one," Nikhil says. "What's the matter? Are you all right?"

"No," the voice responds. "There's water in my house. I'm not sure how deep, but it's well past my knees. Is there any in yours?"

Nikhil glances at me. "I'm not sure, Alan. We're on the second floor. We haven't checked."

"What's going on?" another voice chimes in.

"Jenny, it's Alan. You have a one-story house too, right? You doing okay?"

"Yeah, we're fine," Jenny replies. "So's everyone else on this side of the street."

I picture the street. And Alan's house. I remember him gesturing toward it. It's right at the center of the cul-de-sac. The street has a bit of a slope to it, and I'm pretty sure that's where it dips the lowest. If Alan's house has only one floor . . .

"How fast is the water rising?" Nikhil asks. He's obviously thinking along the same lines I am.

"It was only up to my ankles an hour or two ago."

A muscle in Nikhil's cheek jumps. "You can't stay there, Alan." He gets up and opens the closet door. He takes the lantern with him but doubles back to grab his headlamp.

"I'm going to check the first floor," he tells me as he adjusts the strap around his head. He passes me a flashlight, steps out, and shuts the door behind him.

I wait a second, then follow after him.

"Who's next to you, Alan?" Nikhil asks as he moves swiftly down the stairs. "The Trans?"

"Yes, but they evacuated yesterday morning. Booked a flight as soon as they heard."

"Anyone else around?"

"No. Laura and Jody are on the other side, but they took the kids and went uptown to ride out the storm with Jody's parents. Her parents are getting older, and they were worried about the two of them being alone during this. Pretty kind of them, if you ask me. Sometimes I wish I had family in the area. Well, I guess there's my sister, but you know she and I don't really get along . . ."

"Hey," I whisper, trying to get Nikhil's attention as Alan keeps going, sharing details about the rift between him and his sister.

Nikhil turns, something flashing across his face when he notices I'm right behind him. Disbelief? Or maybe . . . concern?

"Go back upstairs," he says, not offering any additional explanation.

"What are you doing?" I ask.

The first floor is clear. No water anywhere as far as I can tell, which is a huge relief. But even though everything's fine, Nikhil hasn't turned around. He's not climbing back up the stairs. Not retreating to the closet. He's still down here. And from the grim expression on his face, I can tell he has a reason.

But the moment his mouth twists into that familiar pained smile, I know he's not going to share it. "Nothing," he says. "Go back upstairs. I'll be back in a moment."

Fire travels through my veins, hurt and anger from the past bleeding into the present. "You know you always did this."

His eyebrows jump. "What?"

I wave my hand at him. "*This*. When something was hard or you

got hurt or you were worried, you'd just . . . brush me off like this.
As if I couldn't tell something was wrong. As if you didn't think I
could be there for you or that I could help. You just pushed me to the
side. Like I was too delicate or fragile—"

"That's not— I didn't do that."

"Really?" A harsh sound escapes me. "I guess we remember
things very differently then."

He stares at me, his jaw clenched. Then he shakes his head. "I
have to go."

"Go *where*?"

"I'm going to get him," Nikhil says.

Alan's still talking, something about how his sister was always
the favorite child. How not even going to space was enough to impress his parents. And I'm just watching Nikhil, my mouth slightly
open. Judging from the sounds traveling through the window, the
intensity of the storm has waned. The wind is quieter. The rain less
fervent and fierce. But it's still no condition to be going outside in.

Nikhil opens the coat closet, pulling out a thick waterproof
jacket and slipping his arms through the sleeves. He's really going to
do this.

"How are you going to get there?" If Alan's house is flooded, I
doubt we can just drive right up to it. And I'm sure we can't walk
there either.

Nikhil goes up to the front door but comes to a sudden stop.
We've boarded up the front windows. He can't see outside.

"Alan," Nikhil says, interrupting Alan's passionate accounting of
sibling rivalry. "How flooded are the streets? Can you get a good look
at them?"

Though I'd always evacuated instead of staying through hurricanes in the past, you don't grow up here without going through a
number of flooding events. It doesn't take much to overwhelm these

streets. The whole city is flat. Basically at sea level. There's a system of bayous and waterways and reservoirs that are supposed to help, but sometimes they overflow. I remember some city official on TV during one of these floods saying that the streets are part of the drainage system. I don't know if that's really true or just something they said to calm the public, but I've seen it happen. I've seen water flood the streets to the point that the roads start resembling rivers. Sometimes the water is stagnant, and sometimes an actual current forms.

I'd thought it was cool when I was a kid. When I was maybe six or seven, there was a particularly heavy rainstorm, one that flooded our area. The idea of swimming in the street had sounded fun, so I'd asked my sister if we could go out and play. But since she was a good nine years older than me, and therefore wiser than me, she'd just wrinkled her nose in disgust.

"Do you know where that water comes from?" she'd said. "The sewer. It comes from the sewer. You don't want to be out in that."

"Ew," I'd said. At that age, I hadn't fully understood what she meant, but from her tone I could tell it was gross.

It's one of the few childhood memories I have of my sister. She left for college just a few years later, and shortly after that, had Ritu.

In a lot of ways Ritu feels more like a sister to me than my own sister does. I've definitely spent more time around her. In high school I used to rush home at the end of the day, so excited to see her. She'd toddle around with the funniest expressions and the sweetest giggles. I have so many memories of us playing together. I have only vague memories of my sister coming by our house to drop her off and pick her up. Of family dinners where things were tense. Where I often excused myself, offering to watch Ritu instead.

Alan's voice cuts through my thoughts. "Yeah, I'm looking at them now," he says over the radio. "The streets aren't passable. They look like they did during the Memorial Day floods."

"Shit," Nikhil mutters.

I echo the sentiment in my head. I wasn't here for those floods, but the images made national news. Water higher than I'd ever seen it. Whole sections of highway transformed into giant lakes. Cars abandoned everywhere. Videos of people wading through neck-deep water to get to safety.

"Nikhil," I say quietly, not wanting Alan to overhear. "You can't do this."

His eyes meet mine, his gaze hard.

"Stay put, Alan," he says. "I'll be right there."

He turns away, and I follow after him.

"You don't have to do this. There are rescue teams," I say. "People who are actually trained for these situations. We just call them and . . ."

"They won't come out." He's brisk, in both tone and movement. Still walking away, but at least he's responding to me now. "Emergency services will be slammed," he continues. "Maybe they make it in time, but I don't think they will. Not with the rate the water's rising . . ."

"Why can't someone else go?" My voice comes out high and screechy. I hate it. I hate how desperate I sound. How desperate I feel. Alan needs help. I get that. I want him to be okay. But I also want there to be another way. Some alternative that means Nikhil won't have to leave. That means he can stay here. I don't let myself examine why I want that so much. Why the idea of him going out in the middle of this storm terrifies me. Why it makes dread spread through my body, turning my insides ice cold.

"There's no one else, Meena," Nikhil says. He stops for a second, grabbing a key chain hanging in the hallway, then he takes off again.

He comes to a halt in front of the side door that leads to the garage. He flips the thumb-turn lock and wraps his fingers around the handle.

"Nikhil . . . don't go," I say, giving it one last attempt. "Please." My voice cracks halfway through the word.

He goes still, and for a second I think I have him, but then his shoulders rise and fall dramatically. In time with a loud exhale. "I have to. But I'll be right back. You'll be safe in the closet. It'll be okay and—"

"I'm coming with you." The words slip out of my mouth, soft and hesitant. Because I'm not going to sit here quietly while Nikhil risks life and limb conducting some grand rescue. If he won't stay back where it's safe, I'm going with him.

"I'm coming with you," I repeat, firmer this time.

And finally, he turns around. His brows are knit, three strong, deep lines cutting across his forehead. "What?"

I say it again. "If you're going, then I'm coming with you."

His mouth parts. Only slightly. But it draws my attention just the same.

"Why?" he asks a moment later, once the apparent shock has worn off.

"Because," I say stubbornly. I cross my arms, fully intending to let that childish answer stand alone. I don't owe him an explanation. But without my permission, more words rush from my tongue. "I'm not going to let you do this alone."

The lines bracketing his mouth soften. But the swallow he takes is hard. Firm. Flexing the muscles of his throat. Making mine go dry.

"Okay," he says. But instead of opening the door, he retreats, back toward the coat closet. Hangers clang against one another as he reaches inside, rooting around for a few seconds before he pulls something out. "But I have rules," he says, shaking out a jacket similar in size and color to the one he's wearing. "One, you stay in the boat."

My eyebrows jump. A boat? He has a boat?

"Two," he says, gesturing toward me and spreading his arms wide, telling me I should do the same, "we stick together. And when we get to Alan's house, you don't wander off on your own. And I won't either. Got it?"

"Sure," I say, as he slips first one arm and then the other into the sleeves. "The buddy system. Makes sense to me."

"Good." He moves to my front, clasping the bottom ends of the jacket. He begins to zip me up, his face tense and solemn and entirely too close to mine. I take a step back, waving his hands away. I don't look at him as I pull the zipper the rest of the way to the top.

"And rule number three?" I ask.

"Right. Yes. Number three is . . . is . . ."

He falters, and I shoot a glance his way. "Don't tell me you're all out of rules already."

He glares. "You need to take this seriously."

"I am," I say. "In fact, I have some rules of my own. Like . . . no barking instructions at me."

"I haven't been *barking* instructions at you—"

"Really?" I scoff. "What would you call it then?"

"Trying to *help*. Trying to keep you alive."

"I don't need your help."

He laughs then, but the sound is dry. "Right. Of course. Of course you don't."

I blow out a breath. "I just mean . . . I can help too, you know. I can help with this."

He watches me, his brows creasing, and I sigh.

I don't know much about sailing in storms like this, but I imagine we'll have to work together to get through this. And at this rate we're going to capsize the second we climb on board.

"What kind of boat do you have?"

He blinks, his expression clearing. "Calling it a boat might have been a bit of an overstatement. It's really more like a canoe."

"*Like* a canoe or it is a canoe?"

He rubs the back of his neck. "It is a canoe."

I stare. When Nikhil had said he had a boat, I'd pictured something with a motor. Nothing too large or fancy, but something that would help propel us along.

"It's a good canoe," Nikhil says, no doubt taking offense at the disbelief that must be etched across my face. "A strong canoe. I made it."

That doesn't surprise me. Nikhil was always making stuff. When there were leftover materials from job sites, he'd bring them home and turn them into something new. Wood scraps became bookshelves. Or coffee tables. Or the desk he made for me. And once, he'd transformed spare metal into a garden trellis. It was like alchemy. Pure magic.

He'd tinker away in the garage after dinner. Sometimes for hours. I'd found the noise soothing. From my little hidey-hole in the guest bedroom, while I pored over wills and estates and the intricacies of secured transactions, I'd hear the buzzing of the saw, the dull thud of the hammer, the *shh-shh*ing of the sander. It was the perfect background noise, clearing my mind, helping me to focus. And on the rare occasion the noise broke my concentration, it made me feel safe. Like no matter how stressed I felt in that room, no matter how overwhelmed and worried and lonely I might be, I wasn't actually going through it alone.

"Why did you make a canoe?" I don't remember him having one. I don't remember him ever *wanting* to have one.

Nikhil lifts a shoulder before responding. "So I can go fishing."

"You . . . go fishing?"

"Yeah. Sometimes. I have a . . . There's a place by the water I like to go." He's back at the side door before I can finish my interrogation. The man I knew used to say that fishing was boring. That he could never imagine sitting still for so long. That he'd much rather move. Be active. Do something with his hands.

He always was good with his hands.

I mentally slap myself, cursing my quippy, traitorous brain.

I step into the garage as Nikhil unlatches the canoe from the wall. His craftsmanship has always been impressive, and if he hadn't told me he'd made this, I would have assumed it was store-bought. It's beautiful. The shape of it. And the color. A glistening dark green.

He pulls out a pair of paddles and hands one to me. "Do you know how to use this?"

"Of course." Because really, what kind of question is that? You hold it, put the paddle side into the water, and push. I may not have canoed since I was a middle schooler at summer camp, but I'd learned this once. I'm sure it'll all come back. Like muscle memory.

"You sure?" he asks, and his voice is so sincere it makes me wonder whether this is more complicated than I thought.

Before I can respond, he's demonstrating. "The paddle goes like this. The blade, this flat part right here, needs to stay like this when you push it through the water. That's what'll propel us forward." He stops, twisting the paddle in the air. "And usually, you'd alternate. A few strokes on the left, a few strokes on the right. That's what helps you stay in a straight line. But since there's two of us, I'll do one side and you do the other, okay?"

I nod. It's not as simple as I'd imagined, but it seems doable.

"We need to be somewhat in sync," he says. "With the paddles. We'll want to stroke at the same time."

Nope, I warn my mind. *Don't go there. Don't even think it.*

I think it anyway. A brief image flashing behind my eyelids. But it's not something my mind has created out of nothing. It's a memory. One I'd been thinking about not too long ago. One that makes my skin burn. Makes my toes curl inside my shoes.

"Stroking at the same time," I repeat automatically. "Got it."

Nikhil startles, as if he's just heard the implication. And I want to melt into the floor.

A second later, he clears his throat. "And if it gets too hard, I can always do it myself."

Great. Now my brain is hearing innuendos in everything.

"I was planning to paddle solo," he continues. "Before. So, if you're having a hard time with it, just let me know."

"Yeah. No worries. I will."

Nikhil nods, lifting the hood of his jacket over his head. I do the same.

"The garage door won't open since the power's out. So we'll have to carry this outside." He hoists one side of the canoe and I move forward to carry the other half. And together we awkwardly waddle our way to the front door.

8

It doesn't take me more than a few minutes to realize that my sister was right.

This water is disgusting.

Brown and murky. And surprisingly swift. Debris is scattered across the surface, bits of leaves and branches, all moving quickly along this street-river.

At least dawn is breaking, so there's some light for us to see by. It's not bright by any means, but it's not the pitch-black darkness of night either. Nikhil is counting out the strokes behind me, shouting above the noise of the wind. *One, two, three. One, two, three.*

I look up, but with the rain falling around us, I can't quite tell if any of the neighboring roofs sustained damage, though the felled tree in one of the yards shows just how strong the wind had been. It knocked the tree flat, and it looks kind of sad that way, flailing on its side, its roots all scraggly as they stick out in the air.

Nikhil's count continues, and I face forward again. I'd balked when Nikhil had instructed me to sit in the front, but he'd said the more experienced canoeist was supposed to sit in back. Something about it being easier to steer or control things from there, but since I can't see him, it's making it hard to follow his lead. I have to rely on his verbal cues.

We falter at first, zigging and zagging, unable to maintain momentum. And the current certainly doesn't do us any favors, pushing us in the opposite direction of where we want to go. But after a while, I get the hang of it. Though I can barely hear his count anymore. He's at full volume, but it's no use. The wind is quieter, no longer the angry monster I'd heard outside the guest bedroom window, but it's still a force to be reckoned with. It seems to want to remind us of that, as a sudden gust blows our way, making the canoe rock slightly. It doesn't do more than that. Just a wobble. But it's enough to send my heart into my throat.

I can't help but feel like the storm is toying with us. Like the spider that lured the fly. We stepped into its parlor and now it's going to play with us before it has its meal. It wants to have some fun.

I peer over the side of the canoe as I draw my paddle through the water. I don't know how deep it is here. I can't see the concrete of the street at the bottom. Can't see much at all really. The water's too cloudy to make anything out.

The next stroke takes me longer than normal, but I push through. My fingers are starting to feel numb, my arms burning. For the first time in my life I wish I'd used that strange rowing machine at the gym. I'd never understood it before. Never understood why anyone would want to sit on a bench and pretend to row a boat. Now I get it. I'm never going to skip over that machine again.

"You okay?" Nikhil shouts. "We're almost there."

"I'm good," I try to shout back over my shoulder, but I'm clearly not because my lungs hurt from the effort, the words coming out in a wheeze.

Nikhil slows the count and his pace, but it's no use. My arms are like jelly.

We're off count, zigging and zagging again, being pushed by the current.

"Put your paddle up," Nikhil says. "Take a break."

Relief sweeps through me. I yank my paddle out of the water, placing it across my lap. Nikhil starts alternating strokes, and we continue moving forward, but I barely notice. I slouch a bit, taking deep, long breaths, and getting my bearings.

We're smack-dab in the center of the cul-de-sac. Not as close as Nikhil has said we were. More like halfway there.

The street has never felt this long before. But then again, I've never traveled it by boat.

"Okay," I call out, a minute or two later, looking back at Nikhil. "I'm ready."

His mouth flattens. "I'll get us the rest of the way there, okay?"

I shake my head. "I can do it." I force my fingers around the paddle, trying not to wince at how tender my skin is. My palms are sure to blister tomorrow.

The current takes us a little off course and I turn to see Nikhil stick his paddle in the water. He does something fancy with it. It looks like a normal stroke, but then he keeps the paddle in longer at the end and twists it a bit, like a rudder, which miraculously turns our canoe back in the right direction.

Before I can ask how he did that, he thrusts the paddle back in, resuming his strokes.

I move to do the same, but he's stopped counting. I try to catch the rhythm, try to get the timing right before I begin again, but then he pulls his paddle out, pivots, and begins paddling on the other side.

Oh. He's alternating strokes. He really is planning on doing this alone.

"I can help, Nikhil," I shout. "I'm ready now."

"No. It's fine. I've got it," he calls back.

Frustration flares in my chest. I'm about to yell back that I can do it, but then he says two words that stop me in my tracks. "Trust me."

That's the whole problem, isn't it? The whole reason why we're in this mess in the first place. I don't.

How do you trust someone when they never lower any of their defenses? When they never let you in? How can you trust someone who expects your trust, but clearly doesn't trust you in return? How can you trust someone who pulls away when you need them most?

I stick my paddle in the water and put my whole body weight into it, giving the hardest push I've managed so far.

We careen forward, the canoe shaking slightly, and Nikhil raises his voice. "Meena! Stop." I pivot around and watch his eyes flash, his tone hard and bitter when he says, "I know you think I can't do much, Meena, but I promise you, I can do this. I can get us there."

What is he even talking about? Of course he *can* get us there. That doesn't mean he has to do it without me. I'm prepared to say as much, but the current takes us again. Moving us sideways. Undoing the progress Nikhil had made on his own.

He glares at me, then lifts his paddle. He's probably about to do the same maneuver from before to correct our course. The rudder one. The one I wanted him to show me.

"Wait," I say. "How do you—"

Lightning-fast movement catches the corner of my eye. My gaze follows. Something's traveling across the surface of the water. Moving far faster than the branches and leaves and debris I'd seen before.

I frown. It's strange. It's not moving in a straight line. It's curving. From side to side. Almost like a . . .

"Wait," I shout. "Nikhil, wait."

But he doesn't listen. His paddle slaps the water loudly, accidentally striking the thing that had been heading straight toward us. The creature lets out a hiss, recoiling for a moment before reacting to the blow.

Fear chokes me as I witness the most terrifying sight I've ever seen. The wide-open, completely white mouth of one of the most venomous snakes in North America.

A cottonmouth.

Every muscle in my body goes still.

"Nikhil," I say through my teeth. "What do we do?"

But Nikhil doesn't respond. He doesn't say anything. His jaw is tense, his eyes locked on the snake to our right.

Like me, the snake hasn't moved. It's just frozen in that position. Its head raised. Its mouth open.

It hasn't tried to strike, which I'm taking as a good sign. I scrounge up every memory of every nature documentary I've ever watched. I can't remember any specific ones about snakes, but I do remember the general takeaway lesson about wildlife that was hammered home in almost every episode: animals are more scared of us than we are of them.

That doesn't feel real at the moment. I can't imagine that this wild, fearsome, *venomous* creature could be terrified of two people huddled in fear in a canoe. Clearly, it has the upper hand in this situation, but maybe it doesn't realize that.

"Nikhil," I try again, but he doesn't register the sound. His skin is ashen. Slightly gray.

If I saw a snake like this on land I'd back up. Take a few steps away. I wouldn't freeze in place. I'm pretty sure that advice works only when the predator is a *T. rex* and you're in the middle of Jurassic Park.

But since we're in a canoe, I'm not sure how we can manage it. How we can paddle backwards. And Nikhil doesn't seem like he's in a place where he can take command of the situation.

"We've got to get some distance, Nikhil," I say. "Do you hear me? We need to give it some distance."

After a long beat, Nikhil's chin dips. Just slightly. And relief creeps through me. It's not much of an acknowledgment, but that little hint of a nod is better than the nothing I've been getting from him so far.

"Okay, so how do we do that, Nikhil?" My question is gentle. And soft. He's clearly not doing great right now, and as panicky as I feel, I'm not going to let any of it show.

The current is still moving the canoe, but it's moving us and the snake together, so it's not exactly helping the situation. And I'd try to propel us backwards, but I'm far from a pro at this. I could shift the canoe unintentionally. I could accidentally make us get closer. Or even worse, make us bump up against the snake, agitating it further.

But I don't think Nikhil's going to be able to do this either. His eyes are squeezed shut, a bead of sweat running down his forehead.

"We're going to be okay, Nikhil. You hear me? It's going to be okay. Just tell me what to do."

"The reverse." His voice is hoarse. Scratchy and dry. "Paddle in reverse. Back to front."

"Reverse. Okay."

"On the other side," he adds. "Left of the boat. In a straight line, but you're going to need to twist and push a bit when you reach the end of the stroke. Like a small curve away from the boat. That'll keep us straight." His eyes shoot open. "We need to keep it straight."

"Right." I glance back at the snake. It hasn't moved. Its mouth is still open. In warning. It must feel like we're still too close to it. I wish I could tell it that the feeling's mutual.

"Twist it how?" I ask calmly, even though my hands are shaking.

He walks me through it, describing the motion, how my top hand should pivot, which way my thumb should be facing at the end, and how the blade should move through the water. And even though his voice is a little shaky, the sound of it is reassuring. I repeat his instructions in my mind and try to picture the whole thing.

I lift my paddle slowly, saying a silent prayer as I dip it into the water to my left. Holding the blade the way Nikhil had showed me back in the garage, I push it, back to front. I keep it steady, imagining a crisp, straight line in my head, and then I twist and push it the way Nikhil had described.

The canoe moves back a bit, not in an entirely straight line, but straight enough that we don't collide against the snake, and it gives me the courage to try again. Another stroke. Back to front. Calm and sure. Ending with that same hooklike movement.

The snake's stayed in the same spot, but now that we've backed up, it's more toward the narrow tip at the front instead of the side of our boat. Much closer to open water. Once it sees that path, hopefully it will just swim away, and leave us alone.

"Should I do one more?" I ask, but before Nikhil responds, the snake disappears, ducking underneath the surface of the water, underneath our canoe. I suck in a breath, and I'm still holding it when I see the snake emerge on the other side.

I wait for it to lunge at us, to open its mouth back up, to strike, but it does just as I'd hoped. It darts away, traveling across the brown, murky water the way it came, going farther and farther into the distance.

Nikhil's knuckles are white, his hands clasping the seat beneath him. His eyes are open, but they're glazed over. Slightly vacant. Staring out in the direction the snake left.

"It's gone," I say. A shaky, jittery sensation travels through my chest. And a strange laugh bubbles out of my mouth. "It's finally gone."

Nikhil's shoulders jolt at the sound of my laughter, though his hands remain tightly clenched.

I have the strange urge to place my hands on top of his, so I do. Setting my paddle across my lap, I turn and slowly unpeel his fingers from the bench, entangling them with my own.

"We're okay, Nikhil," I say, squeezing his hands in mine. "It's gone now. We're okay."

He lets out a loud breath. He's quiet for a moment, then looks up at me. "I hate snakes," he says.

"I know." Or at least I know that *now*. He'd never mentioned it to me before.

Shame creeps into his eyes, and it triggers some long-dormant instinct inside me. Something defensive. Or maybe protective.

"But everyone's scared of something," I say. "And snakes are a normal fear. I'm scared of them. A lot of people are scared of them. It's a . . . a . . . dashing kind of fear."

"Dashing?" he repeats skeptically.

"Yeah, you know. Heroic. Like Indiana Jones. *Snakes, why did it have to be snakes?*" I put on my best Harrison Ford impression, which really is me just dropping my pitch a bit lower.

Nikhil's forehead shines with sweat, and his cheeks have an unhealthy pallor, but slowly, one corner of his mouth rises. "Like Indiana Jones?"

"Yeah, absolutely. What would Indy be without his fear of snakes? Just this perfect adventurer-slash-professor, and who would want to watch that?"

His smile grows. "Well, he's not that perfect. Wasn't he basically stealing artifacts from the global south and putting them in Western museums?"

"Uhh . . . huh." He's absolutely right. "Yeah. Good point." I shake my head. "Okay, so not like Indiana Jones, like someone better."

"You think I'm better than Indiana Jones?" he asks, a sly, teasing note in his voice, his thumb gliding across the back of my hand.

My mind unhelpfully recalls other times he used that voice. Other questions he asked me in that tone.

I scoff, choosing evasion instead of a proper response to his question. Because, yeah, the truth is I think Nikhil's hotter than Harrison Ford, even when he was at his Indiana Jones prime, but I'm not going to tell Nikhil that.

"So," I say, nodding toward Alan's house. "You ready to get going?"

He drops my hands, and I tell myself that doesn't sting. That I don't feel the loss of it. That I don't miss that brief shared connection.

"Yeah," he says. "I can take us the rest of the way there. Really, it's the least I can do after you saved us from certain death."

I snort. "Nah. I'm good. I can do it."

"You sure?"

"Yeah. Honestly, I've got some excess energy in me after that deadly encounter. I need to burn it up somehow."

His brows furrow. For a second, I think he's going to argue with me, but then he clears his throat. "Okay. Ready, then?"

I confirm, facing forward again, but Nikhil doesn't start up our count. I turn to check and see he hasn't picked up his paddle. He hasn't moved at all.

"Thank you," he finally says after a few more seconds of silence. "You did . . . I couldn't." He shakes his head, and I can't make out his expression. I can't understand what he *means*. "Thank you," he says again, and before I can tell him there's nothing he needs to thank me for, he resumes his count.

One, two, three. One, two, three.

The paddling's much easier this time. Neither of us is fighting for control, or trying to put in more power than the other, or take on the other's job. It's still an adjustment at first, getting back into rhythm, but soon we find it. Soon, we're in sync.

The rain has started to slow down, which is helping visibility quite a bit. The wind is still loud, still making its presence known, but it's growing more and more infrequent. At least it feels that way to me.

The water level seems the same here. I know that it's deeper in this area only when I look at Alan's house. At Nikhil's the water comes up through the yard, but it's not at our doorstep. The river is mostly contained in the street.

That's not the case here. Alan's house looks like it's partially submerged. None of his front yard is visible. And the bottom part of his front door is definitely underwater. I can't tell by how much, but at least a few inches.

"We're going to head to the gate," Nikhil says. "I'll tie us there, all right?"

We paddle in that direction until Nikhil can reach out and wrap a hand around the metal gatepost. Keeping one hand on the canoe and one on the gate, he steps out, making a small splash as the water rises to his knees.

He secures us in place with a small length of rope, checking and double-checking the knot before letting it go.

"I'm going to try to go through the front. You stay here." He takes another step away, the water rising past his knees, concealing his lower thighs.

"What happened to rule number two?" I call. "The buddy system? We have to stay together."

"Yeah, well, rule number one is more important. You stay in the boat. Remember?" He continues walking, the water steadily creeping up his body.

"I don't remember promising to do that."

"Well, you did," he shouts. He's almost at the door and I tell myself I'll be less nervous once he makes it. Once he gets inside, gets Alan, and gets back. But right when he's within reach of the doorknob, he staggers back, letting out a loud cry.

"Nikhil!" I stand up in the canoe. Foolish, I know, but I'm not thinking straight. The boat rocks, and I grasp at the gate to regain my balance. "What happened?"

He's waist-deep now, swatting his arms at something. But he's turned away. I can't see his face. I can't see if he's okay.

"Nikhil! I'm coming. Hang on!"

"No, don't come out here," he cries. "I'm fine, I'm . . . *OW*. My god!"

That's it. I'm knee-deep in the water before I even realize what I'm doing. I push my way toward him, but it's like I'm walking in slow motion. Or through Jell-O. The water slowing down every step I take.

"I'm coming," I tell him.

He swivels in my direction, a wild expression on his face. "No. Meena, go back. You can't be here. You're—"

Ouch. A sharp pain strikes the back of my calf. I try to look for whatever I hit, whatever hurt me, but I can't see a thing in this water. I shake it off, taking another step. Then another. But now my left arm is stinging. And a spot on my right shoulder. And my lower back. And . . . now I can't keep track. Little pinpricks of pain pop up all over my body. Over and over and over. But they don't just hurt. They burn. Almost like fire. Almost like . . .

"You're allergic," Nikhil continues. "Go back. Go back now."

"Too late," I say, picking up the pace, swatting at the water as I move. The pain is unbearable. My skin is hot. And so, so itchy. Though I know what these bites are going to turn into later will be much worse.

Nikhil's reached the door, but he's waiting for me. Visibly flinching with each new bite. "Hurry!" he tells me, extending a hand in my direction. But I'm still too far away.

"Go inside," I tell him. "I'll be right there."

"Not without you!"

Each step burns, but finally I'm close enough to reach for him. He yanks me toward the door just as a floating reddish-brown mass sails past. "Is that—?"

"Yeah," he confirms.

I stare in horror, a full-body shiver going through me. It's been years since I've seen one of these in person, but I know exactly what it is. Fire ants do something weird when water sweeps through their home. They band together. They lock arms and legs, or whatever their appendages are called, and they form a strange kind of raft. And then . . . they float.

They survive.

And they bite.

I hadn't seen the raft when I'd been pushing my way through the water, but I'd experienced the stragglers. The ones that must have fallen off into the water on their own. Biting at anything in their path. And from the painful, itchy sections of my skin, I can tell there were more than a few.

Nikhil opens the door, dragging both of us into the house, but it's unfortunately not much of a reprieve. The water here is the same level as it was outside, except in here it's dark. Making it much harder for us to make sense of our surroundings.

"Alan," Nikhil calls, just as a beam of light appears.

I turn toward it, thinking it's Alan with a flashlight, but it's just

Nikhil and his ridiculous headlamp. I can't quite make out the look on Nikhil's face, but I can just imagine his smug expression. *See? I told you this thing would come in handy.*

I blow out a breath, taking a step farther into the house. "Alan? Where are you?"

"Alan?" Nikhil tries again. "Hello?"

"Over here," a voice calls back.

We venture toward the sound of that voice. And I blink at what we find. Alan is sitting crisscross applesauce on top of his kitchen table. An assortment of snacks surrounds him, as well as a water bottle, a flashlight, a backpack, and a radio.

"Nikhil made it," Alan says into the radio with a loud whoop. "I'm saved!"

"This is what you get, Alan," a woman's voice replies, fuzzy and unclear as it travels through the airwaves. "I told you to evacuate. In fact, I told you not to buy your house. I told you there was a reason it wasn't selling. If you'd just listened to me . . ."

"It was a good deal, Betty. You know that. And how was I supposed to know the land here was a designated flood zone?"

"The mandatory flood insurance requirement should have tipped you off!"

Nikhil clears his throat. "Alan, if you're done we've got to get—"

"Yeah. Of course." Alan scrambles off the table, now wading through the water like we are, holding the radio and backpack above his head. "Nikhil, this is my sister on the line. Betty, Nikhil's here. And Meena. His . . ."

"Friend," I supply.

"Thanks for saving my worthless brother," Betty replies.

"Hey!" Alan exclaims. "That's uncalled for."

I stifle a laugh.

We push through the water, heading for the front door, and the two siblings bicker the whole way.

"I thought the two of you didn't get along," I say when there's a lull in the fight. Nikhil and I had largely tuned out Alan's monologuing about his sister earlier, but from the few parts I heard, none of it was complimentary.

"We don't," Alan and Betty say at the same time.

Nikhil snorts.

"Yeah, I guess . . . I just assumed y'all didn't talk anymore," I say.

"He *wishes* we didn't talk anymore," Betty says.

"That's true," Alan whispers.

"I heard that!"

We're outside now, getting closer to the canoe, and to my relief, I don't feel any stinging bites this time. The ones from before itch like crazy, and I'm sure they'll double in size later, but at least my allergic reaction isn't life-threatening.

Betty's talking about how Alan should have heeded her advice, but Alan abruptly interjects. "Got to go, Betty. Talk soon." He flips a switch on the radio, places it and the backpack on the floor of the canoe, then climbs inside, shaking his head. "We really haven't talked to each other in forever," he tells us. "But she overheard almost everything I told you guys earlier."

"She's on the neighborhood frequency?" Nikhil asks, his eyebrows raised.

"Yeah. She lives a couple houses down from you."

Nikhil pauses. "That was Elizabeth? Elizabeth Jeffries is your sister?"

Alan gives a loud, long-suffering sigh. "Yeah. That's how everyone reacts."

"How did I not know y'all were related?"

Alan shrugs. "Different last names. And we don't talk about it much."

I remember Elizabeth from before, but her full name . . . Something about it is so familiar. I search my memory, trying to place it, but come up short. "Who is she?" I ask as I settle into my seat and grab my paddle.

Nikhil looks our way, confirming we're all situated before untying the rope connecting us to the gate.

"She used to be county judge," Alan replies.

Oh. Right. She wasn't actually a judge, but for some reason that's the title the county uses for its version of a mayor. I remember her name was bandied around a lot during the last big storm we had. She was on local news constantly, telling us to either evacuate or "hunker down." But that would have been years ago. Back when I was in high school.

"You ready?" Nikhil asks, lifting his own paddle, and I nod. He begins counting, but after a few strokes, we don't need it anymore. We're sailing across the water smoothly.

"What is she up to now?" I ask Alan.

"Betty? I'm not sure. She went back to her old law firm after her term was up, but she's also involved in a lot of nonprofit work. Still, I don't think she wants to do that forever. I'm sure now that Congresswoman Garcia's retiring, she's thinking about that seat, but Betty doesn't exactly share her future plans with me." He sighs. "I should have remembered she'd be tuned in to the neighborhood frequency, but I was so panicked I wasn't thinking straight. She eventually interrupted and asked if the two of us could switch to a different frequency and then . . . we talked." He pauses. "We'd never talked about any of that stuff before, but it was good, I think."

We're halfway down the street, moving so much faster now that the wind's died down and the rain's let up. More light is breaking through the clouds, and it gives me hope. That the worst of the storm has passed. That the worst is almost over.

"I guess it's true what they say," Alan continues. "That communication is key."

Nikhil casts a sidelong glance in my direction, and I pointedly ignore it.

"She asked if y'all could take me to her house, so we could keep talking, but I'm not sure—"

"Oh, it's no problem," Nikhil says quickly. "We can take you there."

The eagerness in his voice almost makes me laugh. He's obviously thankful to have an alternative to being stuck in the house with Alan chattering away. But me? My feelings are mixed. I'm not exactly a fan of Alan's stories, but at least he'd provide some kind of buffer. Something to cut through the tension between Nikhil and me.

I chew my lip, anxiety growing as I think about it going back to being just the two of us. With the storm on its way out and Alan close to safety, there's nothing to distract us anymore. Nothing to distract me from my purpose. From the reason I'm here.

My brain whirs, thinking about possible ways forward. Negotiation tactics. Strategies I can try. Different scenarios. I play them through in my head, trying to envision one that gets Nikhil to sign off on the paperwork in the quickest way possible.

It's only when we reach Alan's sister's house that I process an important piece of information Alan just shared.

Congresswoman Garcia is retiring.

9

Congresswoman Garcia, like so many Texas politicians, represents a thoroughly gerrymandered district. It's a sliver of downtown Houston and a large chunk of a couple surrounding suburbs, but the area is all still firmly within Harris County. And like most of Harris County, the district consistently votes blue. Despite the occasional competitor, Garcia's held the seat comfortably for years.

I met her once at some breakfast fundraiser a few years ago. She was an absolute powerhouse. Her exterior had been deceptive, a frail frame, with a light pink shawl draped over her slightly hunched shoulders. But when she spoke, the whole room snapped to attention. No one could resist the command in her voice. The fervor. A decade-long leader on immigration and refugee policy, she spoke about human rights abuses at the border and fighting to increase refugee admissions. By the end of her speech, I'd wanted to rise to my feet. I hadn't heard anyone talk about public service like that in so long, and it had made me really think about what could be possible.

I want to talk to Shake about all of this. We'd planned on my running for an open state representative seat in Maryland—in conjunction with his state senate run—but this could change things. My long-term goal has always been to run for Congress, and Congresswoman Garcia's seat is in my hometown. I have a connection here that I don't have in Maryland, and I care deeply about the work she's done. It's a legacy I'd like to carry forward. Even if local hero Elizabeth Jeffries makes a play for the seat, these kinds of races can be unpredictable. When a long-term incumbent voluntarily steps aside, sometimes things break in favor of a wild-card pick. We could at least run it by our advisory group. See what they think. That is, if I can get Nikhil to sign off on this divorce. And if Shake still wants to get back together, wants to run together, once all of this is over.

As Nikhil and I tie off the canoe and follow Alan into his sister's house, I remember that my phone is broken. That even though I want to talk with him, I won't be able to share any of this news with Shake until I get home.

"Alan, is that you?" a woman calls, and Alan increases his pace.

"Betty, hi!" he says eagerly. "It's me. And I've brought friends."

"*Friends?*" Nikhil mouths at me behind Alan's back, a teasing glint in his eyes, and I fight the urge to laugh.

A tall, middle-aged white woman with short brown hair comes out to greet us, and I recognize her immediately from all the times she came on local news when I was a kid.

She goes up to Nikhil first, her arms spread out wide as she wraps him in a hug.

"Thanks for getting him," she says.

"Not a problem," he replies.

Elizabeth steps back, clasping Nikhil's upper arms. "You're a good egg, you know? We're lucky to have you on our street. And I hate to do it, but I'm going to be asking you for more help soon.

With Building Better? I know you've already given us a ton of your time, but with the storm we're going to be busier than ever. So many homes are going to need gutting and repairs, and we could use your expertise."

Nikhil nods. "Of course. No need to ask. I'm happy to do it."

She beams, then turns to me, taking my hand in hers and pumping it firmly. "And thank you too, Meena. I appreciate everything you both did for Alan." She gestures toward Nikhil. "You've got a good friend over here. Even with how busy he is, with that huge project of his own, he still finds time to volunteer and help us out. I don't know what we'd do without him. I mean, we get a lot of people who sign up, but most of them are only equipped to paint houses. Not a lot know how to do the real structural work, so he's an incredible asset to our nonprofit."

"Yeah," I say, shooting a glance toward Nikhil. "It's nice to meet you too." Nikhil never mentioned that he actually *knew* Elizabeth Jeffries, but they must talk often. She sounds up to date on everything happening in his life. This huge project of his? All this volunteering? The Nikhil I knew was so bogged down in work he had very little free time for anything else.

It's strange to think that she knows this new version of Nikhil better than I do.

The back of my neck prickles, and I rub the spot.

"Where's Kim?" Nikhil asks, looking around the living room. "Is she working?"

Elizabeth invites us to sit down and grabs some water bottles and snacks from the kitchen. Alan reaches for a packet of pretzels and tears into them before I can blink.

"Yeah, she's working." Elizabeth looks in my direction. "My wife's an ob-gyn," she tells me. "She's one of the more senior ones over there, so she always volunteers to be at the hospital during storms like this. She's worked through a bunch of them, so she feels like she should be there, and I can't blame her. I used to work through every storm too."

"I know," I say. "I remember."

She inclines her head, and the gesture somehow conveys acknowledgment and humility at the same time. It's clearly a practiced move from a career in politics, but it still manages to come across as sincere. I make a mental note to try it out sometime.

"I used to watch local news all the time as a kid," I continue. "City council sessions and local policy votes. It's what really got me interested in public service as a career."

"Meena works in D.C.," Nikhil adds.

"Oh." Elizabeth's eyes spark with interest. "On the Hill?"

I shake my head. "Public interest lobbying. I'm on the Hill a lot though. Just not working there myself."

She watches me for a long second, then smiles. "But you want to," she says.

"Oh, I . . ."

"You want to," she says again, her voice clear, leaving no room for disagreement. "I see it in you too. Running for office, it draws the kind of people who crave what it can give. Power or recognition or influence. Or control. I'm not saying everyone starts that way necessarily, but even the people with good intentions . . . All of it can get warped after a while. I mean, just look at most of the people representing us."

My skin grows itchy. Or maybe it's just all the ant bites on my arms making their presence known. But Elizabeth's words . . . they make me uncomfortable. I've been so sure about this plan, I've been trying to work toward it for so long, but is that all my desire to run for office is? A quest for recognition?

I'd thought running for office would allow me to advocate for the causes I believe matter most. I thought it would be an opportunity to make a difference, but is Elizabeth right? What she's describing, I've watched it happen. I've watched people abandon their principles when they realize sticking with them might cause them to lose their seats. And Shake and I have been so busy strategizing, trying to figure out timing and the right races that would give us the best chances of success. We've talked about policy, but only in dry terms, making sure our platforms are compatible. I can't remember the last time we spoke with the kind of sincerity and passion Congresswoman Garcia had that day.

"Meena's not like that," Nikhil says, and my head snaps in his direction. Elizabeth's expression reveals that she's just as surprised as I am, but as she watches Nikhil, her surprise morphs into something else.

"I didn't say she was," Elizabeth replies, a touch of amusement in her voice.

"To be fair, Betty," Alan says around a mouthful of pretzels, "that is what you basically implied."

Nikhil's eyes meet mine, his expression slightly abashed. "I only meant that's not how you used to talk about it," he says, and something pinches in my chest.

"Yeah?" Elizabeth asks.

"Yeah," Nikhil says, still watching me. "You talked about the local leaders you admired, the ones you grew up watching. People pushing for change, for policies that made people's lives better. You said they inspired you, that they were the reason you went to law school, the reason you wanted to work in policy and be in D.C."

That pinching sensation twists and grows as I remember the many conversations Nikhil and I used to have about this. The way he'd listen, retaining everything I said, and reminding me about it when I had a bad day with bar prep. Reminding me why I was doing this, what I was ultimately working toward.

Elizabeth smiles faintly. "See, I wasn't done before. If you'd let me finish you'd have heard me say that there are also people who run for office because they're hoping to subvert things. Hoping they can change things from the inside. Maybe it's optimistic or just plain delusional to think it can be done, but I'm willing to admit I'm one of those people. And it sounds like you're one of them too," she says, looking at me.

My throat tightens. Younger me would have pushed back against Elizabeth a bit. I would have said it wasn't delusional at all, that I really believed that the law, that the whole system could change. That we could make it change.

But years of working in D.C. have dulled some of that shiny, youthful enthusiasm. I've seen just how much harm the law can do. How inherently flawed the whole system is. How quickly fundamental rights can be stripped and how things can go from bad to even worse in an instant, making people throughout this country—and especially this state—suffer as a result.

"I like to think I am," I finally respond.

Out of the corner of my eye, I catch Nikhil frown, the corners of his lips pulling taut.

"It's a hard road," Elizabeth continues. "And it's certainly not the only avenue by which to pursue change. But I feel like it's work worth doing. Even here, where it feels like there's a lot more losses than there are victories, where every day is an uphill battle, there's nothing else I'd rather do. Texas is my home. My wife's home. And we're not going to give it up without a fight." She reaches for a water bottle and takes a sip. "If you feel even a fraction of that, I hope you do run for office one day."

"Thanks," I say, my brain trying to catch up with how I feel. What Elizabeth's said has ignited something in me, and it's a rush of sensation. One that's not entirely pleasant. It's almost like pins and needles, as if something that's been sleeping is slowly coming back to life. "I appreciate that," I tell her. "I appreciate everything you've said."

I reach for a water bottle of my own and catch Nikhil watching me, his face thoughtful and open. A mix of recognition and something else. Like he's saying *There you are* and *Who are you?* all in one single glance.

And as I look back at him, our gazes locked, I know my eyes tell him the same things too.

"How many bites did you get?" Nikhil asks, after we've dropped off the canoe in the garage and entered the house. He's twisting his arms, scanning both of them. The raised red bumps are clear even from a couple feet away.

"I can't count them all. Feels like a thousand. You?"

"Same."

My clothes, my shoes, my jacket—all fully soaked now—didn't prevent any of the tiny ants from getting inside. My skin itches. Everywhere. My torso, my back, the spaces between my toes.

"I'm going to take a shower," I say. I walk toward the stairs but stop right at the foot of them. The idea of trudging up the steps zaps whatever remaining energy I'd had right out of me. I've been running on a cocktail of too little sleep, adrenaline, and a will to survive, and I've pushed my body past its limits over and over during these last few hours. Now it's rebelling. Insisting that we get some rest and shut it all down.

"You want a piggyback ride?" Nikhil asks, standing next to me, a small, tired smile on his face.

Sudden memories flash through my mind. Nikhil carrying me on his back when I twisted my ankle on a walk. Hoisting me onto his shoulders for chicken fights in the pool. Cradling me in his arms and carrying me to bed whenever I fell asleep at my desk.

"No, no. I've got this." I wrap a hand around the railing, and force myself forward. One step at a time.

He huffs, following my slow ascent up the stairs. "It's not a crime to accept help, you know."

I almost roll my eyes. "I know. I'm not the one who needs to learn that lesson."

He's quiet for a beat. "What's that supposed to mean?"

The words gather on my tongue, but I stop, and shake my head.

Nikhil is an island. A self-sufficient little island. He was like that during our marriage and he's like that now. I tried to get past his defenses once. Tried to get him to let me in. I tried over and over. And I'm done. It's not my problem anymore. It hasn't been my problem for a long time.

"Don't worry about it," I tell him breezily.

"You think I don't ask for help?"

"I said don't worry about it." Trying to sound light and carefree takes a bit more effort this time.

"This is ridiculous," he mutters.

I pretend I don't hear him even though I'm tempted to say that I agree. This whole situation is ridiculous, though not for the reasons he thinks. But it's not worth getting into right now. My priorities are shower and sleep. And then whenever I wake up, food. And after I've achieved everything on the bottom level of Maslow's hierarchy of needs, I can work my way to the highest point of my pyramid: the divorce papers.

We finally reach the top of the stairs, and I feel as if I've climbed a mountain. I'm slightly winded, but I keep my eyes on the prize, hurrying to the bedroom. I steal a clean shirt and some gym shorts out of Nikhil's drawer and stroll confidently into the bathroom, claiming the shower first. But before I can close the door, Nikhil's hand shoots out, stopping it.

"You're the one who never accepted my help," he says, his neutral tone betrayed by the fire in his eyes. "You're the one who never needed me."

I shake my head. I should just let this go, but the words escape me before I can help it. "I needed you, Nikhil. I did. That was the problem."

A line forms between his eyebrows, and even though I'm feeling all kinds of things toward him at the moment, I'm tempted to run my finger down it. Tempted to know what that small groove would feel like against my skin.

Instead, I press on. "How do you think it felt to be the only one falling apart? The one who was always struggling. Always taking. Always needing *something*." A rush of breath leaves my lungs, and my next words are quieter. Small and resigned. "I couldn't do it anymore. I needed you to need me too."

He takes a step back, and I barely register his thunderstruck expression before I push the bathroom door shut.

Our marriage lasted exactly one year. I guess legally it's lasted about seven years, but we had only one real year of living together. One year of calling each other husband and wife. One year of trying to make it work.

It's not hard to pinpoint the exact moment things went wrong. That conversation—that fight—was an explosion, razing everything in its path. Burning whatever love existed between us into ash.

In the time that followed, I blamed everything on that moment.

I picked apart the words I'd used. The words he'd used. I imagined different phrases. Different tones. Even different locations for that conversation. I wondered for months if a different approach would have rendered a different result.

But with time and distance I've been able to examine that entire year under a microscope. I see the fault lines that existed before that moment. The tiny cracks that made the ultimate fracture inevitable. Nikhil and I were always doomed to fail.

There was the honeymoon phase, of course. But that wasn't enough to sustain us. It wouldn't be enough to sustain anyone. I was always supposed to move to D.C. And Nikhil's job was here in Houston. I was supposed to be doing things, achieving things, and instead my failure forced me to stay still. Stay home and study. While Nikhil left the house every day and worked. From morning to evening. He took on extra shifts. Extra responsibilities. Working Saturdays and Sundays too. I knew he was miserable. It was clear he was miserable. But when I asked, he always hid it, covered it up with that pained smile I grew to hate, until I stopped asking. Even when the loneliness grew and grew and grew, and his expression grew darker and sadder and more withdrawn, I stopped pushing because I knew why he was doing it. Why he stayed at a job he clearly hated. I wasn't bringing any money in. I had student debt and meager savings. I couldn't help much with the rent. Or the bills. Or anything. Nikhil had to provide.

It felt so regressive. So backwards. So wrong.

I'd told him I'd find a part-time job. Find some way to contribute, but he'd refused. He knew how much time I'd spent studying for the bar exam the first time around. He knew it was basically a full-time gig. That I wouldn't have the time for anything else. He'd reassured me. Told me that he understood.

He'd had dreams of his own, but nothing that he'd ever share in detail. He talked once about creating something of his own. Maybe opening an interior design company. Maybe branching into something else altogether. But whenever I tried to bring it up, he'd say that none of that mattered right now. That he didn't mind putting that on hold.

But he'd said all of that with the assumption that this was a temporary phase. He'd been so sure that I'd pass the bar the next time. That I'd get my job offer back. That I'd get back on track and get everything I always wanted. And he'd said that he'd wait to pursue his dreams until I'd achieved mine.

At first it had been sweet. His faith in me. His belief that I could do it.

And then it had felt heavy. Suffocating. This expectation. This pressure. This weight. Pressing in on all sides.

I *had* to pass. I *had* to do this. I *had* to make this marriage work. I *had* to do it all.

I had no other option.

Because he was supportive, he was willing to put his dreams on hold *for now*, but what would happen in the future? I knew he loved me *now*, but I wasn't sure if that love could withstand another failure.

I don't know when the spiral began, but by the time I realized it was happening, I was too deep in it to know what to do. And it didn't help that Nikhil was always . . . fine. Smiling through every setback. Working twice as hard to make sure we were okay. While I was just a crumpled mess, crying on the floor. I'd tried to tell him how I felt, and he'd comforted me, reassured me that everything would be fine, but my vulnerability was never reciprocated. He refused to lean on me, refused to look to me for support the same way I looked to him, and it made everything feel so unbalanced.

I was taking, and he was giving, and I didn't want it to all build up. For him to resent me, or leave me, so, after some time, I stopped sharing. Started wiping my tears when I heard the garage door open. Started pretending things were okay as soon as he got home.

Just like I'm pretending now. I exit the bathroom, my chin lifted high. No hint of how I'm really feeling on my face. Not that my charade is even necessary. Nikhil doesn't look at me as he passes by, barreling into the bathroom as soon as I exit. He doesn't say a word. Though at the last moment he reaches in my direction quickly, discreetly tucking something in the palm of my hand.

I wait until the door shuts to examine it closely. It's some kind of tube. I squint, angling my flashlight toward it.

1% Hydrocortisone Anti-Itch Cream. The generic Walgreens version.

I'm not sure why that part sticks out to me. Maybe because I'm almost positive I know the Walgreens Nikhil bought this from. It's just up the road. It's the same one where he bought all those reading glasses. And where we'd run if we needed just a little bit of milk. Or shampoo. Or something small that didn't warrant a longer drive to the closest Target or H-E-B.

I squeeze a generous dollop on my finger and start rubbing it across my itchy skin. Relief floods through me within minutes.

I open the door to the closet, more than ready to finally get some rest, but the king-size bed in the middle of the bedroom catches my eye. It's so tempting. Large and lush and inviting. It's not the same bed frame we had when I lived here. This one's a rich dark wood. Maybe something like mahogany. The comforter isn't one of the bright chaotic patterns I'd picked out either. It's all one solid color. Kind of between a blue and a gray. I run a hand over it and almost shiver. It's so soft. I can just imagine how it would feel against my skin.

I shoot a wary glance toward the boarded-up windows. Outside it had seemed like the storm was moving on. Even from in here I can tell that the wind has lessened. That the rain's lighter. There's no more terrifying snap and crackle of branches breaking or trees hurtling to the ground.

But we've come this far. There's no point taking any unnecessary chances now. My father's voice echoes in my head. Something he taught me when I was learning how to drive: "Most accidents happen close to home." He'd explained that when drivers start to get within five miles of their house, they let their guard down. They get too comfortable once they're in the homestretch. Toward the end of their journey.

He'd drilled that into my brain. Along with a million other instructions about not taking unnecessary risks. About following the rules. About not deviating from the straight and narrow. Though he'd never said it directly, I'd always known what his lessons were actually about. The undercurrent of fear in his voice had made it abundantly clear.

My sister was a junior in college when she got pregnant with Ritu. I'd been only twelve at the time, but I vividly remember the fallout. My sister having to drop out of college, having to abandon her dreams of medical school. My parents being utterly distraught. Disillusioned. Dismayed. Ultimately, they supported my sister. When Ritu's father made it clear he wouldn't be involved, my parents stepped up. They were at every doctor's appointment. They stayed with my sister at the hospital. And when Ritu was born, they showered so much love on their new granddaughter. But as loving as they were, there was always a lingering sense of sadness. And the community's reaction certainly didn't help. Snide comments and constant judgment and whispers about how my sister not only wasn't married but also had no plans to *get* married, from the aunties and uncles who were supposed to be my parents' friends. I've always suspected that part of the reason for my parents' move up north was to escape some of that shame.

My parents were never really the same after that. And there'd been a new unspoken rule in our home. An unspoken expectation. *You will not end up like your sister. You will not end up the same way.*

I give the bed one last longing look before crawling into the closet and slipping into my sleeping bag. I must be truly exhausted—and possibly borderline delirious—because this bag feels ten times more comfortable than it did before.

I sink down into its warmth, my body relaxing, a delightful haze taking over my mind.

The bathroom door opens with a loud creak, the sound traveling all the way in here. I close my eyes, hoping Nikhil will think I'm asleep. Hoping he'll switch off the lantern so we can put an end to this day and just start fresh tomorrow. I don't open them, even when I hear the sleeping bag beside me rustle, even though I can feel the weight of his gaze on me.

"I needed you," he says softly. So softly I'm not sure whether I heard him. So softly I'm not sure whether he *wanted* me to hear him. "I needed you," he says again, even quieter. "And then you left."

Oh no. No. He doesn't get to do that. He doesn't get to pin all the blame on me.

I flip over, and watch as his eyes widen in surprise.

"I didn't just leave," I say. "I asked you to move with me."

"You didn't."

"I did!" I'd not only asked him to move to D.C.; I'd practically begged him.

"You said it, but you didn't *mean* it."

"Oh, wow." I sit up, my legs folding underneath me as I turn to face him fully. "So now you're telling me you have some magical ability? You know my own thoughts better than I do? You think you can read my mind?"

He sits up as well, looking directly in my eyes. "I didn't have to. Your face that day said it all. And if you'd really wanted me to move with you, you wouldn't have shouted it at me in the heat of the moment. Like an afterthought. You'd have planned it. Methodically. That's who you are, Meena."

He's right and he's wrong. Normally I would have. I'd have presented a whole plan to him with a time line and ideas of places we could live. But all my carefully made plans tended to fly out the window when I was around Nikhil. And more than that, I'd been terrified to actually plan the move. It had felt like tempting fate. Tempting the powers that be. I hadn't wanted to bank on passing the bar. On getting my job back. I hadn't wanted to plan a move contingent on those things only for it to all fall apart. Again.

"You're just making excuses now," I say. "Bottom line is I asked you to come with me and you said no."

"I didn't say no."

I scoff. "Oh, really?"

"You left before I could give you my answer."

"Well, you didn't move with me. You didn't call me or text me or contact me at all after I left. So, I think it's pretty clear what your answer would have been."

"You'd be wrong." Indecision flickers over his face for a moment, but then something hard and sure settles into place. "I came to D.C., you know?"

A cool wave of surprise washes over me, scattering every half-formed argument in my head. "What?"

"Stupid, right?" He lets out a sad, humorless laugh. "I don't know what I was thinking. Maybe I wasn't thinking."

My mind whirs. "When . . . when did you—"

"Three months after. After you left."

Three months. At that point, I'd barely unpacked my new apartment. Barely found my footing at work. I'd been so new to the city. So new to everything. And so heartbroken.

"I didn't know. You never came to see me."

"I did."

I shake my head. That's not possible. I never saw him there. Not once.

"I went to your office," he continues. "And they told me you were on the Hill."

That sounds . . . probable. I was there more days than not. Lobbying for causes. Pushing for the votes my clients wanted. It had been exhilarating back then. Recently, it's started to feel . . . limiting. We're selective with our clients, so our values tend to be aligned, but I want to be able to advocate for the causes I care about, not just the ones my clients do. It's why I thought about running for office.

"There was a vote that day," Nikhil says. "Proposed budget cuts for WIC."

And now my memory sharpens, the picture coming into focus. I remember that day. I remember being absolutely fueled by anger. This country already lacks a true social safety net, leaving so many to suffer, to fend for themselves. And instead of strengthening the few programs we have, these individuals were trying to cut them further. Cuts that would harm real people.

I couldn't help but think of my sister. My sister, who may not have had the support of our community but had had the support of my parents, and thanks to them, some financial resources. But even with that, she had suffered so much. I was all too aware of the many people who didn't have that kind of support to rely on. WIC doesn't solve everything. It's not perfect. There are still too many hurdles and hoops for people to jump through before receiving the benefits.

But it's one of the only federal programs aimed at supporting pregnant people and young children, and my interest that day wasn't driven only by the fact that I had a job to do. It felt personal.

"I remember," I tell Nikhil. "I remember that day. But you weren't . . ."

"I was there," he says. "And I saw you. You were wearing a blazer. Dark gray. I'd never seen you wear one before. And you were arguing with someone. I wasn't close enough to hear what you were saying, but this guy must have been twice your age. Possibly more. And he was listening. And I could just see it. I could see the exact moment you had him. The subtle shift in his face. In his posture.

"I was so proud of you, Meena. I was bursting with it. I was going to come up to you. Going to tell you how amazing that was, and then you did it again. Confronting someone else. And then another person. And another."

"They didn't all change their minds," I say.

"No, but *he* did. The first guy. I saw it. I watched the vote. You were probably there, seeing it in person, but I was sitting outside, watching it all on my phone. The C-Span feed was slow and buffering, but I saw his vote. And the end result. You won."

"It wasn't just me. There were a lot of people who worked on—"

"But you made a difference," he says, a bit of wonder in his voice. "I . . . I'd never really understood it all before. The things you wanted to do. I mean, I'd heard you talk about it. I knew you were passionate. I knew it meant a lot to you. And I'd admired it, but still, I just . . . I had no clue."

My reality is shifting. I can't make sense of it all. That the narrative of us is different from what I'd thought it was. That Nikhil hadn't just accepted it when I left. That he hadn't just let me go. He'd tried to come after me. Except . . .

"Why didn't I see you? Why would you come all that way and not talk to me?"

"Because I couldn't." His words are raw. Hoarse. "How could I? What could I say? What could I offer you?" He waves a hand around him. "This? A house in the suburbs? Far away from everything you wanted. Far away from the thing you were meant to do?"

"You could have come when I'd asked. You could have—"

"You didn't want me there! And once I got there, once I saw what you were doing, I understood why. What could I, where would I— I wouldn't have fit into any of that."

"I wanted you there. I wanted you there with me. How could you think I wouldn't—"

"You *left*. You asked me to move, gave me barely any time to decide, and then you *left*. You left for your job. You left for something better. You left because Plan A was finally an option. And you didn't need Plan B anymore."

"And what exactly was Plan B, Nikhil?"

He shakes his head. "Me. This. It was always temporary for you. Something to do. A way to bide your time until what you really wanted came along."

I suck in a breath. He . . . he really thinks the worst of me. He really thinks of me as some heartless user who just took and took and took from him. Who disposed of him when I didn't need him anymore.

"You're wrong," I say. "I never thought of any of it that way. Never. I left because you didn't want to come with me."

His mouth opens, but I quickly continue. "You *didn't*, Nikhil. You knew my plan was always to move there, to work there, but every time I dropped hints about it . . . you shut down. You made it clear you didn't want to talk about it. That day I asked you to move . . . that was me putting it all on the line. And I felt so guilty about it. You'd already sacrificed so much, done so much to support me, and I didn't want you to have to leave Houston or this home— I knew how much it meant to you. At one point . . . I even looked for work here. I tried to think about a way to stay, but nothing was close to the job in D.C."

His eyes grow wide. "Meena—"

"But I still asked, I *begged,* because I was desperate. I didn't want to lose you. I didn't want to move without you. But . . . maybe it wasn't right to ask you to come with me, to leave everything behind. Maybe I shouldn't have expected that. Maybe . . . I asked for too much."

"You didn't," he says immediately, his voice low and firm. "I would have come. If I'd known this was how you felt . . ." He swallows, looking down. "There was nothing here that was holding me back. My job, this house . . . None of it mattered to me the way you did. But I was . . . I was so convinced you didn't want me. I thought you were looking for an excuse to end things. A way to let me down gently."

My eyes prick, tears forming at the corners. "If I knew you were in D.C., if I'd known you'd come, if I'd just *seen* you—"

"I wanted to tell you I was there," he says. "But when I saw you working . . . it suddenly seemed so selfish. I thought you wanted— that you *needed*—someone different, someone who would understand your life there and your work, someone who could help you with it."

Someone like Shake.

I mentally flinch.

"I didn't think you wanted me," Nikhil continues. "And I didn't want to try to change your mind. I didn't want you to have to . . . settle for me when you could have something else."

"It wouldn't have been settling," I say, my voice small. "You're . . . you *were* everything I wanted. Back then."

He inhales sharply, and the sound is so startling, so raw, that one of my tears escapes, sliding down my cheek.

His eyes follow the movement, and there's something haunted about the way he looks at me.

"Me too," he says. "You were everything I wanted too."

My chest aches, my mind reels. The past may have been different than I thought, but my present is still the same. Shake and my career and everything I've planned for the future. I don't know how to reconcile all of it. Don't know how to make all these discordant pieces fit back together in my mind.

The silence between us is loud. Heavy. But neither of us breaks it. Nikhil turns down the lantern, and we both lie back on the floor.

After a little while, my tears dry up and I think Nikhil's fallen asleep until I hear him release a shuddering breath, one he tries to muffle.

It breaks me.

In the dim light, I spy his arm outside his sleeping bag, lying in the tiny space between us. I don't say anything, but I shift a tiny bit closer, slowly reaching toward him until we make the barest contact. One he might think is an accident, a movement made in my sleep.

Just the back of my hand lightly grazing his.

10

My tongue is thick and heavy in my mouth.

And I'm cold. I'm so cold.

I shiver, burrowing beneath the covers, wrapping them closer around me. I'm seconds away from falling back asleep when something wet and icy lands on my forehead. I try to bat it away, but my arm seems stuck to the bed. I can't lift it.

"Get it off," I mumble, shaking my head.

"Shhh," a voice replies, returning the cold, wet whatever-it-was to where it had been. "You're burning up."

"I'm not. I'm freezing."

"Okay, then. You're freezing."

I frown. "Don't make fun of me. I am."

A hand coasts over my hair, leaving a trail of warmth in its wake. I wish it had happened slower. I wish it would happen again.

"I would never make fun of you," the voice says.

I blink my eyes open. There's a man standing over my bed. He looks so familiar. For a couple seconds I can't place him. And then suddenly, it comes to me.

"You look a lot like my husband," I tell him. And for some reason, he laughs.

"Oh really? Are you married?"

I groan. "Yes, but I'm not supposed to tell anybody about it. It's a secret."

He laughs again, perching on the edge of the bed. "I need to check for a fever," he says, showing me the thermometer in his hand. "Is that okay?"

"Sure, Doc."

"Doc?"

I squint at him. "Aren't we in a hospital?"

"Uh, no. Not exactly."

Huh. I squint up at him. I'm obviously sick. I'm fatigued and freezing and hallucinating images of my estranged husband. I figured I was in critical condition. But maybe this is just an urgent care or a doctor's office. Who knows?

I open my mouth, though I'm not quite sure why, and he places the thermometer under my tongue. I stare at him as I wait, and he watches me in return. His lips twitch in the oddest way. As if he's fighting back a smile. Though that doesn't make much sense.

A timer dings on his phone and he pulls out the thermometer. He takes a look at the temperature, and his brows crease. "It's high," he says quietly, like he's saying it more to himself than to me.

I don't really care what my temperature is. I just want to go back to sleep. My eyelids are so heavy. Staying awake is taking every spare bit of energy I have.

"Wait," he says, noticing I'm about to nod back off. "Take these first." He presses a couple pills into my hand and helps me sit up. I grumble the whole way but reluctantly comply. He brings a glass of water to my lips, and I swallow, but he's not satisfied until I finish the whole glass, which is just too much. I tell him he's being bossy, and he laughs in response. I'm getting pretty tired of that laugh. Except there's a tiny part of me that wants to hear it again. Wants to make him laugh some more.

"I'm going to sleep," I tell him, lying down again. I shift back and forth a bit, getting comfortable.

My eyes slide shut, and I almost shiver with pleasure when his hand returns to my hair. He smooths it back, away from my forehead, but again the whole thing is over too quick.

"Do that again. Please," I say. "You're so warm."

He's quiet for a few seconds. And then his hand returns. I sigh with relief.

"So, I noticed you don't wear a wedding ring," he says.

"Yeah, well," I mumble. "I'm trying not to be married anymore."

His hand pauses midstroke, then resumes. "Why is that?" he asks. "This husband of yours . . . is he . . . is he that terrible?"

I'm so tired. My consciousness is slipping away fast, but something swift and defensive rises in me. Something that insists I answer him.

"No," I say. "Not at all."

"Then, *why*—" His voice breaks on the word, and he starts again. "Meena, why—"

He keeps talking, and I try to pay attention. The way he says my name . . . it's almost like he knows me. Really *knows* me. But his voice fades, growing quieter and quieter. Darkness closes in on me and finally, I'm asleep.

· · ·

My legs kick out at the comforter, desperate for space. For air. Why is this thing wrapped so tight around me? I feel swaddled. Like this fabric is tucked into every nook and cranny of my body. I kick harder.

"What's the matter?"

"It's hot," I say, trying to free myself. "It's too hot."

"Of course it is," he says agreeably, with maybe a tiny hint of sarcasm. But I don't mind, because a few seconds later, the covers lift away from my body and a cool breeze travels over my skin.

"Better?"

"Yeah." Except . . . I'm all clammy. Sweaty. The clothes I'm wearing are sticking to me. They're making me itch. I'm hot and tired and itchy and it's all awful.

"I don't feel good," I moan.

"I know. I'm sorry, love. I know."

I turn onto my side, curling into a ball. I don't want to be here. I'm not sure where *here* is, but it's not home. It's not my home. I'm somewhere strange and I want to go home.

"I know. You'll be home soon. I promise."

I feel like crying. This man. His voice is so kind. So soft. I want to fall inside it. I can just tell it would be a nice place to land.

"I'm going to run a cold towel over your skin, okay? And then I need to apply this cream. Can you hold still?"

I don't have the energy to do much else. I try to tell him that, but I can't. My lips are cracked. Chapped and sore and it hurts to move them.

But this towel? It's bliss. It's the best thing I've ever felt in my life.

"The best thing? Really?" He lets out a warm chuckle.

Am I talking out loud? I thought my lips were too cracked to manage that.

"What? What do you mean?" Cool fingers trace over my face, lifting my chin. "Shit. Sorry. Give me a second."

A weight lifts off the bed. He's gone for a while and then he's back, dabbing something goopy on my lips. I don't know what it is, but he's obviously trying to help.

He returns to the towel, tracing it down each leg, and down each arm. Then he starts rubbing something on me. Probably that cream he'd mentioned earlier. All of my skin feels like it's burning, but parts of it feel even hotter than others. And some places sting. The pad of his finger travels over a particularly bad spot, and I flinch.

"Sorry," he says. "Sorry. Almost done. It's going to feel a lot better after this. I promise."

I don't know if that's true. I want it to be true. But the idea of feeling better sounds a lot like a fairy tale right now. Something you tell a kid so that they have hope, even though it's never going to happen.

"Okay," he says some amount of time later. "We're done. You can go back to sleep. Do you want the sheet? As a cover? Or nothing?"

"Nothing." I can't bear the thought of anything touching my skin.

"Okay."

He's quiet after that. Probably waiting for me to fall back asleep, but I want to know . . .

"Will you stay?" I ask. "Will you stay here?"

"Yeah. Yes. Of course. I'm not going anywhere."

I swallow. I don't know why that helps, why it makes my body relax further into the mattress, but it does.

His hand comes up to my forehead, and I remember this. He did it earlier. He sweeps his hand back, traveling over my hair, and I sigh. His hand was warm before, but now it's cool. It feels so good.

I'm drifting off again. Everything's turning that lovely kind of foggy and hazy.

"Don't leave," he whispers. So soft I can barely hear him. "Don't leave me again."

I don't know what he means. I don't know what he's trying to say. But I'm out before I can ask.

"You know I drive by that spot all the time. It closed a few years ago, but someone else bought it and it's a coffee shop now. I don't ever go there so I don't know if it's any good, but every time I see it, I think about that time we went and got ice cream."

I'm not sure who's speaking. I'm not sure if I'm dreaming. I can't fully make sense of the words I'm hearing, but something about this man's cadence, the rhythm of the way he speaks, is comforting to me. Familiar.

"I don't know if you ever think about that," he continues. "But it was basically our first date. Though neither of us really called it that. I'd asked if you wanted to 'hang out' and get ice cream, and I'd kicked myself the whole way home. I should have planned something better. Should have been clearer that it was a date. Should have taken you someplace that would impress you. I couldn't believe you'd said yes.

"And then, that day, I'd been so nervous. My palms were so hot and sweaty I'd worried the ice cream would melt right off the cone, but then we started talking and it was just like all those conversations we'd had in your parents' yard. Natural and easy and fun."

He lets out an amused huff. "You made me laugh so much that night, and every time you did it you looked so surprised. Like you didn't realize how funny you could be, and it only made me laugh harder. You always . . . you always thought of yourself as so serious and focused and intense, and you were—you are—but you talked about it as if it was something to be ashamed of. As if I didn't love that you were just as serious and focused about making me laugh as you were about the bar exam. That you took me just as seriously as all the other, much more important things competing for your attention. That you were just as focused and intense and careful with me.

"Maybe it was selfish of me. To want all of that for myself. That day we woke up in Vegas, I knew you were scared. I'd been scared too, but not because we'd gotten married. I'd felt like . . . like I'd just walked by a winning slot machine that was spitting quarters. I'd done nothing to deserve it, but I knew I needed to hold on to them for as long as I could. I didn't know when the machine would stop, how long it would keep giving them, and I could already feel the cold metal slipping through my fingers, but I still held on, and . . . it wasn't fair to do that. It wasn't fair to you.

"I'm sorry," he says, as a light touch travels over my cheek, the pressure growing firmer when it reaches my forehead. "I'm really sorry."

He makes some kind of noise then, some muffled, half-choking sound, but I slip away before I can hear anything else.

An arm slides around my back. "Can you sit up for a second? Just a second?"

I nod, letting him maneuver me. He sits beside me, propping me upright, and I lean my full weight against him. Not that I want to. It's just that I'm positive I'll slide back down if I try to stay like this on my own. That's the only reason.

There's a light shining from my left. From the lamp on the bedside table. That's strange. It's on.

"How is that working?"

"How is what working?" His arm's still around me, but he's turned away, messing with something on the nightstand.

"That light. How is that working? Did the power come back?"

"Yeah, yeah. It did." He hands me a couple pills. "Mind taking these?"

"Sure." I take the glass of water from him and swallow them dutifully.

He should be relieved I'm such a good patient. He was always such a baby when he was sick. Though it was kind of endearing.

"Done," I say, handing the glass back to him. "And thanks," I add on. "How long was I out for?"

He checks his phone. "Ten. Maybe twelve hours. But you've been up a couple times in between." He glances at me. "Do you . . . do you remember any of that?"

"Not really." I'm not even sure how I made it from the closet to the bed. Well, except for the obvious answer. He must have carried me.

"Is it safe?" I ask, sudden alarm pounding through me. "Safe to be here? In the bed?"

"What do you . . . Oh, because of the storm? Yeah. We're fine. Wind speeds are way down. It's moving slow, weirdly kind of hovering over the area, but it's been downgraded from a hurricane to a tropical storm. There's some rain still, which isn't helping the flood situation, but there's no threat of windows breaking anymore."

He places the back of his hand against my forehead and frowns. "You're still warm. I thought maybe your fever had broken, but I think it's still there. We'll need to check it."

"Okay." If the storm's slowed down, maybe that means flights will resume soon. I guess the flooding would have to go down first and I'm not sure how long that would take. Now that the power's working, I should be able to find out.

I stretch my arms over my head, craning my neck from side to side. My muscles are so stiff. The movement feels amazing and horrible at the same time. And . . . "Oh my god." Giant, angry red welts cover my body. My arms. My legs. And from the itching, I think there's one on the back of my neck.

"They're better than before," Nikhil says. "Believe it or not they've gone down in size."

"Oh, I believe it." I've had worse reactions to fire ants than this. I've had bites swell up to ten times their size, looking like balloons. I've just never had this many at once.

"I don't know if that's what made you sick," he says. "I don't remember you ever getting a fever from them before."

"My body may not have known what to do with this many. Or maybe it was from being outside in the rain that long. Or something I caught on the plane." I'd read once that the immune system is less effective in fighting off infection during periods of high stress. And god knows that my time here has been the most stressful of my life.

I lick my lips, tasting something strange on them.

"Vaseline," Nikhil says. "Sorry. It's just . . . your lips were chapped."

"Oh. Thanks." He's still sitting close to me, his arm draped around my shoulders, his thigh touching mine. I shift just the tiniest bit and he's gone, almost jumping off the bed.

"So, uhh, what else did I miss?"

Nikhil clears his throat. "TV's working again so I caught up on some of the news. Water's pretty high everywhere. And a lot of houses got flooded. They've set up some makeshift shelters around town." He places something on the nightstand. "And I got this out of the guest bedroom for you."

Ah, my horrible, broken-beyond-repair phone. The screen looks like a spiderweb, cracks shooting out in every direction. I bet it has water damage now too.

"I tried plugging it in," he says, "but it wouldn't turn on."

I grimace. "Yeah. I think this thing is toast."

Nikhil rubs his forehead, watching me for a second, and god, this feels so awkward. Him towering over me, while I'm still in bed. I want to snap to my feet. I want to stand eye to eye. I feel so small like this. So weak.

"Are you hungry?" he asks. "I tried to get you to eat something earlier, but you weren't having it." The right corner of his mouth climbs up. "You were pretty fussy."

"I'm sure I wasn't."

"How would you know? You don't remember any of it."

I open my mouth, then close it. He has me there.

"Anyway, I made some soup. Nothing fancy. Just from a can."

My stomach rumbles at the thought. "That sounds amazing."

"I'll bring it up."

I want to go with him. I want to say I can go downstairs. That it's no big deal. But I truly have no strength. Just sitting up takes effort. I don't think I could make it down those stairs and back.

"Thanks," I say. He turns to leave, but I reach out, grabbing the ends of his fingers. "Really, Nikhil. Thank you. For all of this."

"It's nothing."

He tries to pull his hand back, but I tighten my grip. "No, it's not. It's—"

"I owed you," he says. "For that time I had the flu. Now we're even."

I laugh. "Oh gosh. You were such a wreck during that."

He grins, one side of his mouth climbing slightly higher than the other. "I was, wasn't I? I think I must have been the world's worst patient."

I soften, a memory rising. Nikhil curled into the fetal position, his hand gripping mine tight, his body shivering with chills. I'd never seen him that way before. He'd never *let* me see him that way before.

"You weren't," I say. "Not really. You barely asked for anything. The only frustrating thing was that you refused to just lie down and get some rest. I'd turn my back for a second and catch you trying to get out of bed." I shake my head. "You even tried to help me with my studying. Your temperature was so high you were shaking, but for some reason you thought it was the perfect time to try and quiz me on civil procedure."

His crooked smile grows, light and teasing, and so familiar it hurts. "I can still remember all five factors needed for personal jurisdiction," he says.

"Oh no." I laugh again. "Please don't remind me."

His smile starts to fade, and I quickly add, "Not that I didn't appreciate it. The way you helped me study." Most nights after dinner, Nikhil used to sit on the couch with me, open bar prep books on our laps. He'd quiz me or help me write flash cards. One time I accidentally fell asleep early and woke up to a stack of bright pink index cards filled with his handwriting. Neat and precise and careful.

When I left for D.C. I discovered that one of them had found its way into my bag. The corners of it are soft now, the hard card stock somewhat fragile from the number of times I've pulled it out and looked at it.

"It was nothing," Nikhil says.

"It wasn't." My hand squeezes his. For so long I've lied to myself, rewritten the past. I've told myself that I would have passed the bar that first time if not for Nikhil. I've told myself that meeting him and falling in love that summer had been a distraction, that our love had made me lose sight of what mattered, but the truth is . . .

"I wouldn't have passed that second time without you," I tell him.

His cheeks flush. "I don't know about that."

"I wouldn't have," I say again. "But . . . when you were sick, I

wish you would have thought it was okay to just rest and get better."
I think of that time he came home from work with a limp, an injury
he'd refused to tell me about, the way he'd pivoted the conversation
back to the bar instead. "I know the bar exam consumed my life back
then, but I'm sorry if I made you ever feel like it was more important
or more urgent than what you were going through. It didn't matter
more than how you were feeling, Nikhil. It didn't matter more than
you being sick."

He shakes his head. "I . . . I know, but being sick, it was more
that . . . I felt guilty. I hated that you had to take time away from
studying to take care of me." Regret clouds his voice as he says, "I
never wanted that for you. For us."

My heart floats up to my throat. "I *liked* taking care of you." I
pause. "It was really the only time you let me take care of you. I . . .
Sometimes, I wish you had let me be there for you the way you
always were for me."

Something heavy settles over his expression, and I feel it. A tangible weight bearing down on the room. I try to shake it off. "Anyway," I say brightly, "the whole flu episode could have been avoided."

He takes the opening just like I'd hoped he would. "If I'd only
listened to you and gotten a flu shot." He inclines his head in my direction. "You'll be happy to know I get one every year now."

"Good."

He smiles again, the corners of his eyes crinkling, and I'd forgotten. His eyes are so brown, so rich, and dark. But they have these
little flecks of gold. They're not always there, but sometimes, in the
right lighting, they just appear. Almost like magic.

Seconds pass, and the amusement in his eyes begins to fade.

"I'm going to get the soup now," he says.

"Okay," I say, but I don't let go of his hand. I know I should, but
for some reason, I keep holding on.

In the end he's the one to do it. He retreats, and I reel my hand back, awkwardly cradling it against my chest.

The loss of contact is sudden. And now, I'm cold. The comforter's been peeled back away from me, and I reach for it.

"There's an extra blanket right next to you," he says.

And so there is. I grab it, throwing it over my legs.

Nikhil leaves the room, returning in a short while with a tray that holds two bowls balanced in both hands. He sets it down on the dresser, and my mouth begins to salivate. Food. It's been so long since I've eaten. I've slept through the last few meals, and that rescue effort was the most strenuous workout I've had in months. I need calories.

Nikhil wraps a cloth napkin around one of the bowls and uses that to carry it over to the nightstand. "Careful," he says, no doubt seeing the longing in my eyes. The way I'm tempted to grab the bowl sans spoon and just tip it directly into my mouth. "It needs to cool down."

He goes back to the dresser, then returns with the other bowl.

He looks around for a moment, as if trying to figure out where he should sit. I scooch over, giving him enough space to sit on the edge of the bed.

He silently accepts the invitation, though he doesn't look my way.

I blow over my soup, cautiously tasting a spoonful. Chicken noodle. The kind with star-shaped pasta.

"My mom used to make this for me whenever I was sick," I say, no longer cautious, full-on scarfing it down. I can still imagine the small plastic bowl she'd serve it in. It had characters from *The Lion King* on it. And a matching spoon.

He doesn't say anything for a moment. His eyes are glued to the bowl in his lap. "I know," he finally says. "You told me that once."

Oh. My chest is tight. There's some kind of pressure. Something squeezing my lungs. Probably a side effect of whatever infection I have.

We eat in silence for a bit, but once I have food in my stomach and feel the tiniest bit better, I can't help but bring up our prior conversation.

"So," I say, "you came to D.C."

His spoon freezes midair, halfway to his mouth, and he sets it back down in his bowl. "Yeah," he says. "I did."

I pick a loose thread off the edge of the blanket. "Did you like it?"

"Like what? The city?"

I nod. I'd been so worried about that back then. So worried that he wouldn't like D.C. as much as he liked Houston. Houston had been his first real home, the first place he'd been allowed to live for more than a year or two. We'd talked about moving. Even when we were just dating, he knew that I'd been planning to move. That I'd *have* to move for my job. After we'd gotten married, he'd said he was fine coming with me to D.C., but I still hadn't been sure whether he would actually do it. If he'd really be willing to pick everything up and leave the first home he'd ever known. And I guess in the end he hadn't.

"I don't know," he says. "I didn't see much of it. I wasn't there very long." He glances over at me. "Finished?" he asks, gesturing for me to hand him my empty bowl. I pass it, and he gathers everything back onto the tray and leaves the room.

I rub a hand over my eyes and sigh. He clearly doesn't want to talk about that anymore, and now I'm not even sure why I brought it back up. The fact that Nikhil came to D.C. years ago doesn't change anything. It doesn't change the fact that he never tried to talk to me once all these years. It doesn't change the fact that the two of us were not meant for each other. It doesn't change the fact that I need this divorce, that I need him to sign the papers, that I need to end all of this to get back on track with my career, and with Shake.

I miss how logical and rational Shake and I were. How things made sense when we were together.

Our plans for the future, our joint runs for office. We're on the same page about everything. Together, it really seemed like all of that might be possible.

I wonder again what he would think about the Texas seat. Elizabeth is probably running, so it might not even be worth it to bring it up, but for some reason, it still has a hold on me. Being here, spending time on this street, it's reminded me how much I once loved this place. And hearing Elizabeth's passion was inspiring. This place was once my home, and the way she'd talked about it made me want to be here, to fight for this place and the people who live here too. I'm not sure whether it would even be possible, but I want to at least try to find out more.

But I'll deal with all of that later. Right now, I have more pressing matters to attend to. I'm all grimy. I feel so gross. And I really need to brush my teeth. I swing my legs out of bed, and the floor rises up to meet me. *Whoa*. I catch myself in time, avoiding a fall. I'd underestimated how slowly I need to take things. Underestimated how weak my body is. I wait a moment before trying again, taking small, tiny steps to the bathroom. Once there, I'm shocked by what I find in the mirror.

I hadn't expected to look great, but it's even worse than I'd feared. My hair has taken on a life of its own. A bird's nest with a hair tie trapped somewhere inside it. And my arms look strange and unfamiliar. Like they don't even belong to me. Dotted with scrapes and scratches and red bites and welts, though fortunately those aren't as itchy as I remember them being hours ago. And my eyes are all sunken in, the shadows under them dark and deep and purple. I can't believe I've been out for hours. I look like I haven't gotten any sleep in days.

I do what I can to repair things, splashing cold water on my face and stealing some of Nikhil's toothpaste. I somehow find the hair tie amid the tangles and manage to smooth the mess of hair back into a low ponytail. This usually makes me look like a Founding Father, but with everything else going on, it's somehow an improvement.

"Feeling better?" Nikhil asks, catching me as I exit the bathroom.

"A bit." I'm still tired, but the moving around helped me wake up. Helped me cut through some of the fatigue.

I settle back under the covers, and the two of us are quiet for a while. Awkwardly avoiding each other. He's messing with things in the drawers. I can hear them open and shut repeatedly. I'm pretty sure he's taking clothes out, refolding them, and putting them back in, but I don't watch too closely. I don't want him to catch me looking. I'm pretending to be busy, examining the cracked screen on my phone intently. As if staring might bring it back to life.

I don't know how to broach conversation with him. Before I got sick, we both peeled back layers, exposing our truths about the past, but he rebuffed my earlier attempt to bring it back up. And now I'm scared to mention it, unsure if I even *want* to. Maybe he regrets telling me all the things he did. Or maybe we're just both experiencing vulnerability hangovers.

What we probably need right now is space, but that's hard to find when you're trapped in a house together. Though at least we're no longer confined to the closet. In fact, why *is* he here? There are plenty of other rooms he could be in. I'd dart out right now if I could. If I had the strength. I'd run to the kitchen or the living room or the guest bedroom. Though I guess the guest bedroom isn't really an option anymore. I wince, feeling a touch of guilt.

"How's the guest room?" I ask.

Nikhil turns around, his hands clutching a balled-up pair of socks.

"When you went to grab my phone earlier," I clarify. "How did the guest room look?"

"Oh. Fine."

"Really?"

"Uh, no." He separates the socks, then refolds them back together. "But it's better than I thought it would be. Some water got in, but nothing compared to if it had flooded. And there's some glass and stuff, but once I clean it out and replace the window, it'll be fine."

I clear my throat. "Good. I'm glad to hear that." I'm about to offer to help with the cleaning, and then remember how I almost collapsed earlier just trying to get out of bed. I won't let him clean it alone though. I'll just have to make sure he stays here until I'm back to full strength. So he doesn't try to sneak off and do it by himself.

"Since the power's back we can watch some TV, right?" I nod toward the flat-screen on the wall.

He grunts in response. I'm not sure if it's meant to be a positive or a negative sound until he hands me a remote a few moments later.

The screen turns on, showing a local news channel. There's a reporter standing in the middle of the street, water up to her knees.

"Though the storm's lost some of its intensity," she says, "a lot of streets throughout the city are looking like this. As you know, it's not abnormal for us to get some flooding during a storm, but city officials have no estimate on when the water might recede. In the last press conference, they explained that due to the significant amounts of rain we experienced before the hurricane, our groundwater levels were already high. With the level of rainfall we received in the past twenty-four hours, there's simply no place for the water to go. So, if you've evacuated, stay put. The worst of the storm may be over, but with these roads, there's no way for you to get back right now. And if you stayed, well, you'll be staying in place a little longer. We'll do our best to keep you updated on any developments and—"

"That's been the only update for the last few hours," Nikhil interrupts. "That no one has any idea on when the flooding will go down."

Great. My odds of getting home soon are looking slimmer and slimmer. I flip through the channels, desperate to find something else. Something to take my mind off of things. But every channel seems to be showing the same images. Flooded streets. Abandoned cars. Homes partially underwater.

"Do you have Netflix?" I ask. "Anything streaming?"

He walks over, taking the remote from my hand and pressing a few buttons until that familiar red logo appears.

"Thanks," I say, as he hands it back to me.

To my surprise, he doesn't return to his pretend organizing of the dresser. Instead, he walks around the bed and sits on the very edge of the side farthest from me.

"What are you going to watch?" he asks.

"I'm not sure." I'm scrolling, trying not to seem too curious, too interested in what Netflix is recommending to him. Or what it thinks he needs to "continue watching." What are his tastes now? Have they changed? When we were together, Nikhil was always insistent that he could never watch anything too serious or too dark before we went to bed. Otherwise, the images would stay with him, and he couldn't fall asleep.

I'd thought it was so cute. But either he's changed that rule or he's been watching stuff in the mornings or afternoons because there are a lot of documentaries in his queue right now. History. Investigative reporting. Politics. And is that . . .

"You're watching *Gilmore Girls*?"

"Uhh . . . yeah."

I look over at him, and he shrugs. "It's a good show."

"I know that," I say. "It's a *great* show."

A smile plays at the corners of his mouth. "Yeah. It is."

"What season are you on?"

"Three."

"Ahh, we're getting into the Jess era."

"Yup," he says. "But I'm more of a Logan guy."

I gasp. "Logan? *Logan?* No. Absolutely not. He's the worst!"

"But he's the only one who really fit into her life. The only one who was on her level."

"*What?*" I ask. "No, Logan was so entitled and spoiled. He wasn't right for her at all and—" I pause. "Wait, does this mean you've seen this before? Nikhil, are you . . . are you rewatching this?"

He lets out a breath, something between amusement and embarrassment. "Like I said, it's a good show."

I shake my head, pressing play. The familiar theme song washes over me, immediately putting me at ease, providing comfort. The snappy, fast-paced dialogue is the exact kind of distraction I was hoping for, keeping my mind busy for a while. But the second there's a lull, a wandering thought intrudes: *Why did Nikhil and I never watch this together? How did I not know he was a fan? What else is there about my husband that I don't know?*

I startle, jumping slightly.

My husband. Every time I've thought those words there's been a bitter taste in my mouth. My husband. The guy standing in the way of what I want. The guy who won't sign a simple piece of paper. The guy who drives me up the freaking wall.

But just now, the words didn't taste bitter at all. They were tentative. Wondering. Soft and unsure. More than anything, they were curious. I'm tempted to try to find out all the things I don't know about him. The things I maybe never knew about him.

"When did you start watching this?" I ask.

"Umm. I'm not sure. Couple years ago? Whenever they added it to Netflix. I never saw it when it was on TV the first time."

"And what exactly do you like about it?"

His brows scrunch. "Why?"

"I'm just making conversation."

He looks at me skeptically, but eventually gives in. "I like the small town. The way everyone knows each other. And how everything's walkable. The diner and the dance studio and the inn. We don't have that here."

I don't say anything for a moment, and his shoulders stiffen. "Why? What do you like about it?"

"Oh, I like that part too. The small town and sense of community. I do. I don't know if I've ever thought that much about it though. I usually think about the relationships and the family dynamics. And the pop culture references."

"Those are fun."

"Yeah. It's just . . . I guess where I live, it's pretty walkable, but it's not like the show, you know? When I'm walking to work, when I pass by people . . . it's not like anyone knows who I am."

His eyes aren't on me anymore. They're fixed on the screen. But I can tell he's not really watching.

"That sounds a little lonely," he says.

My throat constricts. "Yeah. It can be," I admit softly. I hadn't meant to say it, but it's the truth. I've lived in D.C. for six years and lived in the same area that whole time. But outside of work . . . I don't have much of a social life. My friends from law school are pretty much all over the country. There are a few in the city and we get together for drinks occasionally, but they're not the kind of people I'd turn to if I was feeling down. Or if I needed something. I'm not sure I have many friends like that left at all.

After I took the bar exam the first time, my closest friends had planned a group celebratory trip to Vegas. Most of our classmates took big international vacations for their "bar trips," during that period of time when we'd all finished studying but were waiting to get our results back, but those classmates were all headed to lucrative corporate firm positions. They could afford it. The public interest students were on a budget, and a long weekend in Vegas was already stretching it a little too far.

I'd asked Nikhil to come with me, not having any idea things would end up the way they did. After we'd woken up married, we'd extended the trip, staying behind when my friends went back home, turning it into a minihoneymoon. Not that my friends knew that. I hadn't told them about the wedding. And when I failed the bar, I didn't tell them about that either. They'd started their brand-new jobs and I'd lied, saying that I'd be working remotely. That I had a family emergency. That I wouldn't be moving to D.C. just yet.

As time passed, the lies only piled up. When I finally moved to the city, I couldn't confide in them. Couldn't tell them that I was heartbroken. Couldn't explain why I wasn't in the mood to go out. The distance between us only grew until we became the kinds of friends whose main form of social interaction is watching each other's stories on Instagram.

"It can feel lonely here too," Nikhil says, his words halting and tentative. "Everyone in the neighborhood is nice, and I've gotten to know all of them better over the past few years, but . . . sometimes it feels like something's missing." He glances my way, and for a moment something wild and unsure breaks across his face.

It makes my lungs constrict, all the oxygen stuck in one place.

"Do you ever wonder," he says, "if we'd taken the time to get to know the neighbors back then, if we'd had a real community around us . . . Do you ever wonder if things would have been different?"

Different? I stare at him, confused and uncertain. "I'm not sure what you mean."

He fidgets a moment, and I can feel it through the mattress, a small jolt as he settles back into place. "We didn't get to know everyone then, and I know we were both busy, but sometimes I think about how . . . how it was just the two of us. Your friends weren't here, and we weren't particularly close to my family, not that I really wanted to be. But the people who live here . . . even the ones you haven't met, I think you'd like them. Elizabeth's wife and the Trans and—"

"I remember Mrs. Patterson," I say. She's really the only neighbor I remember. "I used to see her sometimes, when we went on walks down the street? She used to garden in her yard. She always waved when she saw us."

"Yeah," he says, some of the tense lines around his mouth relaxing. "She moved recently. Her husband passed and she moved to be closer to her kids. But they . . . they had a great marriage, the two of them. I got to know them better the last few years. I got to know everyone here better, and it just made me think . . . if we'd known them then, if we'd had some kind of support, some advice from people who had been through the same kind of things . . . I don't know." He swallows. "I know you didn't want me to meet your parents, or your sister, or Ritu back then, but sometimes I wonder if—"

"They wouldn't have been that for us," I interject. "My parents? They wouldn't have been that kind of support you're talking about."

His expression falls slightly. The smallest of movements, but I catch it, the beginnings of his retreat, and I want to stop him. I want to *explain.*

"My sister," I say, and he looks back at me, giving me his attention, "when she dropped out of college, when she had Ritu, my parents supported her financially and with their time. They helped take care of all the practical things, and they helped take care of Ritu, but emotionally? They withdrew. From her *and* from me." Old, lingering hurt creeps back up, and my chest tightens. "They were always happiest when I was successful, so . . . they wouldn't have been happy with things then." *They wouldn't have been happy with me.* "But maybe you're right. Maybe we should have made more effort to get to know the neighbors back then."

He watches me a second. "You'd have liked Mrs. Patterson," he finally says.

"Yeah?"

His mouth curves into a gentle smile. "Yeah. The two of you would have hit it off. She was always full of opinions, just like you."

For a moment, I can see this alternate world. One where the two of us had dinners with the Pattersons, with others on the street, people who might have lifted us up when we were both down. Who might have been there for us when we couldn't—or didn't know how to—help each other. People who might have shown us how to walk through rocky times, how to make it out on the other side.

Regret builds inside me, the sensation heavy, a stone sinking in my chest.

"Anyway," he says, "sometimes I wish we'd done that differently."

"Yeah," I say. "There are things I wish I'd done differently too."

Our eyes meet, and I'm not sure if he's been moving, or if I have, but we're closer than we were before. He's no longer on the edge of the bed. He's just a few inches away from me.

If I leaned toward him, we'd be touching. It would hardly take any effort. Part of me wonders what would happen if I did it. If he'd stay completely still or if he'd meet me halfway there.

A loud fight breaks out on the television, disrupting my thoughts, and I shift away. "But there's no use replaying the past," I say. "It's not like we can do anything about it now."

He leans back against the headboard, creating more distance between us. "Yeah," he says. "You're right."

"Though maybe we should have held some town meetings back then," I joke, referring to the silly meeting that's taking place on-screen, trying to lighten the mood. "Maybe we could have met the neighbors that way."

He watches the show for a few minutes, then shakes his head good-naturedly. "I don't know," he says. "Those meetings didn't really seem to help the neighbors grow closer together. The drama only seemed to tear them apart. Though I have been thinking about . . ." He stops, pausing a moment. "You know when Lorelai and Sookie started that inn?"

"Yeah," I say, slightly puzzled. "I remember that."

He nods, and the gesture strikes me as off. Almost like he's nervous. "Well, the first time I saw that, saw them buy that broken-down old place and repair it and fix it up, I thought . . . it seemed like a nice idea. You know, taking an old property and turning it into an inn."

"Yeah?"

"Yeah. I liked the idea of it being this place, this home for people to stay in when they're visiting. But it would also be a spot for people who lived in town. For them to gather. Or have lunch. And last year, I came across this property." He rubs the back of his neck. "It's, umm, a little farther from here. Closer to the coast, but not quite all the way in Galveston. It doesn't have a view of the sea exactly, but there's this inlet. More like a bay, really, but it overlooks some water. It was pretty beat up. In bad shape, but I . . . uhh." He trails off, clearing his throat. "Anyway, it reminded me of the show. And I thought maybe someone could turn it into an inn. I don't know. It sounded nice."

My heart squeezes. I can understand why this idea appeals to him. Why he'd want to create a space that makes others feel at home. "It does sound nice," I tell him.

He relaxes a bit when I say this, reclining his head against the headboard.

I'm curious, filled with a thousand questions, but something tells me to approach this carefully. "I can see you running an inn," I say. "Being an innkeeper." From the way he responds, I can tell this was the right thing to say. His mouth forms a tentative, unsure smile, and my pulse skips a beat.

"Thanks."

We return to the show, and fifteen minutes later, I'm fully absorbed by the love triangle taking place onscreen.

"Okay, I know you said you're Team Logan, but what did you think about Dean?" I ask.

After an extended silence, I peek over at Nikhil. His rigid posture has eased. He's still sitting up, but he's slightly slumped over now. And his eyes are closed, his chest rising and falling evenly.

"Nikhil?" I ask, just to check, but other than an incoherent mumble, he doesn't respond. He's completely out.

I lower the volume on the TV and turn closed captions on.

Nikhil's full lips are slightly parted, his thick brows drawn together, a now-familiar wrinkle forming between them. I wonder what he's worried about. A nightmare or our situation or me. I reach out, smoothing the wrinkle away with the pad of my thumb.

The muscles in his face relax as I stroke the spot, and he makes some kind of noise. A sigh mixed with some mumbled, incoherent words. I continue the movement, and his long lashes flutter a second, before coming back to rest.

There are deep shadows under his eyes, dark gray and purple. Almost like bruises.

I didn't think about it before, but Nikhil was probably up the whole time I was sick. Watching my fever. Taking care of me. He probably didn't get much sleep.

I reach for the spare blanket and throw it over his legs.

Netflix autoplays the next episode, and though I'm watching it, my mind wanders, filled with contrasting images of the Nikhil I knew years ago and the one sleeping beside me now.

W hen I wake up in the morning, the TV is off. And the space beside me is cold. Empty.

I stretch, my fingers gliding absently over the sheets and the spare pillow. In this hazy moment between sleep and waking, I almost roll my face into it, almost allow myself to follow the faint hint of vetiver lingering. The faint hint of Nikhil lingering.

But I quickly snap to my senses, and when I spring out of bed, I'm happy to see that the extra rest helped. I don't wobble or sway like I did before. My body almost feels back to normal. I wash my face, then search the house for Nikhil, eventually finding him downstairs, crouched on the ground, rooting around under the kitchen sink.

"What are you doing?" I ask.

He startles, his head ducking out of the space, bumping up against something with a loud *thunk*.

I move instinctively toward him, my hand reaching out to rub the top of his head. "Oh gosh. I'm sorry. Are you okay?"

"Fine," he says. "I'm fine. You just surprised me." His eyes widen slightly as he looks up at me. "How did you get down the stairs?"

"I was feeling up to it," I say, my hand continuing to rub circles against his scalp.

He frowns. "You shouldn't push yourself. You should get back to bed."

"Maybe *you* should get back to bed. You're the one with a head injury."

"And whose fault is that?" he says lightly, without any real bite. And maybe I imagine it, but I think he's leaning just the tiniest bit, pressing his head more firmly into my palm.

It's only then that I register the position we're in. Him kneeling on the floor in front of me. My fingers intertwined in his hair.

Heat spikes through me as I remember other times we were just like this. And for a brief second, my mind gets carried away. I imagine yanking him up and pressing my lips against his. I imagine his hands finding my waist, lifting me up onto the counter. His thumbs tracing circles on my thighs, his jaw nuzzling the curve of my neck.

"I've missed this," he'd say, and I'd tell him the same.

I've missed this. I've missed you.

The thought pings through me, and I pull back immediately, retracting my hand as if I'm reacting to an electric shock.

Nikhil watches me from the floor, a crease forming between his brows. Then, he scrambles to his feet.

"You feeling okay?" he asks. "Do you need to sit down?"

"Nope. No, I'm fine," I say, even as my mind buzzes. The rational side of my brain tells me I'm just being nostalgic, and I try to listen, but that sensible voice fades away as Nikhil steps toward me. The back of his hand comes to my forehead, and his mouth flattens, growing grim with concern.

I close my eyes at his touch, trying to shut myself off from all of it. From the sensation of his skin on mine, from the tenderness and care I feel radiating off of him, from the fantasies running wild in my mind.

"I'm okay," I say. "Really."

His fingers travel down from my forehead, coasting over my cheek, where the glass of the guest bedroom window had scraped me. "Is this any better?" he asks.

And it's not. He's still touching me, and I need it to end. Because I don't trust myself. I don't know what I'll do—what I'll *ask* for—if he doesn't stop.

I step away. "Yes, it's much better. I'm doing much better." I clear my throat. "So, what were you looking for in here?"

His eyes linger on my face, stopping for a moment at my mouth.

Does he feel this too? This pull between us? The one I've been trying to deny ever since I got here?

My pulse increases, and for a moment the air in this kitchen feels charged. There's potential swirling, gathering. I watch as something builds in his eyes, something dark and intense, but then he blinks, and it all vanishes as he bends back down.

"I was grabbing some cleaning supplies so I could get started on the guest bedroom," he says, his voice carrying up from under the sink. He pops back out with bottles and rags, and I take some from him.

"I'll come help you," I offer.

He looks as if he's going to disagree. I brace myself for it as he opens his mouth, but he closes it almost immediately, as if he's swallowing the words down. "Okay," he says.

He stops to grab a broom from the closet, and we head upstairs.

The gaping hole where the glass used to be gives us a clear view of the street. Unlike the last time we were outside, it's bright now.

Midday. But the water's still high, the sun glinting off the brown, murky surface.

Without the rain and the wind—and ignoring a felled tree or two—it almost looks peaceful out there. Nothing like the disaster in here. Shards of glass litter the floor, the carpet and mattress are still damp to the touch, and there are water stains splattered on the wood furniture.

I pour some polish onto one of the rags, reaching for the desk in the corner first. I don't want these stains to set in. I don't know about the other furniture in this room. We didn't have the rest of it when I lived here, but Nikhil made this desk, and I don't want to see it ruined.

Nikhil pauses in the doorway for a second, then begins sweeping, gathering the broken glass into a pile.

We work in silence for some time. The only sounds in the room are the swish of his broom, the glide of my rag against the desk, and I realize I like this, us working together. It feels like it did when we were back in the canoe. At first, it had been hell, neither of us understanding the other, pushing when the other pulled, but after some time, after some give-and-take, we'd found the right rhythm. We'd trusted each other, and our journey back home had been so much easier than that first stretch on the water.

I finish my task, turning to start on the bed. "We'll need to get this mattress out of here, right?"

Nikhil's bent over, gathering the glass into a dustpan. "Eventually, yeah. Mold will set in if we don't do anything, but I don't know how we'd dry it. We can't stick it outside in the sun with all the water still around. I may just have to toss it."

"We could lift it together," I say. "Whenever you need to do that." *Trust me, let me help.* He didn't see me as a teammate, as a part-

ner, back when we were together, but I want to know if the way
we'd canoed back home was just a fluke. I want to know if it's possible he could see me that way now.

"That's all right," he says. "You don't have to."

"I *want* to." My voice comes out sharper than I mean it, and
Nikhil's gaze snaps to meet mine.

"Meena, what—"

A crackly voice breaks through the room. "Ten-four, ten-four.
Do you read me?"

Nikhil straightens. He leans his broom against the wall and
reaches for the radio. "Alan, the power's back now. You can just text
me."

"Negative," Alan replies. "My phone's dead. Betty's only got one
charger and she's not letting me use it."

Nikhil looks over at me and playfully rolls his eyes. The familiar-
ity in that gesture infuses every corner of my body. The warmth
melts my insides, making me feel all sloshy.

"You all doing okay?" Nikhil asks.

Alan heaves a loud sigh. "Still fighting like cats and dogs, but you
know, I think we might be on the verge of a breakthrough. See, it
was really our parents who pitted us against each other. Who made
us feel like we had to compete for their time and attention, and even
their love, and I think if I can just make her realize that, she'll see—"

"That's great, Alan," Nikhil says. "But everything else is okay?
No flooding at Betty's house or anything?"

"Oh. Nope. All good here."

"Great."

"How are you two? You and your . . . friend?"

Nikhil pivots slightly, half turning to face the wall. "We're fine.
We didn't get any water on the first floor, but we did have a window
break—"

"She seems really familiar, but I don't think we ever met before."

"No, you wouldn't have met her."

"And I didn't know you were seeing anyone."

"I'm not," Nikhil says sharply.

I feel a weird sort of pleasure-pain at the words. A sensation I don't want to examine too closely.

Alan's quiet for a second. And then a sharp noise travels through the radio, as if he's snapped his fingers. "Oh. Wait. I know where I've seen her. I know who she is. You never mentioned her name before, but I can't believe it took me this long to put it together. She looks just like the girl in that—"

"Thanks for checking in," Nikhil interjects. "But we've got to run. We'll talk to you later." Nikhil flips a switch, then sets the radio on the nightstand. He picks his broom back up and starts sweeping again, as if nothing happened. As if Alan hadn't just said something strange about me.

"What was that about?" I ask moments later, when it's clear Nikhil doesn't plan on addressing it.

"What was what?"

"What Alan said. About knowing me from somewhere. That I look a lot like . . ."

"I don't know," Nikhil says. "I mean, you've met the guy. He's not exactly the most . . . the best . . ." He waves a hand. "Who knows what that guy is thinking?"

"Uh-huh."

"And you're on TV every now and then. Maybe that's where he recognizes you from."

TV? I'm never on . . . Oh. "I occasionally appear in the background of C-Span 3, Nikhil. I'm not exactly a television star. I don't even make the cut for C-Span 2."

"That's still TV."

"Okay. Technically. But I doubt Alan's a big C-Span fan."

Nikhil's eyes are fixed on the floor, his concentration on the glass he's gathering into the dustpan. "You don't know that," he says. "Maybe he likes C-Span."

"No one *likes* C-Span."

"You used to watch it."

"Yeah, but that's not the same. I was a huge policy nerd."

"Still are," he says, but it's like he's testing it out, not quite sure if he's right about that or not.

"Still am," I say, and he nods.

"Well, maybe Alan is too."

I blow out a breath, trying to keep my frustration at bay. There's something Nikhil's not telling me. Something he doesn't want me to know.

Most people don't react well to being needled. They need to be coaxed. Cajoled. Lulled into a false sense of security. I know this. I just seem to forget it when I'm around Nikhil.

"Maybe you're right," I say, rubbing the polishing cloth against the headboard a little harder than necessary.

A bewildered expression crosses his face, as if he can't believe I'm letting this go. And I am about to let it go. Really, I am. Until something clicks.

"How did you know I was on C-Span?"

Nikhil's cheeks flush red. His skin's a bit paler than mine, and though my face gets hot when I'm embarrassed, I've got enough melanin that it never really shows. But not Nikhil. He blushes. Full-on blushes. I'd forgotten that about him.

"Oh. Uhh . . ."

"I'm not even actually on it," I say. "Not like on one of those talk shows or anything. You can't find it if you search my name. I'm just in the background sometimes walking around."

"Right. Yeah. Well, sometimes I put on C-Span."

I snort. "You do not."

"I do. Just to have something playing. Background noise. While I'm doing something else."

"Like what?"

"Cooking. Cleaning. Working on a project." He shrugs. "I like leaving it on. It's soothing."

"But you never used to like watching it with me."

"I know." The tips of his ears are turning red now. "I didn't really get it then. But now . . . it's just nice to have it on."

"Why?"

"Because it . . ." He closes his mouth abruptly. Then, clears his throat. I give him some time, but seconds of silence pass and he doesn't complete his thought.

"Because it what?" I ask.

He shakes his head. "It's nothing."

Curiosity burns inside me. "Because it's free? Because you're interested in policy now? Because you enjoy watching paint dry? Because—"

"Because it reminds me of you," he snaps.

My heartbeat thrums loudly in my ears. I stare at him, absolutely stunned. He's no longer looking down at the broken glass on the floor. He's looking right at me.

"I watch HGTV," I blurt out.

His brows knit, creases forming in his forehead. "What?"

"For the sounds. The woodworking sounds. Like the sounds you used to make in the garage while I was studying. I used to . . . I found it soothing back then. So, whenever I'm working on something and need to concentrate, I turn on HGTV."

He blinks, confusion still on his face, and then comprehension dawns. His eyes soften. "Really?" he asks. Quietly. Tentatively. Like he's unsure if he heard me correctly. Or like he's worried I'm going to take it back.

"Really," I say. I'm not sure if I'd fully understood *why* I'd been doing it or if I was just in deep denial until this moment, but everything I'm saying is the truth.

Nikhil shifts his weight, still watching me. And then he resumes his sweeping. "So, what's your poison? *Property Brothers* or that couple that flips—"

"Oh god," I say with a laugh. "Might be an unpopular opinion, but I can't stand that couple."

He looks up with a grin. "Me either."

The threads of tension in the air unravel. "They're annoying, right? And do they really need a line of merchandise at every single store? It's like no matter what I do, no matter where I go, I can't escape them."

"Not to mention their advice on house flipping is usually dead wrong. They strip all these beautiful wood finishings, paint everything white—"

"Ha!"

His shoulders jump in surprise. "What?"

"Ha!" I say again, my finger pointed at him. "J'accuse!"

"*What?*" He's looking at me like I've lost all my marbles, but I've never felt more alert.

"You hate all the white paint on the house too. Admit it!"

His confusion melts away, and something else takes its place. Surprise and . . . maybe embarrassment?

"I do," he finally says.

"So, why do it?" I ask. "Why paint all the brick white? It looks so wrong. It looks so . . . so . . ." I grasp for words, but the only one that comes to mind is not a word at all: Un-Nikhil. The whole thing is so Un-Nikhil. Because Nikhil is old school. He's warm red brick that's stood for ages. He's midcentury furniture made by hand. He's a house that somehow survives the winds and rains and floods of a hurricane. He's not shiplap and white paint slapped on top, covering up what was there before. He's steady and stable and firm and . . .

"Resale value," Nikhil says.

I jump. "What?"

"I painted it for the resale value. My realtor suggested it. She said the fresh coat of paint has really helped some of her older homes sell."

"Your realtor," I repeat blandly. "You're . . . you're selling the house?"

He rubs a hand against the back of his neck. "I'm just looking at options."

"Options for selling. For selling the house."

"Yes."

"Why?"

He swallows, the muscles in his throat flexing. "I'm doing some work on another property. Some repairs. And I could use the funds."

Nikhil needs money. The thought lances through me, accompanied by a sharp pinprick of guilt. I hate that my mind turned in this direction first. Coldly analyzing his words, finding the weak point. Finding the one thing I've been searching for all along: leverage.

I don't want to be this way. I don't want to see everything through the lens of negotiation. Not with him.

"What kind of property?"

He's quiet a moment. "An older building. Really old. It needs a lot of work."

I nod, an idea growing. "I'm only asking because there are certain kinds of loans out there. The normal building and construction ones, sure, but if there's any chance the property's old enough to be considered historic, there are special grants you could apply for.

Some of them are true grants. You don't even have to pay them back."

He clears his throat. "Elizabeth mentioned something like that, but she's so busy, and I didn't want to take up more of her time or ask—" He stops, but I know what he means. He didn't want to ask her for help.

"This is the project she mentioned, right? The one you're working on?"

"Yeah. It is."

"I could help you with it," I say. "I'd be happy to do the research and put the grant proposal together. I'm sure someone I know has ties to the local preservation board or committee. I'm sure Elizabeth does. We could start there." My wheels are really turning now. "There might even be some community development grants available. If it has some kind of commercial purpose, we could argue it benefits the community in some way. I've got a friend at HUD who could walk us through a lot of this. I could set up a call for the three of us, or even just do it myself and get the information first. But what's the project exactly?"

"It's an inn," he says. "Or it will be once the repairs are done. That's the hope anyway."

"An inn," I repeat. He was serious before, then.

"Yeah. You know I've . . . I've always loved design and for a while now I've been wanting to design a place from the ground up, and when I saw this place . . ." He fidgets. "That's actually where I was earlier, before the storm. I had to board it up, and it took more prep than I thought. I'd stripped some of the roof a couple weeks ago, so it's pretty exposed." His forehead creases, worry creeping into his eyes. "I don't know if I did enough. It's closer to the coast than we are, so it probably got more of a storm surge. It may not even have made it, so maybe it doesn't even matter anymore, but—"

"It'll be fine," I say. "Even if there's damage, you'll be able to fix it. I'm sure of it."

He looks at me now, a carefully neutral expression on his face. "If you wouldn't mind sharing more about, you know, any grants or loans the property could be eligible for, I'd . . . I'd appreciate that. I could use the help." He swallows, his hands growing tight around the broom handle, his knuckles turning pale. "I *need* your help."

My mouth grows dry.

"And maybe . . . maybe it would be helpful for you to see it. After the storm, we could stop by there. It still needs a lot of work and it's nowhere close to being done, but it could give you a better sense of the place," he says. "Not that we have to. I don't know what your plans are or when you'll go—"

"I'd love to see it."

"Yeah?" he asks, a hint of vulnerability in that word.

"Yeah. I can't wait."

He smiles then, his teeth flashing. It's beautiful and wonderful and disarming, and I can't pretend anymore. I can't pretend that I'm helping him just to have leverage, to have the upper hand in negotiations. I can't pretend that I'm doing this for any reason other than I *want* to. I want Nikhil to be happy. And this project, it's making him come alive in a way I've never seen before.

Even more, he's telling me he *needs* me. I've wanted to hear those words from him for so long. I've wanted to know that he felt even a fraction of the wild, desperate need I'd always felt for him.

A breeze travels in through the broken window and a nearby branch rattles, drawing my gaze outside.

Nikhil leaves, grabbing a blue-green tarp from the hallway, the fabric waving behind him like a banner. He moves toward the window and tries to stretch the material over the open space but isn't able to do it fully. His arms, as long and impressive as they are, can't cover the distance.

I rush over, grabbing a corner of the tarp, and he steps back to let me in.

I pull it to the part of the window frame he'd been aiming for and feel him staring at the side of my face when he asks, "So, you're thinking about running for office?"

"Uhhh." I secure the blue-green material in the upper right-hand corner, unsure how to go about answering. Everything about this is tied up in Shake. The two of us have been talking about wanting to run for office for years, but we only recently started exploring it seriously. Shake's probably had that meeting with the political advisory team during the time I was here. I wonder what they talked about. I wonder if I'll ever meet with them. I wonder what Shake's thinking after the breakup, or if the news about the Texas seat would change anything for us. For me.

"It's a little complicated," I tell him.

I move to the lower corner, but the tarp snaps back, the area I'd just secured unraveling.

"Whoa," Nikhil says, his arm sliding behind me, grabbing hold of the tarp before it unfurls all the way.

His chest presses against my back, and his thighs bracket mine as he leans forward, taping the material down.

"There," he says, turning toward me, his face only an inch away. "Close call." He smiles, soft and easy, but that smile fades as he registers that his body is flush against mine.

He could move. I could *ask* him to move. But I don't.

He exhales, and I can feel the hot breath traveling over my ear.

"Why is it complicated?" he asks, his voice slightly hoarse, and I close my eyes.

"I don't know which race I'm running for." The words slip out of my mouth, plain and honest. "I thought I did. There's a state race in Maryland, and it's what I've been planning and thinking about for a while, but—" I stop. Is it even worth getting into all of this with Nikhil? This idea of mine is barely half-baked. Basically still raw dough.

"But?" Nikhil prompts, his hand coming to my shoulder, clasping my upper arm. He presses lightly, until I've turned around. Until I'm facing him.

We're so close. His face hovers right above mine, and our breaths are shallow, our chests rising and falling against each other. I lean back the tiniest amount, needing some air, some distance, some space to *think*, but Nikhil's hand slides to my lower back, bringing me toward him.

"Careful," he says roughly. "The tarp."

I swallow, my heart pounding.

I'm scared. I'm scared to move an inch, and not just because of the open window behind me. I'm scared by how much I want this. How much I want to be close to him. And I'm terrified by his earlier question, terrified to put words to this idea. But when he asks again, his voice soft and gentle as he says, "But what, Meena?" I realize I *want* to tell Nikhil what I'm thinking. After spending so much time hoping and waiting, he finally let me in, sharing about his project and his dreams. I want to do the same.

"But I can't stop thinking about what Alan mentioned," I tell him. "That Elizabeth might run for that open congressional seat. That there's going to *be* an open congressional seat."

"You're talking about the seat *here*? Congresswoman Garcia's seat?"

I chew on my bottom lip. "Yeah," I reply.

Nikhil's eyes zero in on my mouth, and I involuntarily mirror the movement, my gaze drawn to his in return. His lips, the shape of them is so familiar, though that stubble lining his jaw is new. I wonder again how it would all feel. The soft pull of his mouth coupled with the rough slide of his skin.

A shiver travels through me, and I rise on my toes, moving closer to him, not quite sure what I'm doing until his head lowers to meet mine.

"You'd move to Texas," he murmurs.

"I don't know," I say, my words escaping on a breath even as my lips brush against his. "I don't know."

Then his mouth captures mine, and I truly don't know anything. I don't know anything beyond this room, beyond this place, beyond right now. There's only the slide of his hands down my back, and the way he pulls me tight against him. The way his mouth opens mine, the taste of him flooding my senses.

Spearmint.

When we'd first met, he'd always chewed cinnamon gum. Spicy and hot. After our first kiss, I'd told him I hadn't liked the taste of it. He'd switched flavors then, and I guess he never switched back.

I reach for the back of his neck, pulling him closer, and he gasps, ceding control in an instant. I run my hand along his jaw, shivering at the way his stubble pricks against my palm. I tilt his head, moving him exactly how I want him, claiming him the only way I can. I take, and take, and *take*, hoarding as much of him as possible, but it's not enough.

Because this . . . It's familiar, but different from all the memories I replay in my mind. It's real. And somehow it feels new. I'm not satisfied with just a taste. I want *more*.

Slowly, he pulls away, and for a second my mouth chases after his, not ready for this to end. Not ready to let go of him.

"Meena," Nikhil breathes. "I need . . ." He lowers his head, resting his forehead against mine. "Tell me there's no reason that we shouldn't . . . tell me there's no reason we have to stop. Tell me that there's no one . . . that there's nothing—"

A rough, jagged sound escapes him, and my heart beats wildly.

Shake and I aren't together anymore. I came here wanting to change that. I came here with a plan, but right now, I can't think. There's nothing I care about except *this*.

"Nikhil," I say, leaning back, letting him see all the want in my eyes. Letting him see all of me. "Take me to bed."

Joy, bright like the sun, flashes across his face, and he bends down, lifting me, wrapping my legs around him. And just like he's done so many times before, he carries me out of the guest bedroom and into our room.

12

Nikhil lays me down on the bed, and our clothes come off in smooth, effortless movements. Nothing's hurried. Nothing's rushed. We take our time, slowly undoing buttons, shimmying out of pants, raising our shirts over our heads. We watch each other all the while, as if we both need the connection. As if we're each reassuring the other. *You're still here. This is real. We're actually doing this.*

I toss everything on the floor and lean back, stretching along the bed, sinking into the mattress. Nikhil's eyes flare with desire and longing, and I reach for him. "You can touch me, Nikhil. Touch me." I take his hands, lacing his fingers in mine, and tug him toward me.

He settles over me, the dips and hollows of his body slightly different than I remember. The same hard muscles press firmly against me, but *more*. There's more of him now. The contours of his body have changed, just as mine have, and I grieve for a moment, sad that I wasn't here to feel the gradual change of him. That I didn't get to witness the day-to-day transformation that took him from the Nikhil I once knew to the man he is today.

The man whose lips are traveling over my neck, his mouth open. He tastes me, and the blunt edges of his teeth bite down on the same sensitive place he always managed to find. The spot he always marked me. He presses harder, and I cry out, my hands rising to his head, holding him fast against me.

But he doesn't stay in one place. He moves, his mouth skating down and down and down. He parts my legs, and proves that even though it's been years, he hasn't forgotten anything. He knows exactly what to do, exactly what I need.

But I want to see him. I want his eyes meeting mine. I want to know he's with me. I clutch at his shoulders, wordlessly asking him to come back, and he listens.

His mouth returns to mine, and his hands cradle my jaw. Kissing him is lightning, a shock of electricity that crackles through me, but the weight of him, the pressure of his body on top of mine, soothes the singe. In this moment, we're fire and rain and it's everything I've been missing, everything I've been *craving* for all these years.

His hips move, the hard length of him brushing the most sensitive part of me, and I hiss. "Meena, are we—" Nikhil pulls back, the gold in his eyes incandescent. Every part of him burning and alive. "Are you—"

"We're good," I say, arching toward him, desperate for contact again. Desperate for his hot skin against mine. "I'm sure. I want this."

He exhales harshly, and then his palm presses into the mattress beside my head. His other hand reaches for my leg, wrapping it around his waist. We're so close like this. So close to what we both need, but for some reason, Nikhil's holding back.

"Do I . . . Do I need to get a—"

I shake my head, finally understanding the reason for his restraint. "I'm on the pill and I . . . I've been tested since my last time."

"Okay," he says. "Right . . . that's . . ." He swallows roughly, the muscles in his throat flexing. "That's good. I have too, but it's just . . . It's been a long time for me."

"That's okay." I reach for him, kissing him slow, and tender, and sure. "We don't have to do anything you don't want—"

His fingers tighten around my thigh. "I want," he says, his voice like gravel, as he brings his mouth back to mine. "I want everything."

What starts as a slow, languid exploration, turns fast. His hips roll against me, our bodies sliding in a familiar rhythm, and his hands find mine, anchoring me, keeping me in place.

And it would be good like this. I know it would be good. But I want something else right now, and I'm not afraid to show him.

I encircle his wrists and flip us around so I'm on top, my legs straddling his waist. Raw heat and want emanates from him, and when I move, when I take him inside me, all the air escapes my lungs. *Mine,* I think. *Mine.*

"God, Meena," he breathes, his face transformed by pleasure so intense it resembles pain. And when he opens his eyes, when he whispers again, he begs me to *move.* I set the pace, rocking against him in slow, even movements. His hips buck, and his hands fight my grip on him. He's stronger than me. I know he could break this hold if he wanted to, but he's letting me take the wheel right now and it's intoxicating. Exhilarating.

"Please," he says, after a few minutes, the word coming out strangled. "I need to touch you. Please." And I release him, knowing that neither of us is truly in control. We're both here, and present, and reduced to our barest selves. Each of us desperately needing the give-and-take of the other.

His hands come to my waist, his grip tight, the imprint of his fingers sinking into my skin. He moves my hips, moving me faster against him, and as good as it feels, as much as I need this friction and rhythm, for a moment I want to slow down. I want this to last. I want to remember everything. Because I'm not sure if this is our last time. I'm not sure if I'll ever have him like this again.

He must feel the resistance in my body because he starts to loosen his grip, but I don't let him. I meet him where he's at, our bodies in sync, both of us climbing higher and higher, in tune with each other.

We're both close, and maybe it's been so long I've forgotten, but I'm not sure if it's ever felt like this. I hold out for as long as I can, but one of his hands slides down, his thumb finding the very center of me, and lightning flashes behind my closed eyes. I come apart as Nikhil's pace increases, his strokes quick and true, until he makes a ragged, wonderful sound I usually hear only in my dreams.

I hold him tight, my legs around his waist, my head tucked in his neck, as we both catch our breath.

Neither of us says anything. For a long while, neither of us moves, but then Nikhil's hand comes to my hair. His fingers run through the mess of it before traveling down my back and repeating their path all over again. I close my eyes, settling deeper against him, content to stay just like this. We'll have to break apart eventually. I know that. We can't live in this moment forever, but right now, it almost feels possible.

It almost feels like all of this could actually be mine.

We find each other again in the middle of the night. And again before the sun rises. Our last time is hurried and rushed, as if we're trying to beat the dawn. As if we both know everything will change once the daylight returns, but refuse to acknowledge it. We barely talk to each other, only saying words like "more," and "please," and "faster." Communicating with only our hands, our mouths, our bodies.

After, Nikhil places his ear to the center of my chest, listening to my heartbeat, and I'm thankful he can't see the tear that escapes from the corner of my eye. His lips brush my breast, and he murmurs something, the words vibrating against my skin. I'm tempted to ask him what he said, but his breaths grow even and slow and I'm sure he's fallen asleep. I hold him to me, trying to commit every little part of this to memory, but sleep takes me too.

In the morning, I wake to Nikhil sitting up in bed, a large book open on his lap. There's a steaming cup of coffee on the nightstand beside him, and when he notices that my eyes are open, he passes it to me.

"Good morning," he says warmly, and I take a sip. It has the exact amount of oat milk and sugar I've always preferred. He remembers, and I'm no longer surprised by that. I've discovered I'm not the only one who's been holding on to memories of the past. I'm just not sure what that means for us going forward.

"Good morning," I respond. The comfort and ease from last night has faded. It's not awkward exactly, but there's a note of caution, of uncertainty, in the air that wasn't there before. "What are you reading?"

He answers wordlessly, flipping the cover in my direction.

Foundations of Business.

That's not what I was expecting.

He places the book back on his lap and opens it to where he had it. "Did you sleep okay?" he asks, and my cheeks warm, memories of last night flooding back.

I scan his face, looking for traces of regret or hope or concern.

Anything that would give me a hint of what he's feeling, but his expression is careful, blank in a determined, purposeful sort of way.

I have no idea what he's thinking. And I'm not sure what I'm thinking either.

I want to do this again. I want to never leave this bed. I want to stay.

Stay? An alarm sounds in my mind, faint and distant, and I ignore it, hitting snooze. It'll come back eventually, but I can't deal with it right now. I don't want to.

"I slept fine," I say. I put the coffee down and stretch, my skin heating even more as I register how delightfully sore I am.

Nikhil watches me for a long moment, his gaze conflicted, as if he's deliberating something, then he lifts an arm toward me, pulling me closer.

My body nestles against his, and his face turns toward mine, his movements slow and measured. He's giving me time to retreat, to say no, but I don't pull back. I meet him halfway, and this kiss, it's different. Soft and sweet and light.

When we separate, his lips spread into a smile, and I can't help but give him one in return.

"Hi," he says.

"Hi."

I settle against him, enjoying the way my head fits in the curve of his neck, the way his hand plays with the ends of my hair.

"Are you okay?" he asks. "After . . . Do you want to talk about it or—"

That same alarm blares, and I mentally slam the snooze button again. "Not right now," I say. "Soon, but not right now."

I look down at the book still on his lap, watching as he turns the page.

"Why business?" I ask.

His shoulders tense. He stays quiet for a little while, his jaw so stiff I think he's clenching his teeth. But then he forces out an exhale, and I can feel the muscles in his body relax.

"I'm studying," he says. "I went back to school to study business."

"Oh." From the shiny, slick cover I'd thought this was a textbook. Maybe I should have assumed this, but from the way Nikhil had always talked about school . . . I never thought he'd go back. He'd made it sound like school wasn't for him. That he preferred working with his hands, being active, instead of sitting in one place reading a book. He'd never said it in a mean way. Like he was judging me for studying all the time. He just made it clear that he couldn't imagine ever doing the same.

"You're finishing your degree?"

"No. Well, kind of. I'm getting my associate's. Not a bachelor's. I'm just at a community college. Not a four-year or anything."

"Why?" I ask, still a little confused.

His shoulder tenses again, and I pull away to look at him.

"There's nothing wrong with going to community college," he says, the words flat.

I blink. "No. Of course there's not. That's not what I meant. You just . . . you never seemed that interested in going back to school before so—"

He's quiet for a beat. "I didn't choose to drop out, Meena. I had to. I had to leave when I learned . . ." He traces the corner of his textbook, his thumbnail flicking the edge of the page. "I only got into college because of my mother. Because she worked there. I should have figured it out sooner. I mean, I barely made it through high school. I came so close to failing senior year." He swallows roughly. "I'm not like you. I'm not . . . School doesn't come easily to me. It never has.

"I was always behind," he continues. "Moving from place to

place, uprooting every school year, it took a toll on me. I couldn't keep up, and my mom didn't get it. She'd sit with me at night, trying to help me with homework, but nothing clicked for me." He looks down, not meeting my gaze. "Some of my classmates gave me a hard time about it. Joking that I should be doing better. That I must be the only Indian kid who struggled with math. Or that it was because I was only half, that I must have gotten too many of my father's genes and not enough of my mom's."

Anger streaks up my spine, and my hands curl into fists. "They were wrong," I tell Nikhil. "On top of being horrible and racist, they were just plain wrong. You know that, right?"

Finally, he looks at me, and the doubt, the insecurity on his face, makes me want to find every one of those bullies and tell them Nikhil is ten times the man they'll ever be. It makes me want to avenge him. It makes me want to fight.

"You're smart, Nikhil. And it has nothing to do with school."

He flinches, but I push forward, forcing him to hear me. "You know one of the things I first noticed about you, the thing that made you different from so many of the people I was surrounded by in law school, was that you're comfortable not knowing something. Whenever we'd talk about things, you actually listened, and if there was something you didn't know, you'd admit it. You'd learn more about it, and wait until then to form a conclusion and that . . . that's such a gift. It's a *strength*.

"And the way you see things. The connections your mind draws. The way you can look at slabs of wood and see the future, see the bookshelf or coffee table they can be. The way you look at a room and see exactly how to make it come alive, to bring in the right pieces and change it from a space with four walls into a home. The way you find a run-down property and can picture it as this flourishing inn. The way you look at me and see . . ."

I break off. I hadn't meant to say that, but sometimes . . . it had felt like Nikhil was the only one who'd seen past the front I'd presented to the world. Who'd seen past the stressed-out, terrified girl who was afraid of failing and seen . . . someone else. The kind of person I hoped I was underneath. The kind of person I wanted to be.

I turn away, but his hand comes up to cup my face. His eyes are bright, and they draw me in, just like they always have.

"I see the woman who listened to me like everything I had to say mattered. Like what I thought meant something. Like it was valuable. This woman whose mind was . . . is . . . ridiculous." He laughs lightly. "Brilliant and sharp. Driven and ambitious and sure of the future in a way I never have been. And the idea that she thought *my* words were important, that she thought *I* could be a part of that future, that she could feel just as sure about me . . ." His thumb strokes against my cheek, and I close my eyes.

I've missed this. I've missed being with someone who sees me this way, who *knows* me this way.

But the *future*. The alarm from before blares, loud and brash.

All the things he's talking about, the person he saw, the way he *felt*, that was all back then.

I pull away from him, catching how his face falls before his guard goes back up.

"I think it's great you've gone back to school," I tell him.

He clears his throat. "Thanks. I'm hoping it'll help with running the business, you know? With running the inn."

I nod, the reminder helping. His business is here, his home is here. And mine is not. I have plans back in D.C. Even if I were to run for the seat in Texas, I don't know if that would change anything. I'd probably still try to be based out of D.C. I'd probably still try to do all of this with Shake.

I think.

I scoot toward my side of the bed and push my hair back from my face. From the second I got here, nothing has gone according to plan. I need a second to regroup. Some space to figure out what all of this means. "While you're studying, would it be okay if I borrowed your phone? And your computer? I haven't checked in with work in a few days, and since we have power back . . ."

"Yeah," Nikhil says. "Of course." He reaches toward his nightstand, not quite meeting my eyes as he passes the phone to me. "I left yours plugged in too over there. I know it wasn't working before, but I swear I saw it light up for a second, so you may want to check it. And the laptop's downstairs on the coffee table. No password." He gets up, looking around the room. "I'll just change and then I'll do some work in the garage, so feel free to use this room, or the living room, or wherever." He ducks into the bathroom quickly, then leaves, and I'm not sure exactly what it is I feel.

Relief, I tell myself, as I reach for my phone. I'm sure this strange, jittery sensation traveling over my skin is relief.

13

My phone miraculously comes to life, but the screen is covered in blurry notifications. With all the cracks, I can't quite make out the text, so I instinctively tap my way over to voicemails, pressing around until they begin to play.

> Meena, I can't find any other flights out, but I have a client with a jet. Don't start, I can hear you grumbling already, and yes, I know it's horrible, and it likely contributed to climate change and maybe this very storm, but that doesn't mean you should have to suffer through this. I'm working on it now and I'll call if I can get confirmation on the jet.

> It's me, again. No luck so far. No one's willing to fly to Houston right now. I think it's too close to the storm landing, but . . . call me when you can. I've talked to your office, and they know what's going on, so you don't need to worry about any of that. Just focus on staying safe. I'll talk to you soon.

Hi, Meena. I don't even know if you're getting these. Considering I've left about a dozen I'm going to assume your phone isn't working, like you said before, and it's not that you're ignoring me. Though I wouldn't blame you if you were. I probably shouldn't be calling like this. I know I'm the one who cut things off, and we talked about giving each other space, but it's just . . . I've been following the news and watching everything in real time and I can't help but feel like this is partly my fault. If I hadn't pushed you, if I hadn't ended things like that, if I hadn't given you that ultimatum, maybe you wouldn't have gone to Houston. I'm about to head over to that meeting with the political advisory team, the one that was supposed to be for the two of us, and . . . I don't know. If you're getting these, call me. Please. I just . . . I want to make sure you're okay.

Oh, god. I put my phone down, my hand slightly shaking.

Just last week a voicemail like this would have given me so much hope. I'd wanted Shake back as a teammate. I'd wanted us to run for office together. I'd wanted all of it.

But now?

So much has happened, and I have to tell him about it. I have to.

My finicky phone refuses to let me make calls, so I pick up Nikhil's and call Shake.

"Shake, it's me," I say, knowing he won't recognize this number. "It's Meena."

"Meena!" His voice is bright, eager. "Are you all right? I tried calling you a bunch, but I could never get through. Is everything okay?"

"Yeah, yeah. I'm fine. It's been a whirlwind, but I'm okay. And I got your voicemails. Well, some of them. It sounded like you maybe left more, but my phone hasn't been working properly. That's why . . . I'm calling from Nikhil's."

"Oh. Okay." He pauses, the sound of papers rustling traveling through the phone. Shake may be one of the only people under forty in D.C. who orders a physical newspaper, but he insists that he retains information better when he reads that way. I've always given him a hard time about it, but now the familiar noise reminds me of another life. The two of us at our usual coffee place, his large newspaper spread out on the table as we update our shared calendar, discuss the latest gossip on the Hill, talk through issues at work. "And uhh, how's that been? Have you all had time to talk about things? Were you able to wrap everything up?"

"Not exactly. It's been a little tough with everything going on." Power outages, windows breaking, canoeing through a hurricane. "We've just been in survival mode for a bit."

"Right," he says. "That makes sense." He pauses. "I went to the meeting. I don't know if you got that voicemail, but I told them about you, about our plan to run together, and they loved it. They have possible endorsements in mind, and they think they can time the announcement with some big media coverage. *D.C.'s Desi Power Couple.*" He lets out a nervous laugh. "Cheesy, sure, but they think it's a good idea and . . . Anyway, once you're back, maybe we can talk about it more."

"Shake, I—"

"I just . . . I've missed you. And I have regrets, about the way I handled things. You shouldn't have had to go down there alone. I should have offered to help you with this. We should have done it together. I'm sorry about that. But in the future, we can do things differently, and—"

I squeeze my eyes shut. "I appreciate that, Shake. Really, but you should know that . . . we slept together. Me and Nikhil."

Shake doesn't speak for a long moment. "Okay," he finally says. "Okay. That . . . that makes sense. I get it."

"You do?"

"Yeah. I know we're not together right now, and I know that's my fault, and you're in a high-stress situation with the man who used to be the love of your life. It's fine, Meena.

"Really, it's probably a good idea to get it all out of your system. Get closure or whatever."

I pause. Last night didn't feel like closure. It didn't feel like the end of something. It felt like . . .

"I don't know if that's what we're doing," I tell Shake. "I don't know *what* we're doing."

He goes quiet, and I rush to fill the silence. Because he deserves to know everything. We'd been set on running together in Maryland, and I don't know if Shake would still want to be with me if that changed.

"And I'm sorry to switch gears like this, but there's something else you should know. I heard Congresswoman Garcia's retiring. Not sure if it's been formally announced and I just didn't see it since I've been down here without power, but—"

"Garcia? From Texas?"

"Yeah. Nikhil's neighbor mentioned it. She's actually pretty well connected in local politics. She used to be county judge when I was a kid."

"Huh. I haven't seen it announced anywhere."

"Really? That's great, actually, because I've been thinking about it and this would give me more time to do some research. But maybe when I get back, we could talk about it some more? Maybe even run it by the team and see what they think?"

"Are you . . . You're not thinking about this for you, are you? A Texas congressional seat?"

"Yeah, I don't know. It's just an idea right now, but I think it's worth exploring."

"I don't . . . I— Sorry, I'm just trying to wrap my head around this. I thought you never wanted to go back to Texas."

"I didn't. Not before, but I mean, I'm from here. This is my hometown. I could get a place here and meet residency requirements if I wanted to. And you know how unpredictable these kinds of races can be. I'm not saying it's not a long shot, but I want to talk about it more. I mean, it's Congresswoman *Garcia's* seat. You know how much her work has meant to me. The changes she advocated for on immigration and refugee policy alone—"

"I get it," he says. "I can see the appeal. The seat's a good fit for you. I bet if we ran your policy platform on top of Garcia's they'd match up exactly. Not to mention, you'd get to run for Congress instead of a state seat. It's just . . . I thought you were set on staying in D.C. I thought that *we'd* stay in D.C."

"I could still do that. If I win, I could travel back and forth, but I can spend most of my time there."

"Is that even something you want anymore? Is this . . ." He lets out a rush of air.

"Meena, is this about Nikhil? This newfound interest in Texas and running there? I mean, do you even want to run together anymore? Or get back together? Are you still going through with the divorce?"

The back of my neck prickles. "I am," I say, not entirely confident in my answer. "This has nothing to do with that."

"Are you sure? Because . . . Just think about what you would tell me if I announced I was going to get back together with Geeta."

"I know, but—"

"Actually, I don't even have to imagine what you'd say. I remember what you said. You said I deserved more. That I deserved better than someone who would treat me that way. Who'd take me for granted. You said I deserved a true partner. A real teammate. Some-one who understood me and put me first."

"Yes," I say, "but what happened between me and Nikhil—it wasn't the same. And there are things I didn't know before. Things about Nikhil that I—" I stop midsentence, unsure what I'm even try-ing to say.

"You deserve that too, Meena," Shake continues. "A true part-ner. That's what we were, and that's what we can be again. We're equals. We can be there for each other. We can help each other. Nikhil couldn't give you that then, and he can't give you that now."

"My wanting to run in Texas has nothing to do with Nikhil," I say.

Shake scoffs. "Really?"

My temper flares. "Are you sure this isn't about you?"

"What do you mean?"

"You not wanting me to run in Texas? You sure this isn't about you? About your ego? About the possibility of me running for the U.S. House while you're running for a Maryland state seat?"

"Please," he says with a huff. "You think my ego would take a hit about something like that? That I'd have some weird toxic male reac-tion to my partner running for . . . what? A position people might consider more prominent than mine? You should know me better than that. And I never said I didn't want you to run in Texas. It's just . . . running for the U.S. House of Representatives is a whole dif-ferent ball game. State rep would be a part-time gig. You could keep working at your job. If you do this . . . you realize you'd probably have to quit, right? To campaign in Texas? I'd hardly see you."

He goes quiet for a moment. "I want to be clear about this. I want to get back together. But if we do that, I'd need us to *actually* be together. I can't . . . You know how I was after Geeta, after everything

that happened. I can't go back to that, to wondering what my partner's doing when they're not around, or worrying about whether
their work trip is actually a work trip. I don't want to be like that
again, and if you're splitting your time between here and Texas . . . I
don't know, Meena. I'd need to know this is really just about your
career and what's best for you and not about anything else. I'd need
to know things with Nikhil are completely final. And not just on
paper."

I let out a breath, my anger slowly deflating. Shake's not a bad
guy, and he's not wrong. He's been hurt before, and I'd never want
to see him hurt like that again. I'd certainly never want to be the
reason for it. Besides, we had agreed on a plan, and I'm the one trying to change it at the last minute. The seats in Maryland are safe
bets. The team Shake met with seems on board. I can see the path
ahead for us if we got back together. I can see us both continuing
down this road, achieving everything we wanted, doing it side by
side.

"I hear you," I tell him. "I do. I'm not saying I have to do this. I
just want to explore it." I rub my arm, suddenly feeling cold. "Maybe
we could talk it through some more. After I get back?"

"Okay," he says. "Let's do that. And . . . I really think you need
to use this time to work out whatever you need to work out with
Nikhil, but you should remember that whatever you're feeling, however you're feeling, may not be the whole picture. You've been
through a lot the last couple days. It's not a normal situation. But
there's a reason you both separated all those years ago. He wasn't the
person you needed, and one night can't change any of that. You always told me being with him derailed all of your plans, and I don't
want to see you go back to something that wasn't good for you before. You deserve more than that, okay?"

The proper response tastes sour, but I say it anyway. "Okay."

"And be safe, Meena. I've been looking at flights back, but nothing's available yet. As soon as I see something, though, I'll let you know. I ended up getting permission from that client to borrow his jet, so I can even bring that down and—"

"You don't need to come here," I say quickly. "Not that I don't appreciate it. I do. But I can figure out the flight back on my own. Once things open up again."

He pauses. "Okay. If that's what you want."

"But, umm, if you do need to reach me, maybe you could email me? I'd rather you not text me on this phone."

I don't want Nikhil seeing messages from Shake pop up on his screen. "I can use Nikhil's computer to check my email. All right?"

He agrees, and after discussing a few more details from the meeting, he hangs up. I pull the phone away from my ear and stare at it for a second.

Shake and I really were good partners. We were on the same page about all the important things. We showed up for each other during hard times. We supported each other's goals. Even when we fought, even when he dumped me, he was honest with me. I never had to guess what he was thinking. Even just now, he was vulnerable with me, sharing his concerns, his worries, how he felt.

Shake is safe. Secure. Predictable. My parents love him. If we get back together, if we one day get engaged, I know they'd be more than excited. They'd be *relieved*.

I have a feeling my sister wouldn't feel that way. My parents had pushed her to consider marrying Ritu's father when she first found out she was pregnant in college—not that he was offering, or offering to be involved as a co-parent in any way—but my parents didn't give up after that. They've tried to matchmake on her behalf a number of times over the years, always insisting that Ritu should have a father.

I know that's been hard for my sister. Not that she would tell me that herself, but it's been obvious. At least to me. I can always tell from the way she tenses up when my parents mention it, from how distant she grows.

If Shake and I ever get married, I don't think she's going to be excited for me. I doubt she'll even care. My sister's never reacted the way I've hoped anytime I accomplished anything. Every graduation—from high school, from college, from law school. My first job. Every success I've had at work. All of those milestones have been met with dull words, tense smiles, rote congratulatory statements devoid of any emotion.

My parents always made up for it, hugging me warmly, telling me they were proud of me each time I achieved something, but no matter how hard I've tried, how hard I've worked to be who my parents wanted me to be, who they *needed* me to be, it hasn't been enough. None of it helped me bridge the gap between me and my sister.

Sometimes, I'm tempted to tell her that I understand. That I'm sorry. That I feel the weight of all of that too. That I know our parents mean well and I love them, but that their expectations have also been hard for me. That sometimes I felt like they approved of me or loved me only *because* I was achieving these things. That I wasn't sure what would happen to that love if I failed, if I couldn't accomplish everything they wanted.

I wonder if my sister would relate. I wonder if we have any of this in common. But we don't talk like that. We barely talk at all.

I head to the living room and grab the laptop off the coffee table. I check my work email, quickly skimming through it, but pause when I look up.

One of the things I'd liked most about this house was the brick fireplace in this room. It had seemed so classic. So grown-up. But it looks different now. It takes me a couple minutes to figure it out, to realize what's changed, but suddenly it clicks. The space above the mantel has nothing on it. It's empty.

When we'd first moved in, Nikhil had made me stand right in front of the fireplace. He'd asked me to wait for a moment, then returned minutes later holding something behind his back.

"I know just what we should put here," he'd said, nodding toward the wall. He'd let the anticipation grow, then pulled the surprise out dramatically, placing a large picture frame on the mantel with a flourish.

I'd stared at the black-and-white charcoal sketch, processing for a moment, then dissolving into laughter when I'd realized what it was. "You . . . you framed that? You actually got that *framed*?"

His smile had grown wider than I'd ever seen it. "Of course I did."

The sketch was something between a caricature and an accurate depiction of the two of us. Some features were slightly exaggerated: Nikhil's large nose, my thick eyebrows, the pointed tilt to my chin. But our expressions were what had been exaggerated the most.

We'd stumbled across this street artist in Vegas after we'd fully recovered from our post-wedding hangover. I can't remember which one of us had insisted on sitting for the drawing, but the result had made us both snort with amusement. And maybe a bit of embarrassment. The result had been so vulnerable. So raw. The artist had all but drawn literal hearts in our eyes. We'd looked absolutely besotted with each other, our hands clasped, our gazes locked, the swooniest, lovestruck smiles on our faces.

It was an exaggeration of what we really looked like, but it had also felt shockingly real. Like an X-ray of the two of us, showing what lay beneath the surface.

"Are you sure?" I'd asked Nikhil. "Are you sure you want to put it up here?"

His smile had fallen the tiniest degree. "Why? You don't want to?"

I'd winced. I hadn't wanted him to think I was embarrassed by the picture. Ashamed of it. But this depiction of the two of us was so intimate. It made me feel so exposed. It seemed strange to display it somewhere so public.

But Nikhil clearly wanted to, and besides, this was our home. *Ours*. It wouldn't be that public. No one else would really see this. This was just for us.

"No," I'd told him. "I do." I'd reached a hand out, grabbing onto his. "It's perfect. I love it."

His smile had returned then, and I hadn't been able to stop the goofy grin spreading across my face. His mouth had met mine, and his hand had threaded through my hair, his body suddenly flush against my own. Kissing Nikhil had always been electric. Every nerve of my body had sparked to life in a way I had never experienced before. I'd thought that connection between us was love, but . . . maybe all this chemistry between us is just attraction. Hormones and chemicals tricking our brains. Maybe that's all the artist had captured in that sketch. Lust and infatuation and the adrenaline high of doing something reckless and impulsive.

Maybe that's all last night was. Maybe that's all that's ever been between us.

I don't know where that picture is now. I haven't seen it anywhere. He probably got rid of it years ago, which would make sense. There's no reason he should have kept a reminder of the two of us hanging in his living room forever, but I am curious why he's left it like this. Completely bare. Why he hasn't hung anything in its place.

I go back to my work emails, reviewing a couple things I missed.

As I read, I hear Nikhil in the garage, his power tools at full volume, and the sound is just as comforting now as it was back then.

Nikhil's phone vibrates, and a text from Elizabeth flashes across the screen. I pick it up, slightly pleased to have an excuse to head to the garage. Once there, I knock on the door.

Something buzzy and electric sounds in response. I knock harder, and the noise stops.

"Nikhil?" I call. "Can I come in?"

A few seconds later, the door swings open, and Nikhil stands there with plastic safety glasses perched on top of his head.

I smirk. "Those are cute."

"They're not supposed to be," he says with a grin. "They're for safety."

"You always were a bit of a nerd about safety."

"And you always were a bit of a nerd about everything."

I laugh. "Well, that's certainly true."

"I liked it," he says. "Just to be clear. I've always liked that about you."

We watch each other, and slowly the light, teasing note in the air begins to shift. His smile fades, and his throat flexes as he swallows. "Meena, we should probably talk—"

The phone in my hand buzzes, and I quickly thrust it in his direction. "Elizabeth texted," I say. "That's why I came to find you."

He takes it from me, barely glancing at the screen before putting it in his back pocket. "Oh," he says. "Thanks." He takes a step back, hesitates, then asks, "You want to see what I'm working on?"

"I . . . Yeah. Sure."

I follow after him, and as he opens and roots around in one of the drawers, I take in how much the workshop has changed since I last saw it. Even though I'd been in the garage earlier, when we'd grabbed the canoe for our rescue mission, I hadn't really been paying attention to my surroundings. I'd been a ball of energy and adrenaline and fear, and everything had been a blur.

Now I take my time, inventorying everything. He's added a few new pieces of equipment. I'm not sure of their purpose, but I know to stay far away from them. I rarely spent time in here while he was working, but Nikhil had still insisted on showing me all of the machinery. He'd walked me through each piece, explaining its function, and giving me a basic safety lesson. I'd told him I never planned on using them, but he said I still needed to know so I could be careful. He didn't want to see me get hurt.

There's a stack of textbooks on the side table in the corner, brightly colored tabs and index cards sticking out of them in various directions.

My heart squeezes. He's using the study techniques I used for the bar, the ones we did together.

Nikhil finally finds what he'd been looking for and comes over to me.

"You'll need to put these on," he says, showing me a matching pair of glasses.

I scrunch my nose. "Is this because I made fun of yours?"

"No," he says, a corner of his mouth rising. He steps closer, gently pushing the glasses onto my face. I go still as he adjusts them, making sure they're secure. His fingers brush against my temple, and his golden brown eyes meet mine. His expression is so open, care and tenderness floating right at the surface. It makes my chest ache.

"No," he says again, still smiling. "They're to keep you safe. Just in case you want to take a stab at this." He gestures to his worktable, and I walk over, my curiosity piqued.

"It's a sign," he tells me. "A welcome sign for the inn. I'm hoping to hang it on the porch, or maybe in the lobby. I'm not sure what it'll say yet exactly. I haven't decided on a name for the inn, but I thought I could carve the 'welcome' part at least." He lifts a shoulder. "I had this spare piece of wood lying around and I didn't want to waste it."

Something within me warms. That's just like Nikhil. Turning scraps into something meaningful. Taking pieces others would discard and transforming them into something new.

"I'll just watch," I say, as he reaches for the saw. I cover my ears as the electric buzzing starts up, and he rounds the edges of this square slab of wood.

After, he grabs a pencil, sketching out the letters, and the way he's freehanding this font, the way his hand moves in precise, deliberate movements—I can't look away. He's an artist and it's mesmerizing. I'm tempted to trace the veins on the back of his hand, the muscles in his arm that bunch and flex.

"What did Elizabeth say?" I ask, needing something else to focus on.

He glances at me. "Nothing, really. She's been getting a lot of reports of homes that'll need complete rebuilding, and she's trying to triage and figure out a schedule for after everything clears up. She wanted to talk through it, but I can call her back in a bit."

"This is for the volunteering you do? With her organization?"

He nods but doesn't add anything else.

"When did you start working with them?"

He continues sketching. "Oh, it's been a few years now. Elizabeth was out walking her dog, and she knew I worked in construction, and she asked if I'd come out for a few hours. Now, I help coordinate and pitch in where needed. It's just . . ." His fingers tighten around the pencil, his movements growing a bit stiff. "Losing a home . . . it can be a traumatic experience. And it's something that happens too often here, with the frequent flooding and storms like this. And fixing places up, that's something I know how to do, so if it can help . . ." He trails off, straightening the piece of wood, then sketching again.

I swallow. I don't know if I'd ever realized that this was something Nikhil would like to do. That he'd enjoy using his skills and talents to help people in this way. I don't know if I'd ever realized this was something Nikhil and I shared.

I think about the people on this street. In this city. How much rebuilding will need to happen, and how much change is needed here and throughout the state. I think about all the things Elizabeth said, and how there's something I know how to do, and how I want to be here so I can do it. So I can help.

"That's great, Nikhil," I say. "I'm so glad you're doing that."

He works quietly for a little while, and I let myself picture it for a moment. Living in Texas, working with folks like Elizabeth, advocating for change. Living in this house, with Nikhil, waking up to his bright, joyful smile, and falling asleep right beside his tender heart and hardworking hands.

"Done," he says, showing me the lettering on the sign. "You want to try carving it?"

I don't know why, but I tell him yes. I take the drill from his hands, and he stands behind me, walking me through a minitutorial. He shows me how it all works, and he does the first letter with me, his body firm behind me, his hands steady over mine as we trace the letter together.

He's patient with me, moving more slowly through the process than he had been when he'd been doing it on his own. And I savor the feel of him, this quiet intimacy of the two of us working together.

"You know," he says, as we finish and move on to the next letter, "I think you'd be great in Garcia's seat."

Hope flutters for a moment. Nothing more than a whisper, but I feel it, somewhere deep inside me. "Yeah?"

"Yeah," he says. "After you mentioned her, I did some reading about her, and the causes she's championed, they're exactly the issues you care about. The ones you've been working on all these years."

I startle, but fortunately my hands don't shake, our movements stay slow and smooth. "How do you know what I've been working on?"

A huff of breath travels over my ear. "C'mon. You didn't really buy that I was watching all that C-Span just for fun, right?" he asks, his voice low and amused. "I've followed your career. The bills you've worked on, the laws you've lobbied for, the articles you've written."

"You have?"

He hums in acknowledgment, and the sound vibrates through me. "I liked your op-ed about immigration policy last year," he says casually, as if every word he's saying isn't making me feel like I'm melting inside. "I ended up reading more and watching some documentaries about it. It's partly why I think Garcia's seat makes so much sense for you. Not just because it's in Texas, but because it's what she's always led the way on. Something that really matters to her constituents. And to you."

"Me too," I say. "I thought the same thing too."

"And I know Alan said Elizabeth might run for it, and she might, but I still think it'd be worth doing. If it's what you really wanted." His voice softens. "People here would be lucky to have you."

"Thanks," I tell him, the word small and inadequate, unable to convey how his belief in me feels. It's as if I have wings, as if the impossible might actually be within reach. "I'm still thinking about it, but thank you for saying that. It . . . it means a lot."

We finish another letter, and he switches off the drill, leaving it to me. "You want to try the next one on your own?"

My heart flips in my chest. He's trusting me with this, sharing this with me, showing he's not afraid of me handling this by myself. I nod, and he steps to the side as I move on to the next letter.

I work for a while, and I can feel his gaze on my hands, then my face. He watches me, and I wonder what he's thinking.

He followed me to D.C. He never called me or tried to find me, but he's been following my career all these years, and . . . The question scares me, but I want to ask it. I want to know the truth.

"Nikhil, earlier, before I fell sick, when you told me you came to D.C., you said you would have moved with me if you'd known what I . . . if you'd known how I felt and is that still, is that—"

Out of the corner of my eye, I see Nikhil's shoulders stiffen.

I lick my lips. "I mean, I know you have the inn, and everything here, so things are different now, but then—"

"What are you saying?" he asks, his voice low.

I lift the drill, turning to look at him.

"It's just . . . I did tell you what I wanted back then. I did. I told you I wanted you to move with me, but it's like you didn't believe me. You told me you thought I didn't want you there, and I don't know . . . I'm trying to understand *why*."

His expression shutters, his jaw growing firm, and it hurts to see him this way. It's the way he looked every time he pushed me out. Every time he refused to tell me his thoughts and feelings. Every time he took away his warmth and left me in the cold.

I feel the stitches on a barely healed wound start to unravel, but I clamp down on the sensation before it all falls apart.

"Why would you think that?" I ask. "Why wouldn't you believe me?"

Because there are things I might want now. Things I want to tell him. But I need to know that he'll trust what I'm saying. That he'll trust *me*. I can't stop wondering how different our lives might have looked if he'd found me in D.C. If we'd actually talked to each other back then. I can't stop thinking about an alternate life that could have been mine.

That could maybe still be mine.

But as the silence ticks on, as I wait and wait and wait for him to say something, to say *anything*, that hope begins to deflate. The stitches come apart, slowly at first, then all at once, exposing the raw wound at the surface.

I wince, turning away, back to the sign on the table. I try to move on to the next letter, but my vision blurs, and I know I can't work like this. I confirm the drill is switched off, just like he showed me, then set it down right as a tear escapes, rolling down my cheek.

"Meena?" Nikhil asks, his voice thick with concern, but I brush him off.

Why am I surprised? Why does this hurt so badly? Why did I *let* this hurt?

These past few days, it had almost felt like we'd been taking steps toward each other. I thought Nikhil had been letting down his guard, letting me in, but he still has walls up. He still has fences I'll never be able to climb, and why should I? Why should I fight and beg for his trust if he doesn't want to give it? Why should I settle for scraps when I could have a real partner if I get back together with Shake?

A man who confides in me, who sees me as a teammate, who sees me as an equal. Not like Nikhil, who's still hiding things from me. Who's still treating me like the lost, broken person I was back then. The person who he thought needed coddling, who needed help, who needed support. Who wasn't strong enough to be there for him in return.

"I'm fine. I just need—" I try to leave, walking quickly toward the door, but he blocks my path.

"What do you need?" he asks, his voice raised in concern.

I shake my head, and do my best to take a deep breath.

Those things Shake said . . . He wasn't wrong. Years ago, I wanted Nikhil more than anything, and that kind of love—that feeling—it was all-consuming. It made me irrational. Impulsive. It made me the kind of person who lost sight of my goals and got distracted. The kind of person who failed the bar and got married on a drunken night in Vegas. At the time, I'd thought staying in that marriage was a risk worth taking, that somehow everything would work out, but it ended in disaster.

This way I feel, if I give in to it, I know it'll end the same way too.

Nikhil's hand comes to my chin, tilts it up. "Tell me what's wrong," he says. "*Please.*"

And that's when I break.

"I can't be here. I *can't*. I'm going back and what have we even been doing? What has all of this been? I don't even understand why you want to stay married to me. Why won't you just sign the papers? Why won't you let us go?"

He drops his hand, and all hint of emotion slides off his face.

I wait for him to say something, to give a straight answer, to finally break this silence between us. I wait for him to *try*, but he doesn't say a word. I wish I was surprised. I wish I was angry. But honestly, I'm just *tired*. Tired of all the times Nikhil has retreated like this. Tired of the way he never used to tell me what he was thinking. Tired of having to guess what's on his mind.

"What is it?" I ask. "I don't understand . . . What do you want out of all this? What could you possibly—"

"I want you!" His voice booms, louder than I've ever heard it.

All the blood rushes from my head. The room tilts, everything going sideways.

"I want you to stay. I want you to be with me. I want to live out everything we promised to each other. Those vows, they meant something to me, Meena. They still mean something to me. What we had . . . what we have . . . is real."

My thoughts swirl, vibrant colors blending and twisting so fast I can't grab on to a single one. Temptation and hope start to build again, but it all comes to a grinding halt when one word breaks through: "stay." He's asking me to stay.

Which means he wouldn't come with me. Just like he wouldn't come with me then.

And I still don't really know why that happened. Why he thought I didn't want him with me. He's still avoiding talking about hard things.

My heart slams against my rib cage, and I hate it. These turbulent emotions, these up-and-down swings, I can't do this again. I can't get caught up in this. My career and my dreams and my plans of running for office, I can't afford to let any of that fall by the wayside.

Not when I could have something safe and stable with someone who understands my goals, who shares them, who could help me achieve them.

"How can this be *real*, Nikhil?" My voice breaks, but I push through. "We've been living in a fantasy. Trapped in this house, away from everything, isolated from the real world, but this can't last forever. I can't stay— I've . . . I've built a life of my own. I can't just come back here and go back to being rootless and lost and stuck in this house. I can't go back to being that sad, dark version of myself again. I can't."

"It wouldn't be that." His brows crease. "There are things you want to do here. You told me there are things you want to do here."

"Like what? Run for office? For a seat that might not even be available?" I blow out a breath. "We don't know if Garcia is actually retiring, and even if she is, we both know Elizabeth is probably going to run and what are the chances I'd win against someone established and connected to this city like her? Why would I—why should I give up on the seat in Maryland? That's real. That's sure. All of this . . . it's just adrenaline. Exhaustion. We haven't been thinking straight."

"What about last night? That was real, Meena." A muscle in his cheek jumps, but his expression is raw, deeply earnest, when he says, "It was real to me."

I soften for a moment, even as I feel myself torn in two. "You're right. It was real, but that was never our problem, Nikhil. It was . . . It was the only thing that worked between us, and it's not enough."

"So, that's it? That's all we—"

"What else is there, Nikhil? There's nothing left for me here. Nothing."

He winces, and it almost makes me want to retract the words.

"We can't make this work," I say instead. "You've put roots down here. This is your home. You have community here and things you're working toward and I'm so . . . I'm so happy to see that. Really. But I need those things too. I *have* those things in D.C. My job, the race in Maryland, and I have . . . I have someone waiting for me in D.C."

Nikhil pales. "I thought you weren't . . . You said you weren't—"

"I'm not. Not right now. He ended things, because . . . well, because of *this*. But we had plans. We talked about running for office side by side, about maybe even getting married one day, but I can't do that. I can't do any of that if I'm still married to you."

He's quiet for a long moment.

"That's why you want the divorce?" he says. "So you can marry him?"

"I want to at least have the option. I want to at least have a *choice*."

The disbelieving sound that escapes his mouth cuts like a dagger. "Tell me this, has he met your family? Do your parents like him? Is he everything they wanted for you?"

"Yes, but why . . ." I shake my head, confused by the abrupt change in topic. "What are you—"

He stares at me, the fire in his gaze slowly dying. "It doesn't matter."

My temper flares. He's still shutting me out, still refusing to let me in. "Clearly it does. Talk to me!"

"You never let me meet your family!" The words explode from his chest. All at once. And then there's silence. All I hear is a ringing in my ears, the aftereffect of the grenade he just let loose.

"We . . . we both agreed," I stammer. "We both agreed that it would be best to wait. That we would wait awhile before breaking the news to them."

"How long, Meena? We'd been married for a *year*. How long were you going to wait?"

"I . . . I don't—"

He raises a hand. "I understood it at first. After Vegas. With the way it happened and with everything with your sister. I understood why you would have been a little worried about telling them, but . . ." He shakes his head. "You were never going to tell them."

"That's not true," I say, but I'm not sure if I'm trying to convince him or myself. Nikhil hadn't brought up meeting my family during the first holiday we'd spent together. Or the second. But as we neared the six-month mark, he'd casually asked if we should invite my parents for dinner. Or even just my sister. I'd refused, panicking, and saying this wasn't the right time. My second attempt at the bar exam was only weeks away. We'd do it later. After that.

He'd retreated. Hiding out in the garage, working on something or other. I'd hurt him, but his response had hurt me too. We'd fought the next few days. Over little things, neither of us bringing up the topic of my family again. But we tiptoed around it, our anger building to an all-time high on our six-month anniversary. The anniversary where I gave him the cologne he inexplicably still wears now. But I'd told myself that the tension between us was only temporary. That things would be fine once the bar exam was over. Once I passed.

Once I was able to prove that I hadn't failed, that I was back on track, I'd be able to introduce him to my parents. I'd worked so hard to make sure they never worried about me. I'd followed every rule. I'd achieved every milestone. I'd made plans and backup plans to make sure things turned out the right way. And then it had all gone awry.

But once I passed, I'd be able to show them that I hadn't made a mistake. That the choice I'd made hadn't completely destroyed my plans. That even though I'd gone off course, everything had turned out fine.

"I would have told them," I insist. "I was just waiting for the bar to be over. To find out if I passed before—"

"Really? Even now . . . have you ever mentioned me to them? Have you ever told them the truth? Have you ever talked about any of it? To your parents, or your sister, or Ritu?"

I recoil at the thought. I've never brought it up to them. I've never wanted them to find out that I'd failed the bar, that I'd failed at marriage. I'd wanted to leave all of that in the past, where it belongs.

"And I don't remember you telling them anything after you got your results back. I don't remember us making plans for us to go up there together. For me to finally meet them," he continues.

I swallow, my mouth dry as sandpaper, because he's right. I hadn't.

"We were . . . There was so much we needed to figure out then. We hadn't even talked about where we were going to live and what it meant for my job, for yours, and then when we did . . ."

Nikhil's expression darkens. No doubt he's remembering the same night I am. The last words we spoke to each other. The final fight, which tore us apart.

"But if we'd worked out," I say, holding his gaze, hoping to break him from those memories and anchor him to the present. "If we'd worked out, I would have told them, Nikhil. I would have."

He scoffs, and the sound is cutting, a crisp edge of a page slicing against my skin. "Let's be honest, Meena. After all this time, let's be honest with each other. You were halfway out the door at that point. You didn't *want* me to meet them. You didn't want them to know about me. And I know why. I'm not a lawyer or a doctor. I'm not the kind of person your parents would have wanted for you. I didn't finish college. I just work in construction, and you didn't want them to know that. You didn't want them to know you'd married someone like me."

The pain in his voice pierces through me. "That's not true. That's not why—"

"*Please.* You made it clear I wasn't good enough for you, and I'm not arguing. I wasn't."

"No. Nikhil—" I stop, a lump in my throat forming. "I was the failure. Not you. I would have been so proud to introduce you to my family. Really, I would have. But I couldn't face them like that. I was falling apart. I was barely making it through. I needed to pass first. I needed to show them that I hadn't messed up. That I hadn't made a mistake—"

"That *I* wasn't a mistake," he says flatly.

"No, you're not listening to me. I—"

"You don't have to do this. It's fine. I've accepted it." He shrugs. "You can say that you were going to do it after you passed, but really, why would you have introduced them to your backup plan? Once you passed, once Plan A was in reach, you left. You went back to the life you were always supposed to have. The one you always were supposed to live."

"You weren't Plan B, Nikhil. You were never Plan B. You weren't even part of the plan."

He laughs roughly. "Great."

"No. I'm saying . . . I never planned for you because I couldn't have. I could never have imagined . . . I could never have . . ." I take a deep breath. "You were better than anything I could have possibly planned."

He stares at me, and then he's moving, erasing the space he'd created between us. His eyes burn hot, the specks of gold brighter than I've ever seen them, and I can't tear my gaze away. I'm locked in, and the force at which we meet almost hurts. It's a clash. His lips against mine, his arm around my waist, his hand cradling the back of my head. The stubble on his cheek burns against my skin, but it's far from unpleasant. I want more of it. I want to feel it everywhere.

I pull him closer, clutching at the collar of his shirt, and he responds in kind, his hands sliding down my lower back, pulling me taut against him. This isn't a simple kiss. This is possession. Claiming. This is each of us screaming, *You're mine, you belong to me.* The truth of it thrums through my bones. Through my blood. We've always belonged to each other. Always. Before we exchanged those vows and every day since.

I press my teeth down, gently pulling on his bottom lip, and he moans in response. The sound sets me on fire. I want to hear him make it again. Over and over again. I capture his lip, fully intending to repeat my actions, but before I can my back meets the hard surface of a wall. Nikhil lifts me slightly, and my legs automatically wrap around his waist.

"Yes," he murmurs, his lips traveling down the curve of my neck. "Just like that."

I let my head fall back, enjoying his attentions, but I'm not patient for long. He's too far away and I need him closer. I cup my hands around his face, bringing him back to me. Bringing his mouth back to mine.

After a long while, our pace slows, the initial frenzy fading into something else. Something slow and soft. Something I'm scared to examine too closely. Something I felt last night.

These last couple days have been stressful and chaotic and wild, but somehow, in these moments, there's been an underlying sense of peace. It's a kind of calm I haven't experienced in six years. I'd forgotten how it feels and now that I have it back, I don't know how I've gone this long without it. Being around Nikhil somehow makes everything better. It always has. He's the quiet center in the midst of chaos. My eye of the storm.

His thumb slides against my cheek, so slowly. So tenderly. I don't realize he's wiping away a tear until another one escapes my eye.

"Meena," he says softly, the sound barely a whisper. His lips brush my cheekbone, kissing another tear away.

I reach for him, and slide my mouth against his, tasting the salt of my own tears. I ignore it, and press closer. I tighten my legs around his waist and slide my arms around his neck, but something light and abrasive brushes against my skin. I trace it with the pad of my finger, trying to figure it out. It's a chain, I think. A very thin one.

I frown, breaking away. Nikhil never wore a necklace. He never seemed into jewelry. But that thought crumbles into dust when Nikhil nips at my jaw. He grabs my hands, interlocking our fingers, then presses his firm, closed lips back against mine. A few seconds pass, and I tilt my head, trying to find another angle, trying to coax his lips open, trying to entangle my tongue with his, but he doesn't respond in kind. His kisses are feather light, and no matter what I do, he won't return to our earlier fervor.

He pulls back, confusion and passion warring for a moment, and then his face shutters. He looks down at our hands, at our fingers still intertwined.

"You're not wearing a ring," he says. And for a second, I think he's talking about my wedding ring. Not the one we'd gotten in Vegas, but the one Nikhil had surprised me with a month later. He'd bought two. A matching set of gold bands. He'd said he was saving up for a diamond, and that he'd get one for me soon. That he'd do a real proposal one day when I least expected it, but that we could at least wear these bands for now.

I'd taken mine off, leaving it on the kitchen table before leaving for good. Is it possible he never found it? Maybe it got knocked off and sucked up by the vacuum cleaner. Or maybe it rolled under the couch or into a shadowy corner of the room. I wonder where his is. I haven't seen him wearing it. I don't even know if he still has it. But when he continues staring at my left hand, I realize what he's really asking.

"It's not like that," I say. "Shake and I— It's just something we used to talk about, but I don't know . . . I mean, he says he wants to get back together, but—"

Nikhil releases me, and I disentangle my legs from his body. He steps away, his breaths harsh and quick.

"We can't do this," he says quietly. "*I* can't."

I open my mouth, desperate for words that will convince him that we can have this. That we need this one final goodbye before we're torn apart for good.

"Nikhil—" I try.

"You're leaving." His words are final, but still a little tentative, as if he's testing them out, as if he's hoping I might correct him.

But I can't. I can't stay here. I have to go back.

"I am," I say.

Nikhil's carefully blank expression fades, something desperate and harsh breaking through, but he reels it back in an instant.

We watch each other for a long moment, and then he shakes his head, turning and leaving me alone.

14

We sleep in separate rooms that night. We don't discuss it. We both just gravitate to our respective areas. I grab a pillow and blanket and head for the couch. Nikhil heads upstairs.

"I'm sleeping in the guest bedroom," he says from the top of the stairs. He doesn't turn back to look at me. "You can take the primary."

"What about the broken window?" I call, but the only response I hear is the soft *snick* of a door closing.

The two of us cleaned that room up earlier, but I can't imagine that it'd be comfortable to sleep there with the open window. It may not be raining anymore, but it's still pretty warm outside, and I doubt that piece of tarp will do much to help with that. But if that's where he wants to sleep, I guess that's his prerogative.

I go upstairs, fully intending to go to bed, but a few moments later, I find myself standing in front of the guest bedroom, my hand hesitating above the doorknob. It's late, and there's not much left for Nikhil and me to talk about. Still, I don't want us to go to sleep like this. I don't want us to end the night on such a bitter note. It's far too late for us to consider following trite marriage advice, but for some reason it seems important that neither of us goes to bed angry.

I gather the courage to finally twist the doorknob, but my heart sinks when it barely moves.

It's locked. He's locked the door.

I could call his name. Or knock. But he's clearly not in the mood to speak to me.

I walk the short distance to the primary bedroom, following his lead and locking the door behind me.

Ten minutes later, after staring wide-eyed at the ceiling, I climb out of bed. I quietly unlock the bedroom door, then slide back under the covers.

"We're finally starting to hear some good news," the woman on the television says. "Though it might look like the flooding's at the same level it was yesterday, there are reports that it will soon start to go down. We expect that many streets will be clear by the end of the day, and almost all areas of Houston should be clear by tomorrow morning. Of course, a number of people are still without power, and others are contending with serious damage from the storm, but if the reports are correct, this is the last day Houstonians will be stuck in their homes. If you're seeking shelter or need assistance, please contact the hotline at the bottom of the screen. We're also showing a list of shelters that are offering temporary housing and aid. We'll continue to keep you updated, but as of now, it seems like the end might be in sight."

The reporter continues talking as I enter the bathroom. I can hear her voice while I wash my face and brush my teeth, but I'm not listening to what she's saying. I'm still thinking about the information she just shared.

I can go home. By this time tomorrow, I could be on my way home.

I should be overjoyed at that news. I should be ready to get out of this house. I should be thrilled to finally be able to leave this place filled with nothing but painful memories, but nothing's feeling the way it should.

The last time I left this house for good, I'd been in a hurry. It had been an impulsive decision. A few weeks prior I'd been in a completely different mindset, having just found out that I'd passed my second attempt at the bar. The relief I'd felt in that moment had been overwhelming. I'd texted the results to Nikhil and he'd somehow managed to leave work early. I'd broken down into tears the moment I saw him, and he'd just hurried toward me, wrapping me in his arms. He hadn't asked me why I was crying or why I was upset. He'd just held me, telling me that it was okay, that I'd been through a lot, that however I felt, it was normal to feel that way.

"I passed," I'd whispered to him, after I'd calmed down. "I passed."

He'd kissed my forehead, and his lips had curved into a smile against my skin. "I know."

We'd celebrated that night, just the two of us at home. And I'd never felt lighter. Like all the weight holding me down had been lifted. Nikhil had put on music and spun me in circles, and I'd laughed until I was breathless. Dizzy and joyful and for the first time, so full of hope.

But it hadn't taken long for reality to rear its ugly head. For my brain to start reminding me of all the practicalities I'd been ignoring for too long. I hadn't wanted to think about moving to D.C. before.

I hadn't wanted to think about *anything* that came after passing the bar exam. Really, I don't know if I would have been able to at the time. I was in such a fragile spot back then. I was truly just taking it one day at a time.

But suddenly, there was so much to do. I'd need to notify the firm that I'd passed. I'd need to fill out the paperwork to waive into the D.C. bar. And eventually, I'd need to move.

I'd always known that. Nikhil had always known that. He knew moving to D.C. had always been my plan. But the two of us rarely talked about it.

He'd mentioned moving with me to D.C. once, but it had sounded like such a faraway thing then. We'd talked about maybe trying long distance, about us visiting back and forth for a while, and him maybe moving up to be with me at some indeterminate date in the future.

But we hadn't talked like that since Vegas. So much had changed since then. After getting married, after living with him for months, I'd realized how important this city was to him. How it was the first place he'd ever been able to call home. I knew how much that meant to him after he'd moved so often as a kid, and I knew how hard leaving all that behind would be for him.

When the firm had gotten back to me, congratulating me and officially offering me the job again, I'd told Nikhil. He'd been over the moon for me, insisting that we celebrate all over again, but he didn't bring up what the job would mean. He didn't bring up D.C., and out of fear, I didn't either.

Days went by, and though I started dropping hints, he never took the bait, and my fear only grew. If he was open to moving with me, if he was excited about it, wouldn't he have mentioned it by now? Wouldn't he have asked what our plans were? Wouldn't he want to talk about it with me?

The more time passed, the more I became convinced that Nikhil didn't want to move. That he wanted to stay here.

So while I waited to hear back about my waiver for the D.C. bar, I casually began looking for jobs in Texas. After all, there was good work to do here. Policies that needed to be fought, advocacy that needed to be done. But nothing I found excited me quite like my original job offer.

I was constantly browsing real estate listings and rental properties in D.C. back then. Just to get an idea. I hadn't completely ruled out staying in Texas, but I wanted a better sense of my options. I'd had pictures of apartments and row houses near Capitol Hill on my computer screen that day, not realizing that Nikhil had been standing right behind me.

I hadn't known it then, but that had been the beginning of the end.

He hadn't pushed too hard about it at first. He'd tried to make his initial questions about it sound casual, but things had quickly gotten out of hand. Our emotions and voices had been high. We'd picked at each other's deepest wounds, knowing the right places to hit, knowing exactly what to say to draw blood.

"You never ask me *anything*," he'd said. "You just plow ahead. You just decide. You don't ask me for help or my thoughts, you just . . . You steamroll over everything."

"You think I *want* to be that way?" I'd shot back. "I've tried to talk to you so many times, but you never want to talk about the hard things. And someone has to make plans. Someone has to figure things out. Otherwise, we'll just end up making impulsive, irresponsible decisions. We can't do that again. We need to—"

"So, you regret it? That's what this is all about? You regret getting married?"

"No, god." I'd felt like tearing my hair out. "Why does it always come back to that? I'm trying to plan a path forward for *both* of us. I want you with me. Beside me. I want to make these decisions together. Why can't you understand that?"

The fight had gone in circles. Both of us revisiting the same topics over and over again. Both of us saying the same things. Neither of us budging an inch. Until I'd finally had it.

"I'm moving," I'd told him. I'd been at my breaking point and the answer he gave me would tell me how he really felt. If he wanted to move. If he wanted to stay. If he thought our marriage was worth fighting for. "I'm moving," I'd said. "And I need you to come with me. I *want* you to come with me."

His mouth had fallen open in surprise. "What?"

"You say I never ask you for anything? Well, I'm asking you now. Move with me to D.C. Move with me, Nikhil. *Please*."

He'd been speechless a moment, the muscles in his throat working. "You can't ask me like this, Meenakshi. I haven't . . . I don't—"

"Then how am I supposed to ask you?"

"I don't know. But not like this. It's not supposed to be like this."

I'd thrown my hands up. "How's it supposed to be then? You want things to stay the way they are? Me living here? Stuck all day in this house? Always waiting for *you*?"

His head had reared back. But instead of responding, instead of telling me that he'd move with me, or that he wouldn't, or that he wanted to one day but wasn't ready yet, he'd just left. And that had told me everything I needed to know.

I'd packed that night, checked into a hotel, and made my plans. I did exactly what I'd said I was always going to do. I moved to D.C.

And Nikhil didn't call. He didn't text. He didn't come after me. Except . . . now I know that he did. He came to D.C. He saw me. But he didn't tell me he was there. Why didn't he tell me? Why didn't he ever tell me anything? He was always so closed off. About work, about his family, about key pieces of his life.

Though I suppose I was hiding things too. I was hiding *him*. From my family and friends. From everyone who knew me. I thought I'd been so open. Confiding in him about my career aspirations, about my parents and my sister and my niece, about the bar exam and how scared I was. But I'd kept him a secret, and I'm ashamed to admit I hadn't really considered how that might make him feel.

Though I still can't believe that Nikhil could ever have thought that I was embarrassed by *him*. He was the one with a job. The one supporting us. The one holding me and everything together. I was the one bringing nothing to the relationship. The one who'd failed. If anything, he should have been embarrassed by *me*.

But of course, he hadn't been, because he's Nikhil. Kind and steadfast and patient. He has a caretaker personality through and through. Sometimes to a fault. Sometimes at the expense of his own needs. Though I have more than my share of flaws too. It's taken some time for me to realize it, but it's clear that we both played a role in the demise of this marriage. We both bear some of the blame. And now, all that's left is for us to make it official.

I go downstairs, enter the living room, and flip Nikhil's laptop open. I would have asked his permission to use it again, but I haven't seen him around, which is a little strange. He's usually an early riser. Or at least, he used to be. But with everything that's happened I wouldn't be surprised if his sleep schedule is a little out of whack.

The airline's sent me a message that anyone who had a flight canceled due to the storm can rebook anything in the next two weeks, regardless of price difference. Their website is already showing options out of Houston tomorrow, including an early afternoon flight to D.C. that has only a handful of seats remaining. I grab it quickly, breathing a sigh of relief when it goes through, the confirmation screen flashing like a victory flag.

I email the itinerary to Shake, so he knows not to book something, or even worse, take his client up on that offer of using the jet. I'm doing a quick scan of the news I've missed over the last few days when an email from Shake pops up in my inbox. I'm able to take in only the subject line ("Rescheduled Strategy Meeting—MUST READ") before the screen goes black.

I frantically tap the touch pad and the power key, but nothing helps. Nikhil's computer is dead. I scan the room and the outlets but don't see a charger anywhere.

I wish I could let it go, but that "MUST READ" is tempting me. Part of me wonders if Shake thought about what I'd said. Maybe he was able to confirm the news about Garcia's retirement. Maybe he ran my idea by the group. Maybe they have thoughts on the Texas seat. I'm desperate to know, and it's that desperation that forces me off the couch.

I have to ask Nikhil for the charger, and though he's likely still asleep, there's a possibility he's in the garage. Sure, I haven't heard any noises coming from in there, but maybe he's working very, very quietly. It couldn't hurt to check.

I rap my knuckles against the garage door, and even though I don't hear any response, I step inside just to make sure. I'm disappointed, but not surprised, when I don't find him in there.

Nikhil hasn't hung the canoe back on the wall. It's lying in the center of the garage on top of a large towel, its green paint shiny and glistening. I sidestep around it.

There are a couple objects covered by sheets and I bet those are the other projects he's working on. They're all different sizes, but they look like smaller pieces. At least they're all much smaller than the canoe. A piece of wood juts out from the edge of one of the sheets, and I'm pretty sure it's the sign he'd shown me earlier. I inch closer, trying to get a better view, to see if he ended up working on it any more, and that's when I notice something propped up against the wall.

The size and shape of it triggers a memory in my subconscious. And the brown backing and black spring clips confirm my suspicions. It's a picture frame. The image inside is facing the wall, but I'm almost positive it's the one I'm thinking of. Though it's possible he kept the frame and changed the picture inside. Or left it empty.

There's only one way to find out. I grab the top two corners and turn the frame around, unable to hold back a gasp at what I see.

The glass is cracked. Lines running in every direction. Not unlike the screen on my broken phone.

The broken glass doesn't completely distort the image behind it, though, and after a while I don't even notice the cracks anymore.

Two faces stare back at me. Such young faces. These two don't have crow's-feet when they smile or strands of gray hair. These two don't know the heartbreak that awaits them. These two aren't even aware of what's going on around them at the moment.

Nikhil and I had laughed the entire time we sat for our portrait, the artist constantly admonishing us to sit still, which had only made us laugh more. I don't remember what was so funny. I don't think it was anything in particular. I just remember that the world had seemed so alive. It had been golden hour on the strip, and every casino and billboard and sign had been lit in this beautiful, magical glow.

Nikhil had been glowing too. Bubbly like a glass of champagne. Joyful and effervescent in a way that felt contagious. He was sunshine incarnate, and any stress or anxiety or worry I should have had about our reckless decision, about our impetuous wedding, vanished under his rays.

I stare at my younger self and hardly recognize the girl I see. She's pure adoration, her eyes fixed on the man beside her. And he's watching her in return, his expression so soft. So gentle. So full of hope.

It makes me want to cry.

These two people trapped behind the broken glass look just like us, but they're strangers to me. I'd told myself before that this sketch was a lie. That it hadn't captured a couple in love. That it had just captured infatuation and foolishness and lust. But looking at it now, I know that's not the truth.

I loved Nikhil. And he loved me. We loved each other.

He saw me. He knew me. Until I chose to hide him away, hiding pieces of myself as I did.

And I knew him. Even as he kept parts of himself buried and out of reach, I knew him. At the time I'd thought he'd intentionally drawn a line around his heart. Intentionally raised a wall that I could never get past. But I think he was scared. He might have revealed those parts to me one day. If he'd felt safe. If he'd felt like I was really in this marriage. If he hadn't felt like he was a second choice.

My chest constricts, my vision growing blurry.

How could he think that? How could I have let him think that?

I want to go back in time. I want to find young Meena and tell her to wake up. Tell her that there's a man who loves her and she needs to make sure that he knows she loves him back. That she needs to tell him what he means to her. That she needs to show him, show everyone, instead of hiding him under a rock.

What had I been so scared about? Judgment and disappointment from my parents? From the community? Being on the receiving end of that same shame my parents and sister had been subjected to all those years ago? It had felt like the worst thing imaginable then, but it seems so small now.

I cared too much about the wrong things, and in doing so I lost the man I love. *Love,* not loved. Because as much as I've been trying to convince myself otherwise, I love Nikhil. I don't think there's been a day that's gone by where I haven't loved Nikhil. I loved him when we got married, and I loved him when I left him. I loved him in those early days, when I first moved to D.C., when I spent every sleepless night staring at his name on my phone. I loved him when I googled him every few months to find out what he'd been up to. I loved him even when I tried to make things work with Shake. And I loved him when I sent him the divorce papers.

I have spent every moment of the past seven years loving this man. It's been an ache inside me that I haven't acknowledged until now, and now that I've put a name to it, now that I've called it what it is, it's like a dam has broken. Emotions flood in, barreling through every corner of my body.

I sink to the floor, my eyes transfixed by this picture of us. This impossibly perfect picture of the two of us in love.

I don't know what to do with this brand-new, but not-quite-new, information. I don't know how it changes things. Or *if* it changes things. We're so different now. But I know that the feelings I have aren't just for the Nikhil I once knew. The youthful, grinning, bare-faced man staring back at me. I have feelings for the man who remembered I like chicken noodle soup with stars in it. The man who ran out to help his neighbor even though we were in the middle of a hurricane. The man who's been searching for a place to call his own and dreams about opening an inn, a place others can feel at home. The man who makes me feel known. Like I can tell him anything and be immediately understood.

That thought spurs me into motion. I pick myself up, taking a moment to compose myself before leaving the garage.

I have to talk to Nikhil. I'm not sure what I'll tell him exactly.

Even though I have newfound clarity on how I feel, I'm not sure what this means. For me. For him. For my career. For this marriage. For Shake. For us.

But I can start with the piece I know without a doubt. That I love him. That I've always loved him. I can start with that and let the rest fall into place. I can start with that and find out whether there's any chance he feels that way too.

I rush through the house, my eyes searching for a glimpse of Nikhil. I come to a sudden halt when I find him sitting at the dining room table.

He looks good. He always looks good, but he looks different this morning. His hair a bit sleep-rumpled. His stubble a little more grown-in. He looks like the worn-in leather couch in the living room. He looks like the beat-up desk in the guest bedroom. The one he made for me. The one that didn't wobble no matter how many textbooks I dropped on it, how many tears I spilled on it, how many hours I spent studying late into the night. He looks like woodworking in the garage and cooking in the kitchen and sleeping bags in a closet.

He looks like home.

Nikhil glances up, and when our eyes meet, his lips curve into a smile. But it's not the smile I love. This one is strained. He's trying to hide it, but his mouth is tight. The muscles in his face tense.

My stomach twists.

He has a cup of coffee in his right hand, the steam twisting and curling above it. There's a matching mug on the place mat opposite his. And a stack of papers on the table, lying right between the two seats.

This sight is so familiar to me. It's the layout of every mediation and settlement conference I've ever attended. It's the pretense of peace between the parties before the negotiations begin in earnest.

It's the exact scenario I've been wanting to happen since I arrived here, but now it's a nightmare come to life.

"Good morning," he says.

Emotion clogs my throat. I swallow, trying to clear it. "Good morning," I say.

"Sleep okay?"

I nod. "Yeah. You?"

"Yeah." He extends an arm, as if asking me to take a seat, but I choose to stay standing.

"I was up early," I say, "just exploring the house. Taking a look around."

"Oh?"

"Yeah. I was trying to find you. To let you know that I have a flight back home tomorrow. In the afternoon."

His strained smile falls slightly before bouncing back into place. "Good," he says. "That's good news."

"Right?" I say, the word tasting bitter. There's nothing right about this. Everything, all of this, it feels so wrong. "I checked for you in the garage but got a bit distracted. I, uhh, found that picture of us."

Embarrassment, and maybe a touch of guilt, travels over his features.

I come around to stand across from him, my hands gripping the top of my chair. "I hadn't seen it in a long time and it was . . . it was nice to see it. Though it looks like the glass is broken? Did it fall or did something happen or—"

"It was an accident," Nikhil says. "I knocked it over, but it was by accident." Hesitation flits across his face. A second later, he continues. "It was up for a long time. Years, actually. It's probably why Alan thought he recognized you. I never took it down from the mantel."

My pulse jumps. Dangerous and desperate hope grows within me, but it dies the moment he continues.

"Not until I got the papers." His gaze shoots toward the stack of papers on the table, and then back to me. "But the glass only broke later. I took the picture down and moved it to the garage and propped it up against the wall, and . . . one day I didn't look where I was going, and my foot caught the edge of it. It fell before I could grab it.

"I probably should have taken it down sooner. I probably left it up too long." He rubs the back of his neck, his expression growing uneasy. "That's what I wanted to talk about, actually. I think I've . . . I've been holding on to the past too long. Holding on to us too long. And I think you're right. We both need to let this go. We both need to move on."

My gut constricts, bile rising in my throat.

"I printed the papers out," he says. "It felt wrong to do it the electronic way. To click and have our . . . And have everything wiped away. It felt better to have something physical. Tangible. It felt more real."

The ground shifts beneath my feet, and I finally sit, not sure if I can stand upright much longer.

"I didn't delay on purpose, Meena. Really. I'd always planned on mailing these back. I don't want to stand in the way of your happiness. I've never wanted that. I just . . . wasn't ready. I needed a little time to adjust."

My mouth is dry. I take a sip of my coffee, thinking it might help, but the heat and acidity only make it worse. I'm quiet for a moment, trying to gather my thoughts. "It's not all you, Nikhil," I finally say. "I could have sent these earlier. I could have tried to make it official years ago. But I've . . . I've been holding on to us too."

The corners of his mouth soften slightly, some of the earlier strain lifting.

I want to tell him that we weren't wrong to hold on. That the love between us never died. That we've both grown and changed, but in good ways, I think. That if we wanted to, we could do things better this time. We could at least try.

But then, he clears his throat. "I don't have a lawyer, but I made some changes." He nods toward the papers. "So, you'll probably want to take a look at that. And here." He fishes his phone out of his pocket and places it on the table, sliding it to me. "You can use my phone in case you need to call your lawyer. Though I guess you don't have to. You probably understand all of this legalese just fine."

"What if . . ." I lick my dry lips. "What if I stayed?"

He goes still.

"What if I stayed for a few days so we could—" Could *what*? I'm not even sure what I'm suggesting. So we could date? Go to therapy? See if there's any way for us to come back together? To try to make things work? It all sounds so outlandish.

Nikhil must read all of that on my face, because his expression is gentle but resigned when he says, "What would we figure out in a few days that we haven't figured out already?" He pauses. "You made the right call, Meena," he says. "I was wrong earlier. It wasn't right to ask you to stay like that." He looks away, rubbing the back of his neck. "When I went to D.C. . . . I should have tried to see you. I should have talked to you, but I was just so convinced, so scared that I wasn't good enough for you. I wanted to wait until I could prove myself, until I had something to show for myself, something to show *you*. Something to show your family."

"Nikhil, you never needed to—"

He raises a hand to stop me. "It's fine. I . . . I realize now that I let that fear keep us apart. Even before you left, I was so scared of losing you, of not being enough, that I think I actually ended up pushing you away, and, well, if I could go back in time, I'd do that differently. I'd do so many things differently, but that's not really an option for us, is it?" His mouth curves in a sad smile. "I don't know. Maybe the writing was on the wall for us from the very beginning. Maybe you were right not to bring me home to your parents from the very start."

His words cut through me, painful and quick. "I wish I could have done things differently too," I say. "I wish I had done a lot of it differently. I just— I'm sorry."

He lifts a shoulder, the gesture too deliberate and careful to be casual. "It's all right, really. Those things are in the past, and you were right before. We can't change any of that now. We should have made all of this official a long time ago, but I'm glad we're finally doing it." He stands up, and the finality of that movement coupled with the certainty in his voice is like the banging of a gavel. It signals that I'm too late. That Nikhil meant what he said. He wants this to be over. He wants to move on.

I grab the document, scanning the first page. There are notes scrawled in black ink in the margins, but I can't make sense of them. I'm just reading the words at the top over and over.

Dissolution of Marriage. Dissolution of Marriage.

"I'm going to make breakfast. Eggs okay?"

I'm not sure if I respond, but I must, because he leaves, giving me privacy so I can read through everything.

This is what I'd told myself I'd wanted. A painless, straight-forward discussion of terms. A handshake at the end. And me walking out of here with his signature on the page.

I can do this. I can pretend that I want this again. I can get lost in these words and turn everything else off. I've had enough practice doing it. And maybe that's for the best. I don't need distractions right now. I don't need inconvenient feelings that take me off track, that steer me away from my plans. I'll pretend like this is work. Like it has nothing to do with me. This is a negotiation like any other and I'm going to do my job.

This mindset slips over me like a plate of armor. And soon, I'm flipping through the pages. Making notes, questions, striking things out and replacing them with proposals of my own.

A plate of eggs and toast appears at my elbow, and I mechanically take a bite and continue.

Nikhil hasn't made any big changes. He asked questions about some things and made notes that he wants to discuss about others, but there's nothing that makes me concerned.

I take another bite of my breakfast and slowly come out of my haze, realizing Nikhil's not in the room. I call his name and he steps out of the kitchen.

"I'm done," I say. "Do you want a moment alone to look through it or . . ."

He sits down, taking the document from me. "No. I'll just read them now."

He's quiet for a long time. Deep in thought. When he turns a page, a wrinkle forms between his eyebrows. He's so intense. So focused. I shouldn't be staring at him. I should look away. But I can't.

"Thanks for this," I say, unable to take the silence much longer. "For breakfast. It was really good."

"You're welcome," he says distractedly. He frowns, picking up his pen and crossing through something.

"But I feel bad," I say. "You've been making all the meals. I should make something."

His gaze stays fixed on the papers, but the right corner of his mouth tips up. "You want to make something?"

"Yeah. I can cook."

This time his eyes flit to mine, humor flashing for a brief second. "Really?"

"Yeah," I say. "I took a cooking class. Learned a bunch of new recipes."

"Hmm." He goes back to the document, but a small smile stays on his face.

I conveniently leave out the remaining details. That I attended a grand total of three classes before giving up entirely. That I went to these classes four years ago and barely remember anything about them. And that they taught us ridiculously complicated dishes that I would be able to replicate only if I was suddenly possessed by the soul of Gordon Ramsay, and honestly, maybe not even then.

"What kinds of recipes?" he asks.

"Oh, uhh, it'll be a surprise." For him and me both. I have no idea what I'm going to make.

He shakes his head slightly. "I don't mind cooking," he says. "I've always liked it."

And he had. When we'd lived together, he'd never made anything superfancy, but he'd always done the bulk of the cooking. I'd help with meal prep and stick things in the oven, but anything involving an actual stove was all Nikhil.

"I know," I say. "But really, I can make dinner." I don't know how to explain, but his cooking for both of us, it's always been a way he's shown care, and I want to do the same for him before I leave. I want him to see that same care reciprocated. I want him to know that he's deserving and worthy of receiving it, that he can allow himself to receive it. If not from me, then from someone else in the future.

My insides revolt at the thought, but I force the sensation down. I want Nikhil to be happy. Even if it's not with me.

He looks at me skeptically, then returns his pen to the paper.

"It'll be our last meal together," I say, trying to convince him. "We should do it in style."

His hand slips, his pen shooting across the page in a jagged line. Then, he nods. "Okay. Sounds good."

The room returns to its earlier silence, until finally Nikhil is done. He pushes the document over to me and settles back in his chair.

"I think we're almost there," he says.

I nod. I make a few tiny changes, and when it's all done, he grabs his computer. We input our edits together, and then he goes off to print it. Minutes later, he drops the shiny new version onto the table, the pages still warm from the printer.

We both read through them one last time. The air around us, between us, is still and heavy. Without saying a word, he signs his name on the last page. And then I sign mine.

It's technically not official until we get this filed with the court, but it feels official right now.

Nikhil and I are done.

15

We spend the rest of the afternoon in the living room. After all the up-and-down emotions of this morning, it's rather anticlimactic. I get some work done on Nikhil's laptop, and he sits on the opposite side of the room studying. His classes have been canceled this week and next due to the storm, but he says he wants to use this time to catch up.

We don't talk to each other much over the next couple hours, but it's not as uncomfortable as I would have expected it to be. It's quiet, but in a good way. Almost peaceful.

Every now and then, I go upstairs to peek out the broken guest bedroom window. The water level is lower each time. It really seems like it might all clear up by morning. I'd never thought I'd feel so conflicted about that.

At some point, Nikhil falls asleep on the couch, his accounting textbook open on his lap, his lips slightly parted. He looks younger like this. The lines on his face softer. Smoother. A lock of hair falls over his forehead, and I resist the urge to push it back. He's not mine to touch. He's not mine to care for. He hasn't been for a long time, and now, he never will be again.

Pain pierces through me at the thought, and I escape to the pantry, needing space away from him, but also needing to figure out what I'm going to put together for dinner. I'm still not sure why I volunteered to make it in the first place, but I can't back out now.

After searching for a while, I find a can of garbanzo beans and a bag of spinach in the freezer. I dump both into a pot and whip up the saddest chana saag the world has ever seen. I made the fatal mistake of trying it, thinking it was tasteless, and then adding too much masala. Now it's not just thin and watery, but also so laden with spices I can feel the grit of them between my teeth.

Fortunately, I made rice to go with it, so there'll be at least one thing edible on the table.

To his credit, Nikhil doesn't say anything when he takes his first bite of the meal, though he follows it with a long sip of water.

"It's okay," I tell him, deciding to put him out of his misery. "I know it's bad. You don't have to eat it."

"No," he says. "It's not . . . it's not *that* bad." He swallows another forkful. "At least, it's not any worse than that time I accidentally made chili with cinnamon instead of cumin." He grins. "Any chance that's what happened here?"

I laugh. "It's definitely possible."

We stick to mostly eating the rice, and plucking a few pieces of chana out of the bowl. The gravy and the spinach seem to have soaked up my poor attempts at seasoning, but the chana itself isn't too bad, the flavor somewhat diluted when it's drowned by rice.

"I can take you to the airport tomorrow," Nikhil says.

"Oh. You don't have to—"

"I'm going to be driving that direction tomorrow anyway." His foot taps absently underneath the table. "I want to check on the property. I've been looking up reports from the area, but it seems mixed. Some houses got hit badly, while others scraped by. Not unlike our street, I guess."

Our street. Nikhil said that so easily. He doesn't even seem to notice it slipped. But that "our" causes a sharp pinch beneath my sternum. I rub the spot, trying to erase the sensation.

"If you're sure you don't mind, that would be great then. Thank you," I say.

"Yeah, of course."

We continue eating in silence for a couple minutes, and then Nikhil casually says, "Actually, we could stop by the property first if you want. On the way to the airport? I mean, I know we'd talked about you maybe seeing it, but that was when you were going to help with the grant stuff—"

"I'll still help with the grant applications, Nikhil. I'd be happy to do that."

"Okay. No pressure, though. I know you're busy. And I'm not sure if we even should go there. We'd have to leave a little early so we'd have time and the place is nowhere close to being done so I can just see it after I drop you off if you prefer that."

"I don't mind," I tell him. "I want to see it."

He smiles then, his teeth flashing. It's beautiful, and wonderful, and horrible, all at the same time.

"Have you decided on a name for the inn?" I ask. "What did they call the one in the show? It was, umm, the . . ."

"The Dragonfly Inn."

"Right. Hmm. Kind of generic, wasn't it? I think you can do better than that."

Humor shines in his eyes. "Sounds like you've got lots of opinions about this."

"I've got opinions about everything. You know me."

"Yeah," he says softly, "I do." He shakes his head. "So, let's hear it then. What names do you think would work better?"

I offer up some suggestions, but it turns out naming an inn is a lot harder than I'd thought.

"It's overlooking the water, right?" I say. "Maybe something about that?"

"And that doesn't sound too generic to you?"

I roll my eyes, and he lets out a snort of amusement.

We keep throwing out names, and our suggestions only grow more and more ridiculous as each of us tries to make the other person laugh. When I fall asleep later that night, I swear I can still hear his laughter echoing in my mind, and I'm struck by a strange thought.

I wish I'd recorded it. I wish I'd recorded that sound. Because I'm not sure if I'll ever hear it again.

The next morning, we leave several hours earlier than necessary. One, because I want to see the inn before I leave, but two, because the airport is going to be much wilder than usual. Every flight out of here is packed. A lot of people got stranded here due to the storm, and I'm sure they're just as desperate as I am to get back.

Or, as desperate as I *was*.

I don't let myself think too much about that though. I climb into the front seat of Nikhil's car and deliberately ignore the rearview mirror. I don't want to look back at the house. There's no point remembering it. There's no point reminiscing about the past, or what could have been. The papers stuffed at the bottom of my bag put an end to all of that. Put an end to us.

Nikhil drums his fingers against the steering wheel. After we're on the road for fifteen minutes, he says, "It's not too far from here."

I nod. "Great."

There's really nothing for the two of us to talk about, so I spend most of the drive looking out the window. It's safe to do so now that the house is miles and miles behind us.

It's amazing, really. How quickly things can seem back to normal after a storm. The streets are completely clear of water, but there are still telltale signs of what happened. Large, lakelike puddles in some of the grassy fields. Felled trees and giant branches. Every now and then, Nikhil has to change lanes or drive on the wrong side of the road to get past them.

He's turning now, down a muddy, uneven gravel road. We're on it for a few minutes, and then the house comes into view.

All the air rushes out of my lungs.

"Nikhil—" I say, but he's already out of the car, his door left open.

I unbuckle my seat belt and scramble after him. It doesn't take me long to catch up. He's frozen in place, his eyes fixed on this ramshackle building in front of us, framed by sea and sky.

I know the brackish blue-gray water in the background meets the ocean at some point, but it looks like it goes on forever. The overcast sky only makes it all feel even moodier and more atmospheric, and I can see the vision. I can see this being a perfect place to run from the city. To retreat. To sit on the porch with a book and a large cup of tea. Or on the dock looking over the water, with a fishing pole in hand. In the winter, there'll be a firepit in the front where guests can roast marshmallows and trade ghost stories, and find a sense of community even though they're far from home. I can see all of it.

Only that porch has fully collapsed, pieces of wood railing tossed to the ground. Like a giant ripped into it and scattered the pieces. The windows are boarded up, so those seem to be intact, but that hardly seems to matter. There's a difference in paint color on the house, a line that clearly demarcates how high the water got during the storm.

And from what I'm seeing, the first floor definitely took on some water. There's going to be damage inside. The bottom of the walls, at least a foot of Sheetrock, will need to be taken out and replaced.

I glance at Nikhil, and suddenly, there's a viselike grip around my heart.

I don't know what shape the property was in when Nikhil bought it, but from the shock written across his face, I know it wasn't as bad as this.

He takes a couple steps forward and slowly runs his hand over a wood beam. A low, dark laugh escapes him.

"Guess you don't need to worry about that grant stuff anymore," he says.

"Nikhil—"

"There's no point now. There's no—" He stops, shaking his head. Then, he takes off, walking around to the back, making a full circle of the property. I follow after him.

The back looks slightly better than the front, but then Nikhil lets out a loud groan. He's tipped his head back, so I do the same. And the roof . . . My god. It looks like a slice of Swiss cheese. Several large holes punched through, shingles completely missing.

"I can't fix this," Nikhil mutters. "This is too . . ." He runs a hand through his hair. "I'm going to have to sell."

"What?"

"There are always real estate developers who come in after storms like this. Vultures." He's still staring up at the sky, devastation written across his face. "They look for destroyed properties and flip them."

"But *you* can flip it," I say. I've seen the work he's done before. He's capable of doing it. He's capable of restoring this place. It would be hard and long and cost a lot more than it would have before, but I've promised Nikhil that I would help with that. I can still help with that. "If it's a funding issue, we can work it out. I'll find a way. You were insured, right? That might cover some of this—"

"No, it's not that," he says. "It's just . . . None of this . . . It doesn't—" He kicks a small piece of debris with the tip of his shoe and continues walking.

I swallow, unsure what to say or do. I want to fix this. I want to make it all better. But I can't wave a magic wand and erase the damage from this storm. I can't make it so that it never happened.

We head back to the car in silence, and Nikhil drives out onto the gravel road, leaving the same way we came. Before we turn back onto the main road, our eyes catch in the rearview mirror, both of us taking one last look at the would-be inn behind us.

"You can repair this, Nikhil," I try again. "You can. If you want to, I know you can."

"I can't." He gives a wan smile as he watches me, sorrow etched in every line on his face. "Some things are beyond repair."

We're quiet the rest of the drive, and when he drops me off at the airport, our goodbyes are simple. Muted. Our emotions are suppressed, trapped and hidden somewhere deep below.

I get out of the car and take a few steps away, but I'm half turned, watching Nikhil through the car window.

Say something, I think, but I'm not sure whether I'm talking to myself or to him. Still, I almost think he hears me because he lowers the window, just as a loud voice shouts, "Meena!"

Only Nikhil's lips aren't moving. My heart lurches, and then so does the rest of my body, as a man comes behind me, wrapping his arms around my waist.

This embrace . . . it's familiar, but he feels different. Lean where Nikhil is broad. Smooth cheeked where Nikhil has stubble.

Out of the corner of my eye, I watch Nikhil's brows lower, and I turn to face Shake, my muscles tense and stiff.

His eyes are shining, bright with excitement. They're brown, same as Nikhil's, but Shake's are a different shade. Flatter somehow.

"Shake, what are you . . . what are you doing here? How are you here?"

At my tone, the smile on Shake's face shifts, some of his earlier enthusiasm waning. He licks his lips. "I know we'd planned on waiting to talk until you got back, but I needed to see you. I needed to make sure you were okay. And since my client's jet was still available—"

"You took the jet?"

"I couldn't wait until tonight," he says. "I don't know if you saw my email, but I've scheduled a new meeting with the team. For both of us. To discuss you running here or there. I don't care which it is, as long as we're doing it together."

I blink. "You'd be okay with it? If I tried to run for the Texas seat? You'd be supportive?"

"Yes. I . . . This time apart . . . It gave me a lot of time to think, and I realized that I don't want to do any of this without you. We both have a better shot if we do this together, and as long as there's nothing standing in our way anymore . . ." He pulls back slightly, his eyes on my face. "I mean, you have it, right? The papers? You got them signed?"

I nod. "Yeah," I say, my voice low. "I have them."

Shake's smile returns. "Then let's go home." He lowers his face toward mine, and I freeze, stuck in place. My heart thumps wildly, and at the last second, I turn, so that his lips end up sliding against my cheek.

As I face the street, my eyes meet Nikhil's. He looks shocked, stricken, but my view of him is quickly blocked by a security officer rounding his car, loudly telling him to move out of the drop-off lane.

"Meena?" Shake asks, and I snap back to him.

"Sorry, I'm just . . . It's been a long few days."

"I bet." He takes my rolling bag from me and starts wheeling it. "Don't worry, we can talk about everything in more detail once you get some rest." He reaches for my hand, tugging me toward the airport entrance. "And at least you won't be flying commercial. It'll be a much more comfortable trip back on the jet." I follow, peeking over my shoulder, trying to see past the security officer. But as I enter the automatic glass doors, I realize I'm too late.

Nikhil's car is already gone.

16

TWO WEEKS LATER

He actually listed it. He's really going to sell.

I've been searching Zillow every day since I got back. When a week passed and nothing popped up, I'd assumed he'd changed his mind, but there it is. He's used older pictures of the property, though there's a note that it sustained serious damage recently. The price he's listed it at reflects that. He's practically giving it away.

I close my laptop, and push it away from me.

It's not any of my business. What he does with the property. Whether he sells it or keeps it. Whether he scraps it or rebuilds. I shouldn't care either way.

"Hey," Shake calls, his head popping around my office door. "You ready?"

"Yeah, I'll be right there." I change my Teams status to "out of office," grab my navy blue file organizer, and meet Shake in the hall.

After we'd landed in D.C., I'd told Shake I needed a little time before discussing everything. That I was still too exhausted to talk about it, and he'd understood.

"I ordered from that Greek place you like," he'd said when we'd reached my apartment. "It should be here in twenty, if you want to go take a shower? Relax a bit before it gets here?"

I'd done just that, and we'd kept the conversation over dinner light. He'd filled me in on more details from the meeting, updates on the drama going on at his work, the latest rumors and gossip on the Hill. It was the kind of dinner we'd had countless times in the past. Familiar. Companionable. Comfortable.

We'd sat on the couch afterward and turned on the news, flipping through the usual twenty-four-hour cable news channels before landing on C-Span. After a few minutes of the bland, unexciting roll call vote onscreen, my chest had grown tight, my breathing shallow. I'd retreated, saying I wanted to turn in early, and that I'd like some time alone, but I'd barely been able to sleep. I'd tossed and turned that night, my dreams dark and confusing, filled with rain and shadows, and flashes of a face I wanted to forget.

The following day was slightly better. Shake and I finally had that much-needed conversation about the Texas seat. I hadn't been able to deny that there were obvious advantages for both of us to run for Maryland state seats. That there was a congruency there. One half of a couple running for state senate, the other running for state house. Two Marylanders trying to serve their community.

But I also hadn't been able to give up the idea of Garcia's seat.

Ultimately, Shake and I decided to put the topic on hold until the meeting so we could see what the team thought. It didn't make sense to make a decision about it when we weren't even sure if it was a viable option yet.

Shake and I exit my office building and walk out into the sunshine. This part of D.C. is all concrete and history, and I love it. I love working here. I love living here. I always have. And why wouldn't I? This is exactly where I was supposed to end up. This is where I'd told my parents I'd end up. And they're so proud that it all came true. They're so happy. So *relieved*.

I remember the day I'd gotten into law school. I'd been wait-listed at a few of my top choices, but this was my first true acceptance. When I'd come home and told my parents, my father had let out a loud cry, wrapping me in a hug. "Congratulations, ma," he'd told me, before kissing me on the forehead. "You did it." Later that night, I'd overheard him speaking to my mother in Tamil, his voice full of joy. "We don't need to be worried about her anymore. She's going to be fine."

The sentiment had been sweet, and I should have been happy hearing it, but instead, I'd felt conflicted. Was this truly it? Was this all I had to do to ease my parents' worries? To prove that I wouldn't make the same mistakes as my sister? To prove that I was going to be okay?

My sister had sent me a "Congratulations" text that night, with no punctuation mark at the end of the word. It had stung, but the sweet hug my niece had given me the next day had made up for it. We'd hung out the rest of the day, my sister conspicuously absent. I can't remember where she'd been.

"We'll be a little early," Shake says, with a bounce in his step. "But that's better anyway. The more face time they have with you the better." He glances over at me. "I think they want to start talking about timing and when we'd want to announce. I know there are a few things we probably need to figure out before then, but still, exciting, right?"

I nod, even though my stomach is twisting in knots.

There's something I'd have to do before we announce, but I haven't gotten around to it yet. I tighten my grip on my bag, adjusting the strap around my shoulder. The papers are still sitting down at the bottom, probably a little crumpled by now.

It'll take me exactly two seconds to send them to my lawyer. I just need to scan and email them. Or I could even walk over and drop them off during my lunch break. His office isn't that far away. I don't know what I'm waiting for. Maybe for this meeting. Maybe I need a better sense of the plan before I take the first step. Maybe I need to talk to the advisory group first. Put faces to their names.

I wonder what they'll say about the Texas seat. Garcia hasn't publicly announced her retirement, so we're technically still ahead of the game. I'd prepared some preliminary research. Nothing big, but information about the district, my ties to it, some ideas on messaging and outreach.

I'd run it by Shake, and he'd listened, asked a few questions, told me it all sounded good. He'd been supportive, but things between us haven't fully returned to normal. It's almost as if both of us are trying too hard, walking around on eggshells, working to keep the peace.

There are still things we haven't talked about. He says he doesn't need to know all the details about my time in Houston. He said he just needed to hear that I have the papers, that they're signed, that it's all over with and done.

I'd said those words with false cheer and a breezy smile, but I wonder if he knows the truth. I wonder if he knows how awful it felt to say "over" and "done." I wonder if he notices how distracted I've been these last few days, memories flashing across my mind when I least expect them. I wonder if he notices how sometimes I'm just seconds from falling apart.

Either I'm hiding it better than I thought or he's pretending not to notice.

When Shake and I enter the conference room, the half dozen or so people around the table rise from their chairs. After a brief round of introductions, Alexa Miller, the young Black woman seated at the head, begins speaking.

My first impression of her is that she's much younger than I expected. Probably only in her late twenties. In fact, everyone in the room is younger than I'd expected. I'd imagined a room of old, wizened politicos, but nobody here matches that description.

She's wearing a faded vintage campaign T-shirt, with an oversize black blazer thrown on top. Her hair is up in a loose, messy bun, and behind the thick, dark frames of her glasses, her gaze is direct. Her tone is cutting. She's not messing around, and I immediately like her.

"We've got a lot to discuss today," Alexa says. "I'm sure Shake's caught you up a bit, but we think a joint run is going to attract a lot of attention. We've already gotten some bites from a few outlets, but we haven't been pursuing anything too hard. Just floating ideas. I know there's some stuff you need to sort out before we go public with an announcement. Though Shake's said you were wrapping that up, right?"

I resist the urge to glance at my purse, at the papers I should have gotten rid of by now. I swallow hard. I need to stop dragging my feet on this. Delaying it isn't helping anything. It's not making me feel any better. After this meeting, I'm going straight to my lawyer's office. I'm going to physically hand the papers over, and be done with this. I can't move forward; I can't sit here and discuss the future if I'm still caught up in the past.

"That's right," I say. "Just need to dot the *i*'s and cross the *t*'s and get it filed, but it's practically done."

She nods crisply. "Great. So, let's talk timing."

One of her associates dims the light in the room, and a presentation begins to play on the large screen on the wall. It's incredibly detailed. Thoughts on how and when we should announce, locations to do the announcement, reporters to invite, talking points for our speeches, strategies for fundraising, and proposed policy agendas for the two of us. We'd have shared core issues, but separate platforms with different areas of focus. It all sounds compelling.

As we go through each point, people around the table add their ideas. We ping-pong back and forth, and it's exhilarating. For a moment, the strange, hollow sensation that hasn't left my chest these past two weeks begins to fade, replaced by the energy and excitement in the room. Something that's been a dream for so long is starting to feel possible. This group—these *experts*—think it's possible. Finally, it all seems within reach.

The conversation turns to Maryland and the specific needs of the state, and some of my excitement wanes. Not all of it. I'd been drawn to this plan in the first place for a reason. Shake and I had both wanted to keep our jobs in the district, so our choice was either Virginia or Maryland. And based on the timing of seats up for election, Maryland had made the most sense. It had seemed like a great launching pad for our political careers. A stepping-stone for more.

Though now I know there's an opening in Texas that might make sense for me. One that would let me run for the House immediately, instead of waiting for some indeterminate time in the future. One that would let me help people who live in *my* city. My home.

I fidget in my seat, uncertainty building within me.

I'd planned to bring this up during this meeting. Shake and I had agreed that I would, but I'm not sure it's such a good idea anymore. The team's done all of this research. Shake's made all of these plans. And I signed on to them and agreed with him that Maryland is the safe route. It's the sure plan. It's what makes sense.

But if I ran for Garcia's seat, it would make it possible for me to . . . there at least would be the option to . . .

You'd move to Texas.

Nikhil's soft, low voice bursts in my mind, as unexpected and startling as a crack of thunder.

I blink and realize the presentation is over. There's a conversation in full swing now that I've apparently tuned out. Something about endorsements and who we might want to approach. Shake offers some thoughts about people he's worked with, and when he stops, I chime in before really thinking about it.

"What about Congresswoman Garcia?"

Out of the corner of my eye, I catch Shake glancing my way.

"Why? Do you know her?" Alexa asks.

"Not well. I've only met her once, but I've worked with her people before. I could probably get us a meeting."

"She'd be a great get," someone else says. "She's a legend."

"Yeah," I say, my confidence slowly growing. "She is. And this is something I wanted to get everyone's thoughts about actually, but she's not running again. She's going to retire."

Alexa quirks an eyebrow. "I haven't heard anything about that."

"Meena heard about it when she was down in Texas," Shake says. "It's just a rumor, but—"

"There are potential candidates in Houston taking it seriously," I say. "And I think we should too."

I sit up taller. "Garcia was my representative growing up. I'm from the district. I know it well. And I want to talk about potentially running for that seat."

A couple of people exchange glances.

"I thought you both were thinking Maryland," Alexa says. "Shake, you're still hoping to run for governor there at some point, right? I mean, that's still the long-term plan?"

"Right," he says. "That is still the plan. For me. But Meena's always wanted to run for Congress, and if this opportunity makes sense for her . . . if there's still a way for us to frame this right, still a way to launch our runs together, well, that's what we want to find out."

"I could still be here for Shake," I add. "If I run in Texas. We could still campaign together. I'd split my time between here and there. I'd be willing to come up for any big canvassing or fundraiser events, and Shake could come down for some of my stuff too. And if I won, I'd be here the majority of the time. I think it could be doable."

Alexa watches me thoughtfully for a moment. "Honestly," she says, "you'd be a great fit for that seat."

Shake's eyebrows jump, and a shooting sensation pierces through me. I'm not sure if it's my own surprise or something else.

"You're young, sharp, a great communicator," Alexa continues. "I actually saw you speak at the Keep Families Together rally a few years ago, and the passion in your voice, the way you connected with people. You're going to be great on the campaign trail, no matter what race you run in. Texas might be a tough sell since you haven't lived there in a while, but people like a hometown hero returning to their roots. We could spin it. It's not . . . it's not the worst idea in the world."

My pulse jumps, excitement and a bit of adrenaline coursing through me. I open my mouth, about to say *yes*. Or *let's do it*. Or at least provide some sort of response to Alexa's words.

Because she thinks it's possible, and really that's all I'd been hoping to hear. With all its flaws, Texas is my home. The laws are a nightmare, people's rights are under attack, but it's where I'm from. It's where I want to be making a difference. I'd never thought about going back before. I'd always thought D.C. was where I was supposed to be, where I could do the most good, but things shifted when I heard about Garcia's seat. When I was actually present in Houston. When I let myself imagine it.

When I talked about it with Nikhil.

I close my mouth, my throat suddenly dry, all the words I'd been about to say evaporating.

I want to run in Texas. I do. But can I be in Texas and not bump into Nikhil? Can I campaign minutes away from his house, *our* house, and not see him? Can I be so close—can I be his *representative*—and stay away from him?

Shake had been worried about that, and for good reason, because I don't know if I can. Letting him go has been hard enough these past two weeks, when we've been separated by more than a thousand miles. I don't know what would happen if I flew to Houston. I might cave the minute I land. I might break down, unable to resist the almost magnetic pull that draws me to him. The string that binds us together. The one I've never been able to sever.

The one I still haven't, even though I have everything I need to do it.

Shake's watching me, no doubt sensing the conflicting thoughts jumping through my mind.

"Could we have five?" he asks the team. "Just give us a moment to step out and—"

"No problem," Alexa says, grabbing her belongings and nodding for the rest of the team to follow suit. "You can have the room. We'll check back in a bit." She shoots me a quick, assessing look, then heads out with the others.

We're silent for a moment, then Shake sighs.

"You haven't filed them yet," he says. "You told Alexa you haven't filed the papers yet. I hadn't been sure before now. I hadn't wanted to ask you about it." He pauses. "Maybe because I already knew."

Just minutes ago, I'd been so sure that I'd leave this meeting and go straight to my lawyer. That I'd hand over the papers and walk away, but just the thought of it hurts. Not a sharp, pricking pain, but a dull ache. One that I've felt for a while, always hovering beneath the surface.

"You're still in love with him," Shake says, and I meet his gaze.

His eyes are clear, his voice calm. But he's preternaturally still, as if it's taking all of his effort to make sure he gives nothing away.

"I am," I say, and somehow, though my blood is racing, my voice comes out sounding just as calm as his.

He nods. "And you want to run in Texas?"

"I do."

He turns toward me, the first cracks in his veneer showing. There's some anger, some frustration, but there's something else too. It's almost like there's no fight left in him. Almost like . . . he's resigned.

"If you were sure about Texas," he says, "if it had nothing to do with him, nothing would have to change. We could still campaign together. But if you're saying you want to go back to him—" He stops, shaking his head. "You always told me how alone you felt when you were with him. How there were parts of him you felt like you never really knew. That he never really *let* you know. How would—how would going back to Houston fix things? How would that change anything?"

My mouth opens, but I don't have an answer for him. Nikhil's different now. We both are. That day we signed the papers, he'd recognized that he'd pushed me away. I'd always thought it was because he didn't see me as a real partner, that he didn't think I was capable or strong or competent enough to be there for him the same way he always was for me, but it wasn't that. He'd thought he'd had to prove something to me. My keeping him a secret had made him think that. I'd hidden him, hidden both of us, from my parents. I knew they'd have judged us, judged what we had, and found it lacking, and I hadn't wanted that to happen. I hadn't wanted to bring something so special before them only to watch it crumble.

But I'd made the wrong choice, because hiding him had hurt him so much more.

"He's still that guy, Meena," Shake continues. "The one who set your career back, who wasn't there for you when you needed him to be." He places his hand on mine, his touch light and gentle. "These feelings that you have . . . they'll fade. We've built something better than that, something that's so much more stable. And we're so close to announcing, so close to everything we've been working for. So close to actually trying to make this work. There's no reason to throw all of that away."

I swallow, my throat uncomfortably tight. I can see the exact future Shake is talking about. A life, a career, a marriage together.

A future with him makes sense, and walking away from all of it would come with consequences. I don't know what happens with the advisory team if Shake and I aren't a package deal. I could be slamming the door shut on my political future.

And it doesn't help that my family's met him. That my parents love him. That they've been hoping the two of us would take the next step sometime soon. If I walk away, how could I tell them that those hopes are never coming true?

What do you want, Meena?

Nikhil's voice pops back in my head, filling me with longing. *I don't know,* I'd tell him. And I can just imagine his response. The sad shake of his head. The small, knowing smile.

You, I'd finally say. I *want you.*

But it's too late for that. The voice in my mind must think so too, because it goes quiet. Nikhil doesn't say a thing. Though I suppose the papers he signed speak for themselves. He doesn't want me. Not anymore.

But does that mean I stay with Shake? All the things that drew me to our relationship—the shared ambition and drive, our easy friendship, the fact that he was *not Nikhil,* that he would never make me feel the way I did when I was with Nikhil—none of that feels like enough anymore.

Shake deserves more than I can offer him. And even if I can't have Nikhil, I deserve more than this too.

"I can't," I tell Shake. "I wish I could. You deserve that. You deserve to run for the seat, to get back into politics, and you deserve a partner who'll stand by you and help you achieve all of that and more. But I can't be that person. I can't."

Shake pulls back, his mouth setting into a firm, thin line.

"I think you're making a mistake," he says. "This, our relationship, the way we are together, it *works*. We're not going to find this again." A small note of desperation creeps into his voice. "*I'm* not going to find this again. I'm not going to find someone who . . . who gets me like this. Who would be content with what we have. Who would understand the kind of love we have for each other. Because I do, Meena. I love you."

"I know," I say, because I hear the lowercase *l* in that word. I hear the years of friendship and support and companionship in that word. I hear everything I was once afraid of losing. I hear what could have been enough if I hadn't known something more. "I love you too. And I . . . I just want you to be happy."

His eyes flash, something flickering across his face. "Maybe we don't all get to be happy." And I know what he means. There aren't any guarantees. He may not meet someone else to run for office with, he may open himself up to love again but not find it, or even if he does, it could all end in heartbreak again.

"Maybe," I say, thinking about Nikhil saying that I was right, that our marriage needs to be over. There aren't any guarantees that we get a second chance. I don't know if he'd be open to it, or if it would work. I don't know how any of this will turn out.

"But maybe," I tell Shake, "maybe we owe it to ourselves to at least try."

Shake watches me for a long moment. Disapproval, even a touch of concern, still lingers on his face, but he doesn't voice any of that when we say our goodbyes.

I grab my stuff and walk out the door, passing Alexa's office in the hall. Her door's shut, but her voice is loud and clear from out here. She's in the middle of a call.

I hesitate for a moment, feeling the slightest twinge of regret that I won't get to thank her. She and the team put time and effort and energy into formulating their plan, and I'm sure they'll go on to do great work with Shake. I've made my mind up. I'm sure I've chosen the right path, but I do wish there was some world where I could have worked with them.

I shake my head, deciding to send Alexa and the team a thank-you via email later.

Right now, there's somewhere else I have to be.

17

I pull up to the house, put my car in park, and stare out the window.

I haven't been here in a long time. In fact, it's been so long I can't remember the last time I came by for a visit. Maybe when they first moved to Jersey. When my sister and Ritu got this house that's only a few streets away from my parents'. It's definitely been years since I visited, but I didn't know where else to go.

I need to talk to someone. I need to share all the secrets that have been piling up. I *want* to share them. I can't change the mistakes I made in the past, but I can make different choices going forward.

I can choose to tell my family about Nikhil. About everything.

I'd first thought about calling Ritu, but she's on a graduation trip backpacking through Europe with her friends for the summer. And it hadn't felt right to bombard her with the details of her aunt's messy life. I'd thought about confessing everything to my parents, but the idea had sent me careening down an anxiety spiral. That seemed like too much too fast. I needed a baby step, and confiding in my sister felt like it might be just right. Something in between the comfort that talking to Ritu would have been and the terror of talking to my parents.

But my sister and I have never really had a heart-to-heart like this. I've never really come to her for advice. We've never had that kind of relationship. That distance has always been a little hurtful, but maybe one of us needs to make the first move. Besides, it's not like I have a lot of other options.

I knock on the door, and smile weakly when my sister answers. "Hi, Akka."

"Meena?" She blinks, tying the belt of her night-robe around her. "What are you doing here? What happened? Are you all right?"

The care in her voice, the genuine concern that she has for me sends pinpricks to the corners of my eyes. "No," I say hoarsely. "I don't think I am."

She lets me in, and when we sit on the couch, the words tumble out of me.

"I'm married. And I . . . I'm in love with him."

"With Shake?"

"No."

"Oh, thank god."

My head rears back in surprise, and my sister grins. "What? No matter what Mom and Dad have been pushing, it's always been clear the two of you weren't in love. Not really."

"Yeah," I say. I rub my arm absently. "I'm just more surprised that you noticed that about us. Or that you'd care either way."

Her smile falls a bit. "Of course I'd care, Meena. And I'm glad you didn't give in to the pressure Mom and Dad have been putting on you and . . . Wait." Her eyes grow round. "Did you just say you were married?"

"Yeah." I let out a half laugh, half sigh. "Maybe we should start there."

"Yeah, we should." A loud whistle sounds from the kitchen, and she jumps up from the couch. "I put the kettle on earlier. I was going to make some tea, but it sounds like we need something stronger than that." She ducks out of the living room, returning minutes later with a pair of mugs and a bottle of amber liquid.

"I haven't unloaded the dishwasher," she says, setting the mugs on the coffee table. "So, these will have to do." She pours some cheap cinnamon-flavored whiskey in each of them and passes one to me before settling into the cushions.

"Why do you even have this?" I ask, pointing at the bottle. My sister's taste runs more toward a glass of red wine on a Friday night. Maybe a margarita if she's feeling wild. Fireball is completely out of the norm for her.

She shakes her head. "College leftovers. You don't want to know all the things we found when we cleaned out Ritu's dorm. Her roommates were a mess. We threw out most of their stuff, but this one was still sealed, so I figured why waste it?"

"Weird to think that she's old enough to drink now."

My sister rolls her eyes. "Tell me about it."

I take a sip, the heat burning in a surprisingly comforting way as it slides down my throat. The warmth gathers in my belly, reducing some of my fears. Still, when I open my mouth, nothing comes out.

I don't know how to talk about Nikhil. Except for Shake, I've never told anyone about him. And I've never really gone into all the details of it before. I've never told anyone about everything that happened in Vegas, about how it felt to fail the bar, about all the things that drove Nikhil and me apart.

My sister leans toward me, placing a hand on my arm, squeezing gently.

"Start at the beginning," she tells me. "Or wherever you want to start. It doesn't matter. Whenever you're ready, I'll be here."

The tightness in my chest loosens a tiny degree. I take a deep breath, and begin.

"So, you and Nikhil ended up signing the divorce papers?" my sister asks, about an hour or two later.

I nod. "Yeah, but I haven't dropped them off yet, so technically we're still married."

The room's quiet for a moment, then my sister exhales loudly. "God, Meena. I'm so sorry."

I startle. "Sorry? No, Akka, you don't have anything to be sorry about. I'm the one who should be apologizing to *you*. And Mom and Dad and Ritu . . . I kept all of this a secret from you and—"

"No. I'm just so sorry that you felt like you had to. I mean, I understand not telling Mom and Dad about everything. Believe me. But I'm so sorry you've been dealing with all of this on your own. I'm so sorry I made you feel like you couldn't tell me any of this. I know that there's this distance between us and that it's . . . A lot of it's my fault." She looks down at the floor for a second, before returning her gaze to me.

"We never really got a chance to know each other," she says. "You were still so little when I went off to college, and then I got pregnant with Ritu, and honestly everything in those early years is still such a blur. I was just trying to get through the day and make sure Ritu was all right. I had no idea what I was doing. But . . . I know I kept my distance from you. Even after I managed to get everything together, I still . . . I don't know. Mom and Dad never told me this explicitly, but I always felt like they worried about me being a bad influence on you or something. And at a certain point, it just seemed like I was too late, you know? You and Ritu had this incredible bond. You still do. And I know that's not something I'm a part of. And that's fine. I get it. I'm so happy she has you. She couldn't ask for a better aunt. But because of that, I thought you didn't need that from me. That you had the sister you should have always had, the sister you *deserved,* in Ritu. But if I'd known . . . if I'd known that you were going through all of this by yourself, I would have been there for you, Meena. I would have."

My throat grows tight with emotion.

"But I'm here now," she continues. "For whatever you need. And Ritu will be too."

"Thanks, Akka," I say, my mind still reeling. I hadn't expected her to respond this way. I don't know what I'd expected, but it wasn't this.

My sister's never been unkind toward me, but she's always been aloof. Not that I'm surprised that she's capable of being caring and compassionate and present. I've seen her be that way with Ritu. She's an incredible mom. She's never been that way with me.

"I appreciate you saying that," I tell her. "But I guess the problem is . . . I don't know what I need. I don't really know what I'm supposed to do now. I started the day with Shake and a plan for the future, and now all of that is gone. It was my choice, and I don't regret it, but I don't have a backup plan in place. I don't know what to do next. I'm just . . . stuck."

My sister sighs. "I know that feeling. And I know how terrifying it is. I'm forty-two years old, and for the first time in my life, I don't know what I'm going to do next. Raising Ritu was the best decision I ever made. I wouldn't go back, I wouldn't trade it for anything, but now that she's graduated, I feel a little lost. Like my life is starting over. And . . . I'm scared."

"Of what?"

"Of messing up again. Of letting them down again." She swallows. "Did you know I've been going to therapy? It's been years now, ever since Ritu started middle school. She'd been having a hard time then, so I looked into it for her sake, but I quickly realized I need it too." She watches me for a moment. "Have you ever felt like Mom and Dad's love is conditional?"

Surprise bolts through me. "I . . . I don't know how to answer that." I'm not sure if I've ever thought about it like that before, but something about that word—*conditional*—it strikes a chord deep within me.

Akka lifts a hand. "I'm not saying that it's true. I'm not saying that their love is actually conditional. I'm just saying that sometimes I *feel* like that. You know, I watched the way they were with you. How happy they were at your graduations, when you got your first job, when you achieved all these wonderful things. They weren't like that with me when I got my first raise or my first promotion. I mean, I know it's not the same thing, but their different responses . . . I couldn't help but feel like they loved you more because you did all of these things that I couldn't do. I didn't handle it well, but I was able to work through a lot of it in therapy. I realized how proud I am of myself, of the things I accomplished."

"As you should be, Akka. Everything you've done, for Ritu, for yourself, it's incredible. The way you handled everything on your own, I would never have been able to do that. I would never have been able to do what you did. I look up to you. I always have."

She smiles softly. "Thank you. It's just . . . until this moment, I didn't realize you might have felt the same way. That you may have been so set on achieving and doing all of these things because you were scared of that love going away. And then once you failed for the first time, I don't know how you felt, but I can imagine it was hard.

That you might have been scared not just of what they'd say, but how they might feel toward you."

It had been hard. That failure had shattered me. It had made me question everything. I'd hidden from my parents, from everyone, because I think deep down, my sister is right. I had been scared of losing their love.

And I think I'd hidden myself from Nikhil for the same reason. I'd been so scared of him seeing past the put-together, confident, high-achieving front I showed the world. With every exposed fracture, every time I let him in, I'd been terrified that his love would vanish. And as he'd retreated, revealing less and less of himself to me, I'd thought that was what was happening. When he didn't move with me, I'd been sure it was because he decided I wasn't worth it.

But that's not true. He told me that wasn't true.

"I haven't thought about it in those terms before," I tell my sister. "But I think . . . it's possible. That I was scared of exactly that. I think . . . I might still be. Not just with them, but with Nikhil too."

My sister grabs my hand, squeezing it lightly.

"Can I speak plainly?" she asks, and I nod.

"The way I see it, you've dropped the idea of being with Shake. You're in love with a guy who sounds pretty great. And—what a stroke of luck—you happen to already be married to him. But instead of having some joyful reunion down in Texas, you're here, so . . . what is it exactly that you're scared of? Why aren't you rushing to see him?"

Despite myself, I almost grin. This is the side of my sister I'm much more familiar with. The cut-and-dried, no-nonsense tone. Quick and direct. Always getting straight to the point. Actually . . . she sounds a lot like me.

"It's not that simple," I say.

"I know. But tell me why. Why isn't it that simple?"

"Because I don't know what he's thinking. I don't know how he feels. I mean, he signed the papers, Akka. And he made it sound like he thought that was best. That we both needed a clean break and a chance to start over and—"

"But isn't that what you told him? Isn't that what you told him you wanted?"

"Yeah, but—"

"So, it sounds like he listened to you. My question is, have you been listening to him?"

Shame floods through me in a flash. My sister's words remind me too much of what Nikhil once told me. That I was a steamroller. That I rushed and pushed my wants and desires without considering his.

He'd wanted me to stay. He'd wanted me to be with him. He'd asked me to. And I'd told him that I wanted to come back here to run for office, that I wanted to do it with Shake, so he'd given me that instead.

What am I scared of? Really, the question should be what am I *more* scared of? Because I'm scared that I just blew up my chance at a political future. I'm scared that by not going through with my plans with Shake I've left my dream career in the dust. But I'm even more scared of losing Nikhil for good.

Part of me wants to run to Houston. To show up at Nikhil's doorstep and tell him that I love him, but I want to do more than just tell him. I want to show him that I've been listening. That I've been listening to what he wants, that I *care* about what he wants. I want to support him and his dreams, the way he always supported mine.

I quickly pull my phone out of my purse and enter a website I've visited numerous times over the past two weeks. I only have to type the *z* for the exact link to populate. I wait, but the page loads at a glacial pace.

"What's your Wi-Fi?" I ask my sister. She rattles it off, along with a complicated password, and I enter it in, hoping it'll speed things up.

"What are you doing?" she asks, leaning over my shoulder to peek at the screen.

"Nikhil bought this place. An inn. But it took a hit during the storm, and he's listed it for sale, but he basically listed it for nothing. I'm going to put in an offer. Just so if he changes his mind, he can have it back. And if he really doesn't want it anymore, I'll sell it. I'll help him find a new place. A better property. But the way he talked about this one . . . I don't want him to regret giving it up."

The page finally loads, but my stomach sinks as I read the words under the address.

Off Market.

No. No, no, no. I knew someone would snap it up. At that price and with that location, I'd expected it to happen, but I thought I might have been fast enough. I thought I might have had a shot.

I search, trying to find out who bought the place, but nothing comes up. Whoever grabbed it must have wanted to keep it private. I groan.

"Someone bought it," I tell my sister. My head hits the back of the couch, my body slumping with defeat.

"Who?"

"It doesn't say."

We sit in silence for a bit, my big imagined grand gesture moment crumbling into nothing. When we were together Nikhil rarely talked about his dreams. He was vague those areas of his life. He didn't talk about school or work or his own ideas for the future, but now he has. He didn't have to, but he showed me the inn. He laid his dreams for the future bare. He was vulnerable in a way that I'd never seen from him, and for the first time that I can remember, he asked me for help. And I'd promised him that I would give it. I'd promised to help with securing funding for the repairs. I can't break that promise now.

Nikhil was there for me, through my lowest and darkest moments. When I failed the bar, he didn't let me give up on my dreams. He encouraged me, supported me, and listened to me. He held me while I was broken so I could put myself back together. How can I not do the same for him?

I sit up straight, opening a new window on my phone. "I'm going to Houston," I tell my sister.

"What?"

I check for flights, quickly making plans. "I'm going to go down there. I'm going to find out who bought the place and I'm going to get it back."

My sister's eyes light with surprise. "But how . . . how are you going to do that?"

"I'll check the property records. I'll ask around. I'll show up at the site and see who's working on it. I don't know, but I'll figure it out." I smile, feeling hopeful for the first time in weeks. This might be the worst, least thought-out plan I've ever had, but I've never felt so confident. So sure that things will turn out. I don't know how yet, but something about this feels right.

My sister smiles in return. "I'm sure you won't need it, but I'm wishing you all the luck," she says, clinking her mug against mine.

My flight doesn't leave until early morning, so we stay up late talking, mending the rift between us piece by piece. I wish we'd done this years ago. Now I know that my sister would have understood what I was going through back then. She had felt those same fears and worries; she still feels this burden of being a disappointment to our parents. But like she tells me, that disappointment isn't the end of the world.

"My life doesn't look the way they thought it should," she says. "It doesn't look like yours, but I think it worked the way it was supposed to. I'm not saying Mom and Dad were wrong for wanting our lives to be set and sure and easier than theirs, for prizing stability. I can't blame them for that. But from that good desire came . . . well, this. All this stress and pressure you felt. I had no idea you were going through all of that."

"Yeah, well, I tried to hide it."

"And you succeeded." Her eyes soften. "Are you . . . With your career and job, are you happy? Is this something you really wanted or did Mom and Dad make you feel like you had to? Because you don't, Meena. You don't have to do any of it if you don't want to. You deserve to do something that brings you joy."

I'm quiet for a moment. I'm not sure whether I've really thought about my career this way. About my dreams and aspirations. Do I really want any of this, or have I just been trying to live up to some unreachable expectation? Have I just been trying not to let my parents down? To not lose their love?

"I don't know," I say. "Part of this I chose. I chose law school. Not medical school like they originally wanted. Like they wanted for you. I picked D.C. I picked being involved in politics. I always wanted to help people, and I still want that. But this . . . this pressure, this drive, this intensity. I don't know if that was me. I don't know if I would have always been like that. And I'd be lying if I said my desire to run for office is just about wanting to help people." I think back to what Elizabeth had said, about the reasons why people run for office. "I think . . . part of what I like about it is the prestige. The recognition that comes with it. The idea that Mom and Dad would be able to see me. That they'd see I was doing something important. Something that mattered. Something that they could be proud of. If I take that part away . . . I think I'd still want it, but I don't know. I'm not sure."

I go to sleep that night still thinking about it, unsure how I feel. Walking away from Shake had been the right choice. I'm sure of that. But the idea of giving up on a political future entirely still stings. And I'm not sure if that's because I actually want it as much as I've always thought, because I think it would make me happy, because it would allow me to really make a difference, or if it's rooted in something else. Something deeply ingrained in me. Pride or fear or this pressure I've been operating under for so long.

In the morning, my sister wraps me in a big hug before I leave.

"Whenever you get back, whenever you get everything sorted, you just let me know, okay?" she says. "And whenever you're ready to tell Mom and Dad, I'll support you. And I know Ritu will too." She pauses. "Maybe we can both take a week off sometime and go visit her during her trip? In France or Italy or wherever she happens to be at the moment? Might be nice to spend some time together, just us girls?"

"Yeah," I say, warmth filling me at the thought. "I'd like that." I give her a final hug before heading to the airport.

As wonderful as jetting off to Europe sounds, those plans will have to wait. Right now, I'm going home. To Houston. And somehow, I'm going to make all of this work.

18

When I walk out of Hobby Airport I'm greeted by thick, heavy humidity, but it doesn't remind me of hell this time. Instead, I think of warm summer breezes, the scent of salt in the air, vast expanses of water stretching as far as the eye can see. I think of a building with a porch, a firepit in the front yard, and a dock reaching out into the bay. A home away from home for travelers. An escape from the city. A gathering place for the community.

And standing on that porch is a tall, dark-haired man, greeting people with a wide, heart-stopping smile as they enter his inn.

I tighten my grip around my suitcase handle, dragging it behind me with purpose, resolve coursing through my veins. Come hell or high water, I'm going to make this vision come true.

I climb into the Uber, making a stop at my hotel to drop off my bags before taking another car to the property. I don't really have anywhere else to go. I have no other leads.

I'd searched property records and called in favors, but no one had been able to find out anything about the new owner. There hadn't even been any public documentation about the sale. Everything still listed Nikhil as the owner, though I've been told it's not uncommon for there to be a delay while the new paperwork gets filed. That sometimes it takes a while to update all the records.

I'm not expecting to stumble upon the new owner at the site today, but I am hoping whichever developer bought the place will have started some kind of repair work by now. Sheetrock and flooring have to be stripped quickly after a flood. Otherwise, mold can set in, causing a whole host of issues. Someone should be working there today, taking care of all of that, and I hope they'll be able to give me some insight about the owner.

I haven't told Nikhil that I'm in town. I haven't told anyone really, except for my sister. And I'm not sure I should tell him just now. I don't want to get his hopes up about the property or confuse him. Really, I'm not sure what kind of reception I'm going to get from Nikhil. Maybe I'm just delaying the inevitable. Maybe there's nothing left for us. But I'm going to get him his inn back, even if it doesn't mean I'll get *him* back. I have to make sure he doesn't give up on this. I have to make sure he knows that I see his dream. His vision. That I see *him*.

The car turns onto the rough gravel road, and disappointment creeps through me when we come to a stop at the front of the house.

There doesn't seem to be anyone here. No construction crew ripping out the rotting wood. No one on the roof patching up the holes. I'd hoped to see some activity. Some movement on repairing the place. If the new owner is just letting it sit, there may not be anything left to salvage.

I'm about to ask my driver to just take me back to the hotel when a loud *clang* sounds through the air.

I swing the car door open, my eyes scanning the house from top to bottom, trying to find the source of the sound.

"Hello?" I call. "Is anyone here?"

No one answers. I strain my ears, hoping to hear that noise again, but all I hear is the crunch of tires over pebbles as my Uber drives away.

I stare at the house, unsure whether I should venture inside. The porch is likely not safe to walk on, and whoever owns the place probably wouldn't leave the door unlocked, so I make a wide circle around the building instead. When I've almost reached the back of the house, I hear that loud *clang* again.

I move faster.

"Hello?" I cry.

Another *clang*.

Something bright and shiny propped up against the side of the house catches my eye. A ladder. My gaze follows the line of it up and up and up, until I reach the end. And there near the top of the roof is a lone, solitary figure.

The person is crouched down near one of the holes, though that hole seems a lot smaller than I remember it.

Relief trickles through me. Someone *is* fixing this place up. For a moment I'd been worried that whoever bought it had just planned on scrapping it for the land, but if someone's working on repairs then this place still has a chance.

I squint up, lifting a hand to block some of the sun's glare, but I still can't fully make the person out.

I almost call out again but stop when I see the figure move. It's a quick, sudden swing of an arm and then another *clang*.

I wait until they're done, then give it a try. "Hello," I say, louder than before, cupping my hands around my mouth. "Can you hear me up there?"

Silence for a beat.

"Yes?" a man's voice calls back.

My body almost sags at the staggering joy I feel. I'm not too late. This madcap, absolutely absurd plan might actually work.

"Hi! I'm sorry. I know you probably just bought this place. Or maybe you're working on it for the person who did, but I need to talk to the owner. Or if it's you, I guess I need to—"

"Hold on a sec," the man shouts back. "I can barely hear you. I'm coming down."

He shimmies across the roof, and something about the movement seems so familiar. I guess I *have* watched Nikhil do this a lot, back when I used to visit him while he was working. It's a pretty distinctive kind of dance, which requires you to move slowly and carefully, making sure to find the right footholds. And I imagine it's even harder on a roof like this. One so fragile, with shingles missing here and there.

With his back toward me, the man swings one foot onto the top rung of the ladder, and I rush to hold the base.

There's a pair of ropes tying the bottom of the ladder to a stake, so he must have secured it properly before climbing, but I still feel the need to keep it steady.

We're both quiet as he climbs down. At first, I track his progress, but that means I'm basically staring at his ass, which seems impolite. I shouldn't be ogling some random guy's butt, even if the millisecond glimpse I caught of it made it seem like it's a very good one.

I look at my feet instead, then at my hands clutching the ladder.

"So," I say, no longer able to handle the silence. "Sorry about before. And sorry to make you come down. I didn't mean to take you away from your work. I'm just looking for the owner. I saw the house was listed recently and I was hoping to put an offer in, but someone snatched it up. Or if you're the owner, I guess you did. And you probably wouldn't be interested in selling if that's the case, but I do want to make an offer. And it would be a competitive one, so maybe we could—"

"You're right," he says. "I don't want to sell."

I startle, my heart thudding fast. His voice is so close, and I *know* that voice. I peer up, and realize he's hovering just above me.

I back away from the ladder, giving him space to swing down. He does, then bends over, dusting something off his jeans before straightening to his full height.

Even though I've just figured out that the mystery man on the roof was Nikhil, the sight of him is a shock to the system. Electric and sudden and jarring.

My eyes greedily run over his face, cataloging all the features I haven't seen in days. His stubble is longer. I guess he's let it grow out a little. But otherwise, he looks the same. Though his eyes look a little tired. Fatigued.

I want to wrap my arms around him. I want him to draw me close. I want to feel his heartbeat against mine and his chin resting on top of my head. I want to tell him that I've missed him. That I love him. But his expression stops me in my tracks.

More accurately, his *lack* of expression.

He doesn't look happy to see me. And I can't blame him for that. But he doesn't look angry either. Or confused. His face doesn't reveal anything at all.

"I came because . . . I wanted to—"

"You wanted to buy the house," he says evenly. "I heard that part."

I swallow. "Right. Well, I didn't realize . . . I thought you sold it."

He crosses his arms. "I didn't."

I scramble for words. My barely-thought-out plan is falling apart. I suppose I should be used to that by now, but this was supposed to be my moment. My way of showing Nikhil how much he means to me. Without the plan, I'm not sure how I'm going to do that. I'm not sure what I can say.

I'm stuck in place. My body and mind frozen.

After watching me for a long moment, Nikhil lets out a sigh. "Meena, why are you here? You don't owe me anything. The terms of the divorce are settled. I don't need some . . . some consolation prize. Or some gift from you because you feel guilty or because you pity me or—"

"No, Nikhil. It's not that." I take a deep breath. "I didn't turn in the papers."

His brows knit, and I force myself to continue.

"The divorce papers. I didn't turn them in."

Something bright flares in his eyes, hope or something a lot like it. I hold on to it, even when it flickers out quickly and his face returns to that dull nothing expression, I hold on to it like a lifeline.

"Was there something wrong with them?" he asks.

"No," I say quickly, then shake my head. "Yes, actually. All of it. All of it was wrong." I take a step toward him. "I didn't come here just to find out about the house. I mean, I wanted to buy the house, but only because I thought you were going to sell it. I thought you were going to walk away from all of this, and I couldn't let that happen. You deserve this, Nikhil. You deserve to be happy."

He doesn't react. Not even a little bit.

A lump forms in my throat. "But," I say, "I guess you didn't sell the place, so you already know all of this and—"

"Why didn't you file the papers?" he asks, and for the first time, his voice is gentle; it's lost some of its earlier hardness.

My vision blurs, tears forming at the corners of my eyes. "Because I couldn't. Because I . . . Because I'm . . ." Something hot and wet slides down my cheek. I lift the back of my hand to wipe it, but

Nikhil's already there. His hand holds my jaw, and his thumb slides across my cheekbone.

"Because you're what?" he asks. He's so close I can feel the breath of his words on my skin.

"Because I'm in love with you." I squeeze my eyes shut. "I've always been in love with you."

"Meena," he whispers. Something light touches my forehead. A brush of his fingers, I think, but I don't move. Not an inch. I'm too terrified of what he might say. Terrified of what I might lose.

"Look at me," he says gently, and slowly I open my eyes.

He's no longer watching me blankly. His face is a kaleidoscope of emotion. Vibrant and colorful. With each millisecond, it shifts. From hope to fear to so much joy it makes me ache.

"I love you," he says, cradling my face in both of his palms. "I've never stopped. Never. I've never not been in love with you."

A sob of relief escapes my lungs, and he catches the sound with his mouth. In the days apart, I've replayed every kiss, every touch we shared during the storm, but this . . . It's better. It's not us desperately clinging to a few stolen moments, terrified that each second is bringing us closer to goodbye. There's a certainty to each movement, a rightness. There's no more bitter aftertaste of a looming expiration date. There's just us.

Nikhil's hand sneaks around to the small of my back. He pulls me closer against him, and I melt, the warmth from his body transferring to mine.

He loves me. He loves *me*. Still. After everything.

After a few minutes, he slows, his firm lips sliding one final time across mine before he pulls back entirely.

For a second, I'm worried, but he doesn't step away, and my anxiety melts entirely when he leans toward me, his forehead resting against mine.

"We need to talk," he says, with just a tiny amount of regret, making it clear he doesn't quite want to. That he'd much rather continue as we were, but he's right. There's so much we haven't said to each other. So much we've both buried and neglected all these years.

"All right," I say.

We stay like that for a moment, our breaths intermingling, and then we part.

But as we walk back to the front of the house, Nikhil reaches toward me, slipping his hand into mine.

19

"Where's your car?" I ask. I should have thought about that earlier. I hadn't seen a car in the driveway when I'd gotten here.

"I have a new hire," Nikhil says, his fingers lightly squeezing the back of my hand.

It's the most casual of touches. Nothing, really, compared to all that we've done, but it sets my nerves on fire.

"A new hire?" I repeat.

"Yeah." Nikhil smiles. "Someone really wise pointed out I have a problem accepting help. I'd never put that together, but I mentioned it to Elizabeth, and she almost laughed. She reminded me that she'd offered to help with the grant stuff before, and that she'd sent me résumés of volunteers she knew who were looking for part-time paid work, but I'd always shrugged her off. When I decided to keep the place, I realized just how much help I needed, so I hired one of the people Elizabeth mentioned. I don't have the funds for a whole crew, but something is better than nothing. Anyway, he took my car to pick up some more supplies, but he'll be back soon."

I nod, my throat growing tight. "I'm so happy you did that."

A pleased flush spreads across his cheeks, and I want to say more. I want to tell him how proud I am of him for not giving up on the inn, for accepting help, for working so hard to make it all come true. Even if I'd never come back, he would have been right here, steadily working toward his goals.

I know that's a good thing, but I can't help but feel a little conflicted. In all my imaginings of this moment, I had a role to play. I was part of all of this. I was part of helping Nikhil get the inn back. But he doesn't need me for that, and now, I don't know where I fit into any of this. *If* I fit in.

Anxiety thrums through my veins, increasing my heartbeat.

Fortunately, Nikhil doesn't seem to notice my inner turmoil. He leads us out onto the dock, and we take a seat at the end of it, our legs dangling off the edge, both of us facing the water, my hand still tucked into his.

"I spent years thinking about this," Nikhil says, breaking the silence between us. "Of you coming back here one day. I'd imagined that when you did come back, I'd have something, some successful business of some kind. I thought if I became someone, maybe I could find you. Maybe I'd go back to D.C. and actually have something to offer you. But . . ." He stops, turning to look back at the house over his shoulder, a tinge of embarrassment on his face.

I lift a hand, cupping his cheek, forcing his gaze back to me.

"I'm sorry," I say. "I'm sorry I ever made you feel like you had to prove something like that, because you didn't, Nikhil. You never needed to *become* someone. I didn't need you to be anyone else back then, and I hate that I made you feel like I did." I take a deep breath.

"Hiding you from my family, from everyone, it had so much more to do with me than it did with you."

His body goes stiff beside me, but I continue.

"Really. It did. I cared too much about what my parents would think. I cared too much about disappointing them, about being judged by them, and all their friends. The way they'd all judged my sister. I worried that they wouldn't love me anymore. I worried they'd think I was a failure. That *I* was a failure. Not you, Nikhil. It was never about you. I . . . I felt so ashamed. Every day. You were working so hard, working extra hours, and taking care of everything, and I couldn't contribute. I was helpless. I wasn't supposed to mess up like that. I wasn't supposed to fail. I wasn't supposed to be that person. I didn't know what to do."

He watches me for a moment, and his expression softens, compassion and understanding clear in his gaze.

"Meena," he says softly. "No one expects you to be perfect. I don't. You're allowed to mess up. You're allowed to be a full human person. You're allowed to fail. And none of that"—his eyes flare, bright and intense—"none of that would ever make me stop loving you. Ever.

"And you weren't the only one who didn't know what they were doing. *I* didn't know what I was doing. I . . . I knew you were struggling and I didn't know how to reach you. How to help. You were going through so much with the bar and your family, and I wanted to just be . . . fun. The easy part of your life. I didn't want to come home and dump all my stuff on you. All the stress I had with work and the long hours and how I wasn't sure if I wanted to do it anymore. I didn't want to tell you any of that and make you feel worse. I didn't want to tell you that I had other dreams and thought about doing something else one day. I didn't want to give you a reason to leave me. I thought you had enough reasons already. But . . . hiding everything I was going through, hiding how I felt about things, it wasn't fair to you."

I'm quiet for a moment. "I didn't understand why you were shutting me out," I finally say.

Pain flashes through his eyes. "I didn't know I was. I didn't know I was making you feel that way."

"I mean, I can understand why you kept those things to yourself. I didn't then, but now I understand how you felt. It's just . . . I wanted you to confide in me. I wanted to share the load where I could. I wanted to help."

He pushes a loose piece of hair behind my ear. "I wanted that too. I wanted to do that for you too."

I lick my lips, my mouth feeling dry. "And I'm sorry if I made you feel like you couldn't share those things with me. If I made you feel like my dreams . . . like the things I wanted were more important. If you felt like I . . . steamrolled over you and—"

He winces. "I said that, didn't I? Or something like that."

I nod.

"I'm sorry," he says. "I thought you were leaving me behind. I was hurt and angry and once you passed and had what you needed, I felt like you could leave and go to D.C., that you didn't need me anymore and—"

"I needed you, Nikhil. I've always needed you." I swallow, looking down at the dock. I rub my fingers against the grain of the wood. "And you were right. At least partially. I know I was so laser-focused on the things I wanted back then, but the things you wanted matter too. But I'm so happy you're working toward what you want now. That you decided to keep this place." I pause. "Though you seemed so sure about selling it before. I don't . . . What made you change your mind?"

He looks back at the house for a moment, then leans toward me, tilting my chin up until our eyes meet.

His are misty and shining, the flecks of gold there burning bright. "I figured nothing's ever too far gone," he says softly. "That some things are worth rebuilding. Even if it means rebuilding them from the ground up."

My heart squeezes, and then he brushes his lips against mine.

This kiss contains everything we've said to each other and everything we haven't. Apologies from him to me. From me to him. And at some point, seconds or minutes later, there's forgiveness too. Traveling both ways. Settling deep inside of us. Healing old wounds. Clearing out leftover debris. Creating space to build something new.

My arms fly around his neck, and something rough rubs against my skin. A faint memory strikes me, of the last time we kissed. I'd thought I'd felt something around his neck before. Something rough and abrasive. A chain or necklace of some kind.

I run my fingers over it, but Nikhil stops me, his hand closing around mine.

"What is this?" I ask, but he doesn't respond. Not with words. He just lifts my hand, running it down the line of the chain, until we reach the front. My fingers coast over something hard and round, and I pull his necklace out from under his shirt.

Two small gold loops hang like pendants on his chain, and all the air leaves my lungs.

It's his ring. And mine.

"You kept them?" I ask softly.

"I wear them," he says. A small, almost sheepish smile plays at the corners of his mouth. "I just never . . . I couldn't . . . Even when I stopped wearing it on my hand it never felt right not to have it. I couldn't seem to take it off."

My lips return to his, closing the gap between us, and he returns my kiss with equal fervor.

"I wish I'd kept mine," I tell him. "I wish I'd taken it with me."

"It's yours," he says. "I've just been holding on to it. Keeping it safe. But it's always been yours. *I've* always been yours."

Our mouths meet again, and we stay that way for a long moment, until Nikhil breaks away.

"So," he says, a moment later, slightly out of breath. "We're still married."

"Yeah," I say, in a bit of a daze, still running my fingers over the rings. Still reeling. Still processing everything that's happened.

"What does that mean for you?" Shadows cross his face. "With the race and with . . . your *ex*?" He says the word tentatively, hopefully, and I immediately reassure him.

"Yes. That's . . . I ended things with Shake. And the race . . . Well." I lift a shoulder. "I'm not running for office anymore either."

Nikhil's frame relaxes a fraction, then grows tense again. "What? Yes, you are. Why would that change anything? Why wouldn't you—"

I sigh. "It was kind of a package deal. Me and him. Running together. Working with the advisory group. They were his contacts, so maybe they'll keep working with Shake, but I don't think they'd want to work with just me."

Nikhil raises his eyebrows. "So, that's it? You're going to go back to your old job?"

"No. I'm going to move here. To be with you."

His entire being brightens with joy, radiating pure sunshine. I bask in it for a moment, allowing it to scatter some of my lingering unease. I hadn't fully thought through what might happen after I bought the inn back. I hadn't allowed myself to hope that Nikhil and I might be able to mend things. But in this moment, I'm sure. I don't want to go back to the job I had before. It was once everything I wanted, but I've done it for years now, and I don't want to just advocate for my clients' causes anymore. I want to do more.

Nikhil watches me for a while, and slowly his countenance dims. "But what about . . . Is there a new job you're excited about? Something else you'd want to work on here?"

I falter. "I'll . . . I'll help you with the inn. I'll help in some way. Any way. With the grants, like I said before. And I could . . . I don't know. Do something."

His eyes grow tender, but he slowly shakes his head. "No." His lips curve into a soft smile. "You're going to run for Congress."

"No," I say, even though his words make something leap within me. Make something come back to life. "No, this isn't about me. This is about you. I've let my dreams lead the way this whole time, and I don't want to do that again. I don't want to—"

"This isn't about me, Meena. This is about *us*. I love your dreams. I've always loved them. And I love them even more now that I understand them better. I love your mind and your heart and your strong will. I love your desire to help people and make a difference. I was never upset about you chasing your dreams. I supported your move to D.C. I wanted you to have everything you always wanted. I just worried I was holding you back."

"You weren't. You never could. And I don't need to do this, Nikhil. I don't have to—"

"You *want* to run," he says. "So, you're going to run. And I'm going to help you."

I open my mouth, about to interject, but he keeps going.

"We'll find out more about the Texas seat. Or any other race you're interested in. We'll contact other groups. I'm sure you have connections to some, and if you don't, we'll find others. We'll talk to Elizabeth, and if she's planning a run of her own, we can always talk to Alan." He playfully raises an eyebrow. "Because he definitely won't be able to resist spilling the beans."

I laugh without meaning to, and he laughs in return.

"I don't know how we'll do it, Meena," he says, a moment later, his hand returning to clasp mine. "And honestly, I know you don't need my help. You could absolutely do this on your own if you wanted to, but I want to do this with you. I want to be there. I want to be by your side as you figure it out."

Love swells through my chest, so sudden and forceful I almost feel like I might burst. But reality cuts through like it always does.

"If I made it," I say, "if by some miracle I win—this seat, or any other congressional seat—I'd have to be in D.C. part of the time. I'd have to go back and forth. And you have the inn here—"

"Maybe I open another inn up there once we get this one off the ground. Maybe I hire staff to run this place while I'm away and travel back and forth with you. Maybe we even end up moving there one day."

"But this is your *home*," I say. "I understand how important that is to you, why it would be hard for you to leave it and—"

"*You're* my home, Meena. Out of all the places I've lived, I've only ever felt at home with you." His voice is fervent, the truth of his words blazing in his eyes. "I've been living without that feeling for years now and I'm not going to live that way a day longer. I don't know exactly how we'll do it, but we'll find a way to make it work. Together."

I want to believe him. I want to believe him so badly, but I can't stop the worry climbing up my throat.

"But that's what I thought back then. I thought we'd be able to make things work, but we couldn't. What if we . . . what if we want to, but we can't? What if we try and we just mess it all up?"

"Then, we mess up," he says gently. "And we try again. We're not the same people we were six, seven years ago, Meena. We've changed. We're different. We've grown and we'll keep growing. We'll keep doing better. We'll grow together."

He smiles, wide and full and beaming, and I feel it. Warmth and comfort and this overwhelming sense of rightness. *Mine*. This wonderful gift of a man is mine.

"I love you," I say, the words flying out of my mouth.

His lips return to mine, his kiss firm and quick and fierce. "I love you so much," he whispers.

A drop of water lands on my shoulder. I ignore it, assuming one of us has just started crying again, but then another lands on my cheek. And another on the top of my hand.

I tilt my head up. "Is that—"

Nikhil lifts his palm toward the sky. "It's just a drizzle," he says. "Just a—" A loud boom of thunder cuts him off.

I lean back from Nikhil, my eyes wildly scanning our surroundings.

"We need to get inside," I say, standing up.

"We can't," he responds, coming to his feet. "We haven't gotten that far in our repairs yet. We'll have to wait for the car to come back." He clasps my upper arms, running his hands up and down them. "But it'll be fine, Meena. It's just a normal thunderstorm. We'll be okay out here. Honestly, it's not even that bad."

In that moment, the heavens open up. The rain grows heavier, changing from a drizzle to sheets in a minute.

Nikhil's lips part in shock, and his bewildered expression draws a loud laugh out of me.

I throw a hand over my head, doing my best to shield my eyes from the onslaught of rain.

"You were saying?" I tease. And Nikhil grins.

"Are you laughing at me, Mrs. Chopra-Wright?"

"Oh, I absolutely am, Mr. Nader." I pause. "Mr. Chopra-Wright-Nader? Mr. Nader-Chopra-Wright?" We'd never discussed whether we'd change our names when we were married. We'd both kept our names as they were.

A flash of lightning splits the sky, and Nikhil pulls me closer.

"Don't tell me we're going to be a triple-hyphenate-surname family. Our poor kids. Just think how badly they'll get teased at school." Nikhil's smile grows, the corners of his eyes creasing.

We're both drenched. Our clothes plastered against our bodies. And the rain is pelting, stinging a bit when it hits my skin, but I can barely feel it.

I imagine us back here in five years, ten. The property filled with friends and guests and little ones with Nikhil's gold-brown eyes, and my unruly hair.

A family. Nikhil and I are going to be a family.

"Our kids are going to get teased either way," I say, pushing his damp hair off his forehead. "With me as their mother, they'll probably turn out to be huge nerds."

"Maybe," he says. "But that just means they're going to be bright and sharp and hardworking and intelligent. Like you."

The wind picks up, howling at both of us, but I raise my voice to speak over it. "And kind and thoughtful and patient," I say. "Loving and brilliant and wonderful. Like you."

He cups my face in his hands and we crash together, our mouths colliding with sudden force. I reach for him, grasping his soaked collar in my hand, anchoring myself and changing the angle of our kiss. He responds in kind, letting out a rough sound of approval.

A shiver travels down my spine.

"Are you cold?" he murmurs against my lips. And I laugh, shaking my head.

I skim my mouth along his jaw, planting kisses toward his ear. "I'm burning up," I whisper, and now it's his turn to shiver.

A bright light flashes, illuminating the fire in Nikhil's eyes, but it's not lightning this time. Relief sets in when I see the source: twin beams of a pair of headlights.

The approaching car lets out a quick honk, and I smile.

"Guess your assistant is back," I say, giving Nikhil a quick peck, then turning back to the house.

But Nikhil stops me, his fingers catching mine. "He can wait for a bit," he says, drawing me toward him. "We'll be okay out here a little longer." He smiles as he lowers his head. "After all, you and I have made it through worse storms than this."

I relax into his embrace, quickly losing myself again in the feel of him. In the way I feel when I'm with him. The rain, the lightning, the car honking, the wind whipping around us—all of it fades away.

Because Nikhil is right. We have.

Epilogue

EIGHTEEN MONTHS LATER

HOUSTON CHRONICLE
A Tour of Houston's Newest Inns and B & Bs
By Lina Richards, Staff Writer

Somewhere halfway between the hustle and bustle of Houston and the overcommercialized piers and beaches of Galveston Island sits a small, unassuming, newly opened inn.

In the wake of the devastating hurricane that wiped out a good portion of this area a year and a half ago, it hasn't been uncommon to see newly renovated houses and businesses crop up around here. But as a locally owned and operated venture, M & N's Inn by the Bay stands apart. Its owner, Nikhil Nader-Chopra-Wright, has spent all of his adult life in this part of Houston and bought the property before the storm ever hit.

"It's been a passion project from the beginning," he tells me. "It's taken a lot of work, but it's always been a labor of love."

As he walks me through the lobby, past the cheerful pale green sign saying, "Welcome to M & N's," and up the handcrafted staircase, I can see what he means. From the refinished wood floors to the minute detail in the crown molding, it's evident that Nader-Chopra-Wright has poured a lot of himself into this place. Instead of the neutral white, gray, and beige aesthetic popular with coastal bed-and-breakfasts, he's leaned into deep, bright colors. He explains that this was an intentional choice and that the décor in the bedrooms is heavily influenced by designs associated with the region of India his mother immigrated from.

You might recognize Nader-Chopra-Wright's wife, Meena Nader-Chopra-Wright, from her posters, billboards, and general campaigning around town. Ms. Nader-Chopra-Wright, who insists that I call her Meena, shows me around the exterior of the property, taking me out onto the dock overlooking the bay.

"It's a mouthful," she says with an easy grin. "Our last name. My campaign manager even suggested I shorten it to help with name recognition, but I like it too much." She lifts a shoulder in a small shrug. "It just fits us."

Despite having recently lost the primary election for beloved local figure Congresswoman Garcia's former seat, Meena seems to be in high spirits. I tell her as much, and her smile doesn't fade.

"I'd known Elizabeth Jeffries would be a formidable candidate to run against, and she was. But now that the primary is over, I've thrown my complete support behind her. We need someone who carries Congresswoman Garcia's legacy forward, not someone who takes us back, and I'm proud to support Elizabeth. I know she'll do exactly that."

Meena's husband joins us, mentioning that this is his favorite spot on the property. The view of the water is stunning, and he notes that guests can fish off the dock or borrow one of the inn's canoes and explore the bay—canoes that he happened to craft himself, his wife chimes in—but the reason this is his favorite spot is because it's the place where he proposed to his wife.

"He proposed with a pair of sneakers," Meena says with a laugh. "Can you believe that?"

Nader-Chopra-Wright drops an arm around his wife's shoulders, the casual affection between the pair obvious and clear. He mutters something about how he never got to propose properly the first time around, and when I ask what he means, he waves it off.

"I also gave her a ring," he says, his cheeks turning a little red. "Just to be clear."

Meena nudges him playfully. "He did, but the sneakers were my favorite part."

She insists that Nikhil explain the meaning behind them. He gives her a look, rubs the back of his neck, then sighs. "I'd watched this documentary following different activists running for Congress," he says. "And one of them mentioned that she'd spent so much time campaigning door to door that she'd literally worn holes in her sneakers." He shrugs. "So, I bought Meena a couple pairs of her favorite ones. I bought myself a couple pairs too. It was right around when she was deciding whether she'd put her name in the running, and I just wanted her to know that I was with her. That I meant it when I said I wanted to share every part of our lives with each other."

When I ask whether Meena has any plans to run again in the future, she offers a coy smile. "I loved meeting the voters and hearing about their concerns and hopes and dreams. I still want to be a part of the community. I still want to push for meaningful change that helps people, but I don't *have* to hold office to do that. And I'm pretty happy here. Working with Nikhil. Getting to meet the folks who pass through. And the ones who live in the area. But who knows what the future holds?"

It's the kind of diplomatic, noncommittal answer I'd expect from a polished former D.C. lawyer, but I have to admit that it sounds authentic in the moment. Though I wouldn't be surprised to see Meena announce her candidacy for something else soon.

The Nader-Chopra-Wrights turn the discussion back to some of the repairs they did after the storm, and we step off the dock, continuing the rest of the tour . . .

I scroll to the end of the article on my phone, and my head slumps back against my pillow with a sigh of relief. After a year and a half of intense, grueling work, Nikhil had launched the inn with a soft opening last month, inviting close friends and family and a few members of the press.

My parents had made it, as well as my sister and Ritu. They'd met Nikhil prior to that, of course, when all of us had taken a trip to Europe to visit Ritu during her time abroad. My parents had loved him, immediately calling him the son they'd always wanted, to which my sister and I had rolled our eyes. Light sexism aside, my parents had welcomed Nikhil with open arms, and even my sister had given him a warm reception. Or at least as warm as she could manage.

Even though we've grown closer recently, my sister's prickly exterior has remained firmly intact. She hasn't changed in that regard, but my understanding of her has. She's soft beneath the front she presents to the world. Vulnerable and scared, just like me. Just like all of us.

I reach for my phone again, rereading the article. I can't wait for Nikhil to wake up so he can see this. We've both been on pins and needles this past month, repeatedly refreshing the same search terms in Google, waiting to see our first review, and though I'd had high hopes, this article has far exceeded my expectations. It's an absolute rave.

"Good morning," a gruff voice says into my ear. Warm, firm lips coast over my cheekbone, and even now, after hundreds of mornings together, this is still my favorite way to wake up.

I turn in to him, the news I was going to share temporarily forgotten.

The daylight filtering in through the window casts his skin in a golden glow. He's wearing his beard slightly longer these days, and I run my fingers over it, over his jaw. I always expect it to feel coarser than it is, but it's so soft.

The corners of his mouth tilt up.

"You're supposed to say 'good morning' back, you know. That's considered polite."

I shush him by pressing my lips against his, and he laughs against my mouth. I absorb the sound, and we don't say much of anything for a while. Our hands and mouths roam until my phone falls to the floor with a loud *thwack* and I break away to grab it.

Nikhil grins as I return to him. "Well, that works too," he says. "Feel free to skip the 'good mornings' from here on out."

I roll my eyes, swiping across my screen, returning to the article.

Nikhil reaches for me again, his arm around my waist, his beard tickling the side of my neck, but I don't let myself get distracted this time.

"Soo," I say, teasing out the vowel. "Our first review is in."

To my surprise, Nikhil doesn't perk up or scramble for the phone to see it. He just pulls me closer.

"I know," he says, nuzzling into me. "I got up in the middle of the night to get some water, and I saw it."

I twist around to face him. "You read it already?"

"Yeah."

"The article? From the *Houston Chronicle*?"

"Yeah," he says nonchalantly. "It was pretty good."

"*Pretty good?* They loved it, Nikhil! It was incredible."

"I guess. But it wasn't my favorite review."

My eyebrows scrunch together. "There's another one?"

He nods solemnly, taking my phone from me. He fiddles with it for a couple seconds, then hands it back.

I scroll past the "Google Reviews" banner to the lone entry beneath it. Five stars. And just a handful of words that make me burst into laughter.

This place is out of this world. —Alan M.

I glance at Nikhil and his smile is so wide and mischievous and beaming, I laugh again.

"I guess Alan would know," I tell him. "After all, he's been to space."

"Has he?" Nikhil says, his voice thick with affected shock. "He's never mentioned that before."

I smack him lightly across the chest, and he catches my hand. He opens his mouth, as if he's about to say something else, when my phone buzzes, Alexa's name flashing across the top.

I'd been shocked when Alexa, the political strategist Shake had introduced me to, had responded to my "thank you for meeting with me" email with two curt, ominous words: "let's talk." The next day, she'd informed me, in her classic, no-nonsense way, that she wanted to run my campaign. I'd been floored and overjoyed, and somehow, just four days later, she'd helped me file all the necessary paperwork.

It had been a whirlwind. The whole race had been. Completely exhausting, but exhilarating. I'd loved so much about it. Campaigning. Meeting people. Hearing the needs of the community and the people who live here, with a special ear toward the people this state so often forgets or flat-out ignores or actively harms. People in vulnerable circumstances who need support and care and kindness and deserve to experience all of that with dignity. Even though I'd lost, and that loss had been brutal, every moment still felt worthwhile.

Nikhil's silent as I read the latest text from Alexa. He doesn't say anything until I lift my head, meeting his gaze.

"Still thinking about it?" he asks, brushing a piece of my hair over my shoulder. There's no judgment or pressure or expectation in his voice or expression, but I'm pretty sure I know which way he's leaning.

A couple years ago, I never would have considered running for city council. I was laser-focused on a path to Congress, and a municipal-level seat wouldn't have been on my radar, but now . . . I don't feel that same pressure I once did. That desire to climb and reach and strive for something prestigious. Something that shows or convinces someone else I've "made it." That's not what's pushing me anymore.

I could serve the community in this role. I could help people, the way I've always wanted. It's not the lack of prestige or a lack of purpose that's holding me back.

I rest my hand on the slightly rounder than usual curve of my stomach, and Nikhil clocks the movement.

His eyes soften. "I want to tell you that this shouldn't be a factor," he says quietly. "That you shouldn't have to consider this when making your decision, but I know the reality. That there will be additional hurdles now. New obstacles you'll have to overcome. And I know last time was hard enough as it was, but . . . you know what you want, Meena. You do. And whatever you want, it's what I want too."

I watch him for a long moment, but where I expect there to be conflict, I see only certainty. Resolve. And when I look inward, it's what I feel too.

"Let's do it," I say, smiling at the joy on Nikhil's face when the words register. "We'll make it work. Right?"

"Yes," he says. "We will. Come hell or high water." And I reach for him, kissing him hard and fast and true.

The two of us—no, the *three* of us—are going to be okay. Honestly, I think we already are.

Acknowledgments

I'm writing these acknowledgments six months before this book comes out, and I'm still in shock that it's even happening. It's a dream to get to publish another book and I'm so grateful to everyone who made this happen!

First, to my editor, Kara Cesare: I remember sharing the idea for this story the very first time we talked, and your enthusiasm and support meant everything to me. Thank you for helping me shape that rough idea into the story I always wanted it to be. You showed so much care for Meena and Nikhil, and for me, and I'm so thankful for the work we did on this book together. Thank you too to my brilliant agent, Johanna Castillo. Johanna, you are a powerhouse, a talent, and a trusted partner. Your insight on this book—and on everything I write—is invaluable, and I can't wait to see what we do next!

And to everyone at Dell: Melissa Folds, Taylor Noel, Corina Diez, Jesse Shuman, Gabby Colangelo, Kara Welsh, Kim Hovey, Jennifer Hershey, Debbie Aroff, and Jennifer Garza: it's such a joy to get to work with you! Melissa, Taylor, and Corina, especially, thank you for your genius marketing and publicity support. I so appreciate all of your hard work!

Thank you to everyone at Viking UK, especially Vikki Moynes, Lydia Fried, Ellie Hudson, and Rosie Safaty.

And thank you to Sarah Horgan for designing the most stunning covers! And special thanks to Ali Hazelwood for helping with the cover reveal, and for just being the best in general!

I'd had the idea for a romance novel set during a hurricane for a while, but the premise didn't come together until I had a conversation with Ellie Palmer. Ellie, you are one of my favorite writers, and I feel so lucky that I get to always read your work early! Thank you for that brainstorm session in the Twitter DMs years ago. So thankful that this book and our friendship were the result!

And thank you to everyone who read this book (or parts of it) in its early stages and gave me helpful feedback: my mom, Ellie Palmer, Ava Watson, Scarlette Tame, Maggie North, Amanda Ciancarelli, Mallory Marlowe, Mae Bennett, Alexandra Vasti, and Liana Savari-rayan. Thank you to Kitchen Party, SF 2.0, 2024 Debuts, and so many writing friends who have been there for venting and encouragement and advice. To Jessica Goudeau, a brilliant nonfiction writer and my dear friend: your last book, *We Were Illegal,* really had me thinking about Texas and what it means to live here, and I know those reflections made their way into this story. Thank you for sharing your gifts and thoughts with the world. To Alexandra Vasti, Jill Tew, Laura Piper Lee, Danica Nava, Ellie Palmer, and Myah Ariel, I love our frequent (and often hilarious) chats. I wouldn't have survived the debut experience without you. And to Reapera: Maggie North, Amanda Ciancarelli, Lavanya Lakshmi, and Tania Lan, our group chat has been such a safe place to share highs and lows and I am so grateful to all of you. And an extra thanks to Maggie for helping non-outdoorsy me understand canoeing technique and terminology. Any mistakes are entirely my own.

Readers who found *Say You'll Be Mine* and have messaged me or shared your thoughts via posts and videos and reviews: Thank you so much. I know you have a lot of options when you sit down to read, and I am so incredibly thankful you'd take the time to both read and share about my book. I hope I get to keep writing stories for you for years to come.

And of course, a huge thank-you to my family. My parents, my brother, and my sister, with whom I've experienced three different hurricanes, several tropical storms, multiple flooding events, and a few other natural disasters: I moved back to Houston to live closer to all of you, and even with all the climate and non-climate issues here, I would make that decision all over again. I love you all so much.

And lastly, to the people in Texas who are showing up, through protest, through mutual aid, through community organizing and activism, through political work, through legal challenges: you all make me proud to call this state my home.

VANESSA VELAZQUEZ PHOTOGRAPHY

NAINA KUMAR is the bestselling author of *Say You'll Be Mine*. She lives in Texas, close to her family, whose antics provide endless inspiration.

nainakumar.com
X: @nkumarwrites
Instagram: @nkumarwrites